... captures layer... ...phere and complex emotions bea... ...fully, along-side writing a compulsive tale. I loved it'

Kate Hamer, author of
The Girl in the Red Coat **and** *Crushed*

'Tension comes from the skillful zeroing in and out of Connie's sad story and Marina's desperation for a happy ending ... Clever'   *Daily Mail*

'An emotionally taut, spellbinding, vivid mystery ... This is definitely a book readers won't be able to put down'

Karen Hamilton, author of
The Perfect Girlfriend **and** *The Last Wife*

'I loved *The Hiding Place*. Wonderful writing, mystery and intrigue, and a great story ... I shed a tear at the end'

Emma Curtis, author of
The Night You Left **and** *Keep Her Quiet*

'*The Hiding Place* is a real gem of a book. Jenny Quintana's evocation of the 1960s bursts from the page and the human stories that unfold for the residents of 24 Harrington Gardens are breathtaking and compelling. A gripping plot with characters who will keep you guessing (and break your heart a little, too)'

Eleni Kyriacou, author of *She Came to Stay*

'Another beguiling Quintana mystery ... *The Hiding Place* is about the hopes, fears and impossible choices of ordinary people. It is about the things that connect and separate us. It is a testament to the fragile nature of truth and a masterpiece of storytelling'   **Claire Dyer, author of** *The Last Day*

'A gripping suspense story that expertly interweaves the past and present ... Beautifully written and extremely moving'

Nikki Smith, author of *All in Her Head*

'An absorbi... ...acks with her ini... ...cky

THE HIDING PLACE

JENNY QUINTANA grew up in Essex and Berkshire, before studying English Literature in London. She has taught in London, Seville and Athens and has also written books for teaching English as a foreign language. Her first novel, *The Missing Girl*, was published in 2017 and chosen as a Waterstones Thriller of the Month. She now lives with her family in Berkshire. *The Hiding Place* is her third novel.

Also by Jenny Quintana

The Missing Girl
Our Dark Secret

JENNY QUINTANA

THE HIDING PLACE

PAN BOOKS

First published 2021 by Mantle

This paperback edition first published 2021 by Pan Books
an imprint of Pan Macmillan
The Smithson, 6 Briset Street, London EC1M 5NR
EU representative: Macmillan Publishers Ireland Ltd, 1st Floor,
The Liffey Trust Centre, 117–126 Sheriff Street Upper,
Dublin 1, DO1 YC43
Associated companies throughout the world
www.panmacmillan.com

ISBN 978-1-5290-4042-5

A CIP catalogue record for this book is available from the British Library.

Typeset in Sabon by Jouve (UK), Milton Keynes
Printed and bound by CPI Group (UK) Ltd, Croydon, CRO 4YY

MIX
Paper from
responsible sources
FSC® C116313

Visit www.panmacmillan.com to read more about all our books
and to buy them. You will also find features, author interviews and
news of any author events, and you can sign up for e-newsletters
so that you're always first to hear about our new releases.

For Stephen, Amelia and Olivia,
with love

1

Marina

November 1991

The house is still, like a crypt. Only the maple tree moves, branches swaying in the night breeze, leaves trembling and then brightening as a light in the top window flicks on.

Marina parks opposite and switches off the engine. Heart thudding, she opens the door and steps into the street. The midnight air whips her face. Her breath is wispy, like the remnants of a ghost. In the distance, traffic speeds along Streatham High Road. A siren wails.

She has been in Tooting Bec visiting an author whose manuscript she's editing. Agata is Polish and is writing her memoirs, focusing on the Second World War. Setting off for the drive home to Wiltshire, Marina has taken a detour, speeding through the network of suburban streets, along past the common and into Harrington Gardens.

It's an ordinary street in a nondescript part of London, with the air of a place battened down for winter. Hedges are scruffy, tendrils trail from the tops of hanging baskets. Rubbish nudges the lids of dustbins. On one path, a rusty pram stands discarded along with a broken cot.

The houses are mostly semis but number 24 is different. Detached. It's a double-fronted Victorian home with two gables topped with arrowed finials. Spiked iron railings, with gates either side, contain the front garden with its modest patch of earth, single maple tree and geometric path. Stone steps lead to a massive front door; metal stairs to the entrance to the basement. To the right, a public footpath separates it from the house next door. An estate agent's fallen sign rests on the ground. *Flat 2. To Let.*

Automatically, Marina compares the reality before her to the photographs she's seen in newspapers. But those grainy images were mere reproductions, while this building is solid and stamps its importance on the street.

Marina crosses the road. The house is in darkness save for the light on the second floor and a cobwebbed lantern above the front door, but it's enough to notice the crumbling cornices and cracked stained glass. The bricks need repointing, the ledges need repainting and the maple tree needs cutting back.

Three floors and five windows and then the basement.

The light in the top window is turned off. Marina shivers and buttons her faux-fur coat. Her hair hangs abundantly around her face – rich and dark and warm. She wears thick clothes, boots and fingerless gloves, but still the chill of the night creeps inside her bones. Flexing her fingers, she moves beneath a street lamp as if it might give her heat.

Above her, the sky is heavy. Stray snowflakes are falling. She should go home. She should get into her Mini, turn the heating on full blast and speed away from London.

But she does not.

Warily, she steps forward and peers more closely at the

house. Along with the set of doorbells – five, she counts, for five flats, there's a separate bell for the basement – she takes in the original details: the lion-head door knocker with its gaping mouth; the metal bell pull that hangs like a noose; the guillotine blade of the boot scraper.

She considers the people who have lifted the knocker, jangled the bell or scraped their shoes: tenants and visitors. She imagines the figure of a lonely woman, creeping like a spectre up the steps, pushing open the door and leaving her baby inside.

Who would do that?

A weight forms inside her chest. It's an old question and yet Marina's body bows beneath the hurt because she knows she was the baby and the woman was her mother.

2

Connie

April 1964

It can't be true, thought Connie, breathing deeply as she hurried along the pavement of Harrington Gardens. She had missed another period and this morning she had been sick. Deep, retching spasms before she'd even eaten.

She knew it was a sign because Mrs Kolinski had been sick when she was pregnant. Not that she'd had her baby. She'd lost it, just as she'd lost her husband three weeks before that. Some people, said Connie's father, had the luck of the Devil and some had no luck at all.

Despite the warmth of the morning, Connie shivered. Having no luck didn't come close to what might happen next. To have a baby at seventeen. Her father would be devastated, worrying about how they'd manage to look after it, and fretting about money. His eyes would reproach her. *What about your mother? What would she have said?*

Yet, to have a baby, a miniature version of *him* . . . Would it be so bad? She paused in her stride, thinking about Johnny. His blue eyes, his dark hair.

She quickened her pace, knowing her father would be waiting in the bookshop with a list of jobs. The shop opened at nine, but he arrived early. Sometimes he left the flat before she was even awake.

A line of sweat trickled down her neck. She lifted her

dark hair and twisted it into a ponytail, securing it with the band she found in the pocket of her dress. Her favourite dress, short and bright yellow with black polka dots. She smoothed the front, checking to see if it was visible yet, but her stomach was as flat as ever. That was something. Maybe she was wrong and had miscalculated her dates. Perhaps the way she felt now was because her period was due. The blood would come and the cramps would start. She would be annoyed by the inconvenience and laugh at herself for being dramatic.

Still. Perhaps she should see Doctor Franklin. She envisaged sitting in his surgery and shuddered at the thought. How could she explain to the man she had known since childhood that she suspected she was pregnant? The same man who had seen her with pigtails, had told her she had chickenpox, had pronounced she would grow out of eczema. It was he who had diagnosed her mother. He knew everything about their family.

Walking faster, almost running, she reached the end of Harrington Gardens and turned onto Streatham High Road. People strolled on the common. It was a bright morning, the sky a canvas of blue and white strokes. Johnny had painted sunrises and sunsets, copying the postcards they had bought at the National Gallery. Connie imagined him using words such as *textured* and *intense* and she saw herself listening and yet not listening, captivated by his eyes and the way his face fell into a frown. He rarely smiled. But when he did. *When he did.* Well, that was why she had got into this position in the first place.

Grimacing, she hurried along past the common before

turning off and waiting on the kerb as a bus and a few cars rattled past. Further along, a milk float whirred to the depot. She crossed, dodging the boy on his bike heading for the grocer's where he worked, a few doors down from the bookshop. Harry – seventeen, skinny as a post, wearing drainpipes and a shirt, with a bowler hat perched on his head. Grinning, he lifted both hands from the handlebars and said, 'Connie. You're killing me.'

He said it every time he saw her and she laughed because she liked him and because he had been kind to her mother, Sarah, especially in those last few weeks, when she had insisted on shopping alone. Harry had carried her bags and accompanied her home. Connie had waited and watched them from the window of their flat, her heart filling as her mother's diminished frame rounded the corner, with Harry walking beside her.

The cancer had been quick. Her mother had lain beneath the covers with her long hair spread across the pillow while Connie and her father had kept vigil beside her. Forty years old. Too young – everyone said. She'd died in the middle of the night. Only when the doctor had come and the body been taken, had Connie slipped out of the house and onto the common, where she'd stood beneath the cold moon and the indifferent stars and allowed herself to weep.

A year ago. Connie could hardly believe she'd been alone – motherless – for so long.

Crossing another road, she stifled her sadness and focused on Johnny. She remembered his cool hands on her body, and afterwards, the spark of his frustration each time he talked about his painting and what he wanted to achieve.

Now he was gone. He'd taken the boat train to Paris to start a new life without her. Yes, he'd promised to write once he'd settled, but that had been in January and now it was April and she still hadn't heard.

The bookshop stood on a side street squeezed amongst a row of shops and cafes. Two storeys, it had darkly painted walls and a rusty sign that read:

THOMAS LITTLETON BOOKSELLER

BOOKS BOUGHT AND SOLD

RARE AND SECOND HAND

The window on the ground floor was so crammed with books it was difficult to see inside. Fairy lights circled the pane and a forgotten nativity scene nestled in the corner, giving the impression of a shabby Christmas card or an old-fashioned etching in a book.

Connie opened the door. She blinked, letting her eyes get used to the gloom. Her father leaned at the counter, and so did Victor Wallace. She considered slipping away, but decided against it. If her father was conducting business with Victor, it was better that she stayed.

The shop smelled of ink and old paper. It was narrow, with a wooden counter along the rear wall and, behind that, a doorway to the back room. At the far end of the counter, on the right, a staircase led to the first floor. A fairly reliable grandfather clock and a small cabinet of rare books stood next to the staircase. Black and white photographs hung on the wall to the left, showing south London through the decades.

Nostalgia, according to Connie's father, encouraged the buying of books, and so did free biscuits: often Connie would arrive to find groups of customers reminiscing about closed-down dance halls and tea rooms and wartime rations as they ate digestives and drank cups of tea. Whether they bought any books was another matter, but their talk was a distraction for her father and that was important, especially since Connie's mother had gone.

There were books *everywhere*. They spilled out from the shelves that covered two walls, were stacked on the floor, the counter, the window seat. It seemed like chaos, but her father catalogued and treasured every volume, no matter how valuable or otherwise. Every hardback or paperback – poetry, play, fiction, non-fiction, popular or literary – needed a home, and if it didn't have one, her father would keep it safe. If they ran out of space in the shop, he would store them in the attic at Harrington Gardens. Many books had been in the shop for years – like her mother's favourite, *A Complete Edition of the Poets of Great Britain. Volume the Fourth*. Inside you could read Donne and Fletcher in the smallest of print, on the thinnest of paper. Her mother had pencilled at the front *Not to be sold*, as she always had if it was a book she particularly prized.

Victor turned first and grinned. He gathered books from house clearances or other sources, and there, on the scratched-up counter, next to a sheaf of bills secured by a paperweight, a pile of tattered paperbacks signified his latest haul.

'Ah, Connie,' said her father, smiling. 'See what Victor has brought us.'

Her father was dressed in his usual waistcoat and white shirt, his face adorned by a pair of half-glasses, hair greying and needing a trim. Connie's chest tightened. She should tell him to go to the barbers. He never did anything for himself unless she pushed him, which both irritated and pleased her.

Now he held up a volume of poetry by Emily Dickinson. Connie took it with a tingle of anticipation and noticed with surprise that the rest of the books were by female authors too: Sylvia Plath, Shirley Jackson, Virginia Woolf.

'What do you think?' said her father eagerly.

She smiled, touching the spines. Oh, to be one of these women, to let her thoughts run and slide on every page. She'd wanted to be a writer for as long as she could remember, scribbling stories at an early age. Her parents had read them and taken her ambition seriously, nodding gravely, offering advice. She still wrote, but her ideas were small, her settings confined to south London. She wished she could travel the world and feed her imagination, that she could go to exotic places like Marrakesh and Cairo and absorb the sights and the smells and the sounds. Next door in the second-hand shop, a Remington typewriter had been in the window for months. Gleaming, black and silver and compact. One day she would buy it. She imagined herself clacking away at the keys on a train headed for Venice, shooting back the carriage with a ding.

'They're perfect,' she said, averting her eyes from Victor's grin.

Victor was twenty-five. Good-looking, light-eyed,

smooth-skinned with tawny coloured hair, it was his mouth that spoiled the effect, with lips that were over-red, always damp. They parted when he looked at her, showing pointed teeth like a wolf's. Today he wore an ugly green and orange checked jacket, yet he still managed to look slick. *Slick*. That was the word to describe Victor. Or sleazy. Even though he was the best-read person she knew – apart from her father. Now he leered at her in the way he always did, his gaze travelling over her body. She crossed her arms to cover her chest, regretting her short yellow dress.

'Can you guess who owned these books?' said her father, waving *A Vindication of the Rights of Woman* in front of her eyes.

Connie smiled. 'No. Who?'

'A suffragette, or at least a relation to a suffragette and a very famous one at that. Have you heard of Emily Davison, the lady who died on the track at the Epsom Derby?'

'Of course!' Connie replied.

It was her mother who'd taught her about the suffragettes. She'd also said that women should want more than to be yoked to their houses and their husbands. *Head for the horizon*, she said. *Don't be satisfied with standing still.*

'Which relation?' she said, looking directly at Victor.

'I cannot divulge the identity of my client.' He spoke with mock secrecy and tapped the side of his nose.

She rolled her eyes. Victor was a past master at exaggeration and deceit. He knew well enough that his claim about these books would determine the deal for her father.

In the corner of the room, the grandfather clock struck ten. 'Right,' said Victor, 'Time and tide and all of that. Are we agreed?'

'Indeed we are,' said Connie's father, rubbing his hands and grabbing a scrap of paper. Connie tried to see the scribbled figures, certain Victor would trick them if he could, but her father was already heading into the back room. Connie watched him sadly. His once confident stride had turned into a shuffle. He had become hunched, weighed down by grief. He looked so much older than he was.

She reached for the copy of *Mrs Dalloway*. Opening the book, she read the first line. *Mrs Dalloway said she would buy the flowers herself.* What kind of flowers had she had in mind? Lilacs perhaps, like the ones her mother used to fill vases with. Daffodils like those Connie had laid on her grave. Or violets like the drooping bunch Harry had given her that time they'd gone to the pictures. She smiled at the memory. She suspected he had pinched them, but she hadn't cared. Johnny had never given her flowers although he'd painted enough sunflowers. Sunsets and sunflowers and the occasional attempt at a portrait.

Victor spoke. 'I like your dress. Yellow suits you.'

She was tempted to throw the book at his head, but that was no way to treat any book, let alone *Mrs Dalloway*. She ignored him instead.

'Don't be shy. I don't bite.' He smiled in that way he had, drawing back his lips, showing his pointy teeth. Fumbling in his pocket, he pulled out a hip flask and offered it to her. She shook her head mutely. He took a swig. 'You know, it isn't easy to make conversation with a girl who doesn't speak.'

'I have nothing to say.'

'Ha!' He held up one finger. 'But you have.' He looked at her for a second more and then asked after her boyfriend.

'I don't have a boyfriend,' she snapped. Automatically, she moved her hands across her stomach and then immediately crossed her arms.

'Because if that was the case, I'd understand, but seeing as you don't have a boyfriend – or so you say – I'm bewildered.' He pocketed the flask. 'I'm not saying every girl falls for me, but . . .'

'I told you, I don't have a boyfriend, not that it's any business of yours.'

'What about the boy in your building? I've seen you together. You can't deny it.'

True. They had been in the attic which was where Johnny did his painting. He'd been working on a sunset over Waterloo Bridge, feeling frustrated because everything he did was wrong: the colours, the lines, the light and shade. They had argued. He had told her that she had no appreciation of art – like his mother. She had defended both herself and his mother. Afterwards, he was tearful and apologetic, and when they were leaving, Victor was sauntering up the stairs on his way to see her father.

Victor had a knack for turning up uninvited in their flat. Her father welcomed him because he believed in generosity and respect, but Connie hated every second of his presence.

'He's gone,' she said, finally answering his question.

'Where's he gone?' Victor patted his pocket and pulled out a pouch of tobacco.

'Paris.'

He gave a low whistle. 'Nice. Expensive. Has he robbed a bank? He's not one of those train robbers, is he, and now he's done a bunk?' He rolled his cigarette and licked the edges. 'Two and a half million. Wish I'd thought of a stunt like that.'

'And what about the train driver?' said Connie hotly.

'Yeah, well.' Victor grimaced. 'I never said anything about what happened to him. It's the entrepreneurship I admire.' He flipped open his lighter, changed his mind and snapped it shut. Leaning forward, his eyes shining with approval, he said, 'You know the farmhouse – the gang's hideout after the robbery?'

She nodded. After the men had gone, the police had been tipped off. Searching the building, they'd discovered tins of soup and corned beef, bags of sugar and slabs of cake. There had even been a Monopoly board with the men's fingerprints on it. Imagine playing Monopoly with real money.

'Well,' said Victor, 'I heard the owners of the farmhouse charged half a crown to look round – a shilling for kids. Now that is genius.' He pocketed his lighter and gave her another sly look. 'So, is he?'

'What?'

'Your boyfriend. Is he a bank robber?'

'No! Of course he isn't. He worked at Smithfield, you know that.'

'I'm a salesman, but it doesn't mean I'm not cut out for a different job.' He tucked the cigarette behind his ear. 'I know I'm older than you, but that means I've got experience. And maybe I could help you and your father out.' He waved an arm about, indicating the shop.

Connie took in his meaning and shook her head in disgust. No amount of money Victor could provide would compensate for his personality. The landlord had already waived their rent for this month, but better Kenneth Quip than Victor Wallace.

'We're doing fine,' she said.

'You seem worried.'

He rested his hand on her wrist and her fingers itched to grab the paperweight and bring it down on his knuckles.

'I'm not worried. And if I was, I wouldn't come to you.'

His face darkened and he tightened his grip. 'That's not nice. I'm only trying to help.'

She snatched away her hand as her father appeared holding a bundle of notes. Connie's heart constricted again as she pictured him scrabbling at the back of the safe, or in the petty cash tin, gathering together enough money to pay Victor. He filled in the details of the invoice, using a fountain pen her mother had given him. The shop held countless memories like that: her mother's presence filled the space, even now.

He finished writing and tore off the sheet. Connie turned her head away, hating to see Victor signing the piece of paper and taking the notes. She held herself stiffly as he brushed past, saying his goodbyes, giving her a leer, tempered by a wink.

The door banged shut. She wanted to ask questions,

to check that Victor had charged a fair price, but her father was already absorbed, scratching the new titles into his book.

She looked at him with a fondness tinged with concern. For an intelligent man, he was remarkably ignorant of business matters. Her mother had been the one who did the accounts, checked the outgoings and incomings, balanced the figures and insisted on fair prices.

'Shall I make tea?' she offered.

'Lovely,' her father replied, without looking up. 'There's digestives in the tin.'

She gave him another fond look before retreating to the back room, and while the kettle boiled she rubbed her wrist where Victor had grabbed it. He had left a faint mark, branded her like cattle. Her mind darkened. How dare he touch her? He had overstepped the mark. What would her father say? Not that she would tell him. He couldn't fall out with his best supplier because eventually Victor might find a prize amongst the cast-offs he came across, a rare edition, a literary gem. For the sake of her father she had to put up with him.

She sighed and gazed through the barred window at the courtyard. The crooked houses that fronted it leaned precariously. One day, the buildings would lean so far, they would crush the bookshop. Mind you, if more money didn't come in, the business would fail anyway. The last thing they needed was another mouth to feed. She *mustn't* be pregnant. It would be a disaster for everyone. Pushing away the foreboding that rose so urgently inside her, she turned to make the tea.

3

Marina

November 1991

Marina reads Agata's manuscript. *Early recollections: snow falling, goldfish swimming. My brother racing into the kitchen saying we had to leave.*

She's finding it hard to concentrate, though. It's been like this since she returned from London – memories competing for attention, intrusive thoughts and suppositions. She sighs, twiddles her pencil, fiddles with the mess of papers on her desk: receipts, invoices, notes.

Grabbing a piece of honey cake from a plate, she crams it into her mouth. Sticky and sweet, it's the only food she has eaten all day. Last week, Agata sent her home with a Tupperware box full of cakes and pastries, recipes passed down through generations. Marina wonders what kind of cook her own mother would have been.

Throwing down her pencil, she strides to the window. Snow has given way to rain, and the sky is overcast, smeared with grey. Without any morning sunshine, the fields are dulled to yellow, and the trees and hedgerows seem more black than green. Beyond the church spire on the hill is the Westbury White Horse. It is mythical and magical. Marina imagines the horse taking off and galloping across the plain.

Ruth had told Marina from the beginning how she

and David had come to adopt her. That Marina had been abandoned, left in the hallway of a shared house, dressed in a gown and a neatly pinned nappy, wrapped in a shawl of the deepest blue. Ruth said her birth mother must have loved her very much because she had put her somewhere safe where she would be found.

The media had run the story, nicknaming her *Baby Blue*. It was a Spanish nurse who had called her Marina, which came from the Latin and meant 'of the sea': with the blue shawl and her dark looks, it seemed to fit. David and Ruth had agreed. Naturally, they'd added their stamp, naming her Marina Zoe Alexander – Zoe for 'life'.

Marina had listened to these stories of her birth with her knees drawn up and her face serious. She had stored away the details and conjured an image of the woman who was her mother, imagining her with thick, dark hair like her own and dark eyes too. A tragic figure always intending to return.

Ruth had saved dozens of newspaper articles and had kept them in a box in her wardrobe. Marina liked to sneak into her bedroom and study the photos of the house, which seemed like a mansion compared to the cottage they lived in.

When she was older, Marina had read the articles more closely. She had made notes, gathering information about the tenants mentioned and making a plan of who had lived where in the house. A pregnant woman had been spotted nearby. Could that have been her mother? Where had she gone? Marina had searched newspaper archives for unexplained deaths, but there were no dead young women reported, only the corpse of a man who had been dragged from the lake on Tooting Common.

For want of anything better to do, Marina eats more cake. In a few hours, she is due for lunch at her parents' house. She thinks about meeting a friend for coffee beforehand. It's Saturday so someone will be free, but while she is searching for a dress to wear the temptation fades and dies. She will arrange a drink for later. Now, she makes a strong cup of coffee, adds two teaspoons of sugar and takes it to her desk.

But she can't concentrate, and not for the first time she debates whether editing is what she wants to do. Maybe she should go back to teaching. She had lasted twelve months at a comprehensive school in Bristol teaching French and German. It wasn't the kids that had drummed her out; it was the strict policies staff were expected to abide by. One day, she had downed her chalk and given in her notice. She had ended up in Warsaw for a year, working in a bar and learning Polish to add to her repertoire of languages.

A spontaneous act. Like dyeing her hair auburn when she was a teenager to make herself look more like Ruth. Like visiting a psychic and asking about her mother. Like taking a detour through London streets at midnight to look for a mysterious house. Maybe she'll spend the rest of her life lurching from one decision to the next, living hand to mouth.

Ruth says Marina will settle eventually, but she's twenty-seven, and with no full-time job or relationship on the horizon, there's no sign of it happening any time soon.

She ransacks a drawer looking for cigarettes. Finding an old packet of Marlboro, she lights up, shoves open the window and leans into the cold air. She hasn't smoked for months and the cigarette tastes stale and makes her feel shaky. Still, she draws harder and steadies herself, fixing her eyes on the White Horse.

In the street, a neighbour is unloading shopping from the boot of his car. He waves cheerily at Marina and she smiles at him. They've been out for drinks a few times. He's good-looking in a strong-jawed way, owns a cafe, enjoys travelling. Her friends joke they would make beautiful babies together. Maybe so, but Marina isn't ready for that. Besides, it's too late. There's a blonde woman sitting in the passenger seat of the car. One more opportunity lost.

At her desk, she spots a typo, a misspelling of a Polish town, and smiles wryly. Languages are her strength. Her mind works well piecing together the rules and regulations of grammar and syntax, weighing up words, producing sentences that make sense. Circling the mistake, she scans the rest of the page. One of the tenants at Harrington Gardens had a Polish surname. Marina chews the end of her pencil, remembering. *Kolinski.*

A draught of cold air slips through the open window. She lifts her head and looks around the room. Most of her stuff is in boxes. The walls are virtually empty, as they were when she moved in.

'What does that tell you?' she asks herself, lighting a second cigarette, not bothering this time to lean out of the window. The other night at the house, she'd seen the estate agent's fallen sign, its message half hidden by the maple tree. *To Let. Flat 2.* The wisp of an idea rises like the smoke from her cigarette.

She fiddles with a paper clip, turns a page and picks at the polish of her red-painted nails. What if she made an appointment to look around? Simple curiosity. She shakes her head, tells herself not to be stupid and to focus on the manuscript, but the thought won't go away.

Slowly, she draws the telephone towards her, then taps out the number which she has, without even meaning to, memorised. A woman answers on the third ring.

Marina closes her eyes, opens them again. 'Hello. I'm enquiring about Harrington Gardens.'

'Harrington Gardens?' The woman sounds surprised. There is a pause, and then, 'Can you hold, please?'

'Yes.' Marina drums her fingers on the desk. She can hear the woman talking in the background, conferring.

She considers replacing the receiver. No harm done. But it's too late. 'Sorry to keep you. My colleague, Wayne, is dealing with that property, but I'm afraid he isn't here right now. Can I take your name?'

'Zoe Alexander,' she says, using her middle name on impulse. Marina is unusual and the last thing she wants is to trigger a memory of her story.

A fast drive across Westbury. Careless parking in the drive. Hugs and smiles. They sit at the table. Ruth has made moussaka even though David hates aubergines. She has done it for Marina who loves them.

David eats without complaining. In his sixties, he's a retired housing officer and a part-time musician who plays the cello in a local orchestra. An ordinary man, with dark hair turned grey, and a soft, kind face marked with two deep lines, one on either side of his mouth.

Ruth mentions a new position at the National Trust. She's a tour guide, but promotion would mean working in the office.

'Should I take it?' she asks. 'Is it time for a sedentary life?'

David smiles. Marina shakes her head and laughs. There is zero chance of Ruth accepting a job like that and they all know it.

The clock on the mantelpiece chimes. The dining room is reassuringly familiar. The same dark orange curtains and green geometric wallpaper. David's cello leans in the corner. An old gramophone stands on the parquet floor, its surface covered with photos of Marina doing ballet and music and art; attached to climbing ropes and suspended on a rock face; wearing a wet suit ready to plunge into a lake; visiting Stonehenge with Ruth and her friends one Midsummer's Eve.

Ruth cuts into her thoughts. 'How about that second-hand boutique you like?'

Marina looks blank. What has she missed?

'I knew you weren't listening. I was suggesting a shopping trip.'

'Do you mind if we don't? I need to get on with the work I told you about.'

'Ah yes. The Polish lady in Tooting Bec.'

David sets down his cutlery and glances across at the two of them.

'So, how did it go?' says Ruth evenly.

'It went well, thanks.' She keeps her tone casual,

paying attention to her food, transporting a forkful to her mouth.

'And did you go to Harrington Gardens?'

David coughs. Marina fidgets. 'Yes,' she admits, 'I wanted to see how it looked.' Her eyes shine and she waits for the guilt. It's always been like this – a feeling of ingratitude whenever she alludes to her birth mother.

'I knew that's what you'd do.' Ruth's voice is soft and that makes it worse. 'Are you planning to go again?'

Marina lowers her eyes. 'Yes, maybe, but only if you don't mind.'

There is a pause before Ruth stands. She walks around the table and rests her hand on Marina's shoulder. 'Of course I don't mind.'

Marina leans back, catching the familiar scent of sandalwood. David comes over too. 'Do what you need to do,' he says, before kissing her cheek and leaving the room.

They hear him walking through to the kitchen, opening the door. He will work in the garden as he always does, leaving Marina and Ruth to talk.

Ruth gestures for her to follow and they go into the bedroom where they sit together like they used to on the huge brass bed. 'Do you remember,' says Ruth, taking her hand, 'that time you went to London?'

Fifteen years old. A wet and miserable day in November. She had left without telling anyone, caught the train to Paddington, the Circle line to Embankment, the Northern line to Tooting Bec. She'd never been to London alone and had felt like a runaway hurtling through the Underground. At Tooting Bec she'd followed her A–Z to

Harrington Gardens, cold and tired, yet buoyed up by the idea she would learn about her past simply by dint of being there.

She hadn't – of course – and had returned home with a sense of failure. It had taken twelve years before she had visited again.

'You felt so guilty,' says Ruth, 'when you told me where you'd been, but it was natural then for you to want to know and it's natural now.' Her voice breaks and she pauses.

'It's only curiosity.'

Ruth shakes her head. 'That's not true. It's far more and so it should be. You are my daughter and I love you more than anything in my life.' She stops and smiles. 'That moment when I held you in my arms and looked into your face – a missing piece clicked into place. Yet I knew from the start that you weren't completely mine. I knew there would always be a part of you that belonged to someone else.'

Tears brimming, Marina closes her eyes. 'I'm sorry.'

'You mustn't be. And now I have something to show you.' She fetches the box of articles from the wardrobe, lays it on the bed and takes out an envelope. 'I've told you about the nurse at the hospital. The Spanish lady, Sofía.' Marina nods. 'I've told you that she lived on St Michael's Road, which is parallel to Harrington Gardens, and that we exchanged letters until she moved to Ireland. The point is she wrote to me again not long ago to say she had gone back to her old address in London. I was debating when to give this to you and now seems like a good time.'

She hands Marina the letter. David appears in the doorway. His hair is thinning, lines have deepened. Time passes quickly. Marina goes to him and he tucks her into his embrace, but her mind clouds as she rests her head on his chest, as he strokes her hair like he always does. Familiar feelings collide: gratitude and frustration. Guilt, again. How lucky Marina was to have been found. If only she could banish the uncertainty that follows her around.

It is late afternoon by the time Marina returns home. Ruth gave her the box as well as the letter and she carries it up the stairs to her flat.

The phone is ringing as she opens the door. She hurries across the room and snatches up the receiver.

'Is that Zoe Alexander? This is Wayne from Castle Estate Agents. My colleague tells me you're interested in the flat in Harrington Gardens.'

She pushes the receiver hard against her ear. 'I'd like to look around if that's possible.'

'Yes, of course,' says Wayne. He tells her about the rent. 'It's low for the area. Very low.' He gives her a figure. 'And now you're probably wondering why.'

She is silent, letting him fill in the blanks.

'The building is a little tired.' He pauses. 'The upkeep hasn't been . . . efficient.'

'How long has the flat been available?'

'Two years.'

'Two years?' She frowns. 'Why?'

'Well, there's the decoration as I mentioned.' He pauses as if resigned to her rejection. 'We have other properties, of course, if you'd prefer a smarter option. There's a flat in Clapham Common, non-smoking, professional required, only the landlord is insisting on references and wants a deposit and two months in advance. Or there's a maisonette in Tooting Broadway that only needs a lick of paint.'

Marina rubs her temples and looks out the window. In the dusk, the horse glows ghostly white. If she squints she can almost see its legs moving, ready to gallop across the plain. A foolish fantasy. The horse is tethered, but she is not.

'Thank you,' she says, 'but I'd like to look at Harrington Gardens.'

'Lovely! Right!' A few more exclamations and they arrange to meet on the following Wednesday.

Afterwards she calls a friend and suggests a night out. She pulls on her favourite black dress with lace sleeves and scalloped edges, brushes her hair and applies red lipstick. When she looks at herself in the mirror she frowns. It takes a moment before she realises what has unnerved her: she is exactly like the image she created of her mother so many years ago.

4

Connie

April 1964

'Peppermint?' Doctor Franklin leaned across his desk and held out the tin.

Connie took one. Outside the surgery, a robin landed on the window ledge. Some people believed the appearance of a bird was a supernatural message from a loved one, but to Connie, the robin just seemed like, well . . . a robin.

The doctor folded his arms. He had a heavy build, a large, bald head and a nose that was too small for his puffy face. Connie noted the thick gold wedding band, his rough fingers with their hairy knuckles. How different from Johnny's soft skin and smooth chest. Her breath caught in her throat as it always did when she thought about Johnny. She tried to focus and licked her dry lips. The room felt stifling. An electric wall fire was switched on full.

'What can I do for you?' said Doctor Franklin.

How should she begin? She had rehearsed the conversation, speaking aloud to her reflection in the mirror, but each time the dialogue had turned out differently and she had no idea what to say.

Time had gone by with no sign of her period. For a while she had tried to forget about it. She had worked in the bookshop, cared for her father, cleaned and cooked.

Every day she had searched the post box, longing for a letter from Johnny.

The days weren't so bad because she had plenty to do, but at night she lay awake staring into the darkness, thinking, imagining. She told herself it would be all right. Her period would come. It was only a matter of time. But another night passed, and then another and there was no blood on the toilet tissue.

One night, exhausted from lack of sleep, she had begun to cry. Quietly at first and then more loudly, until she was sobbing. She had tried to stifle the sound, knowing her father in the room next door might hear her, but part of her had *hoped* that he'd hear, and she had promised herself that if he came she would tell him the truth and accept the consequences. But he must have been sleeping soundly because he hadn't appeared. Her tears had subsided and she had slipped into an uneasy sleep. In the morning, she had gone back to believing that it was nature playing tricks. Her period would come. Of course it would.

But now, she could no longer pretend that her body wasn't changing. It was the sickness she felt every morning; the heavy feeling in her breasts; the thirst; the need to rush to the toilet. She clung to the idea that they signified something else, but she had to check. She had to be sure. It was the only way to stop this panic that was spiralling through her, affecting everything she did.

'Connie?' The doctor said.

She looked at the robin for guidance. It hopped and pecked and flew away.

He coughed.

'I've been off colour,' she said.

'Off colour,' he repeated, his hand creeping towards the prescription pad. 'What are your symptoms?'

Connie swallowed. 'I feel sick.'

'Sick?'

She nodded.

'Anything else?' His fingers rested on the paper. 'Any aches or pains?'

'I'm tired.'

'Are you sleeping well?'

'Yes,' she lied. No point telling him how often she lay awake at night, missing her mother, missing Johnny, worrying about her predicament, her fear and loneliness so acute that it felt like pain.

Doctor Franklin pulled the pad towards him. She had never liked him, and neither had her mother. Not that her mother had told her so directly. She would only mutter that he took more interest in his lunch than in his patients. Connie knew too that her father thought the cancer should have been detected sooner. He blamed Doctor Franklin for not diagnosing it in time.

'Is it your period, perhaps?' he asked, smiling a little.

She gripped the sides of the chair, hating his tone. Maybe she should have gone to a different surgery, but where? If there were any other options, she didn't know what they were.

He blinked, glanced at the clock on the desk. It was two minutes after twelve. Lunchtime perhaps. As if to confirm the suspicion, his stomach rumbled.

Connie's gaze lit on a photo of the doctor's wife and three children in a brass frame next to the clock. She remembered a story Harry had told her about his cousin's friend. The girl had been made pregnant by her married neighbour. There had been talk that she had been forced, although nothing was proved, and regardless of that, Doctor Franklin had refused to recommend an abortion. In the end, she had gone to a backstreet. Hot water, carbolic mixtures, douches and knitting needles. The girl had nearly bled to death.

Why would Doctor Franklin make a different decision for Connie? Besides, she knew his recommendation wouldn't be enough. She wasn't sure how getting an abortion worked. She only knew it wasn't easy and would cost money and where would she get that?

The doctor coughed again.

Connie gathered herself. 'Yes. I mean I don't have it now, but . . .'

'Ah.' He rocked gently from side to side as if unsticking the seat of his trousers. A line of sweat had gathered on his upper lip. Connie could feel her own sweat pooling between her breasts.

'You're probably low on iron,' he said. 'It's common in young girls. Are you eating well?'

'Yes. Maybe. I don't know.'

Picking up his pen, he paused and gave her another look. 'And you have no other symptoms?'

She shook her head.

'In that case . . .' He scribbled a prescription, signed it with a flourish, tore off the sheet and handed it across. 'This is a tonic,' he said. 'Take it three times a day and you'll be as right as rain. Your diet is poor, that'll be it. It's not surprising without . . .' He stopped, winced, glanced at his watch. 'Give my best to your father, won't you? Is he recovering, keeping busy?'

It would take more than keeping busy to make her father stop missing her mother, but she told the doctor he was fine.

Outside, she ran, her feet pounding on the pavement. How stupid she was. How cowardly. Seeing the doctor had been a waste of time. But if she hadn't had the courage to confess to him, who *could* she tell?

There was no one. If only her mother were alive. She would know what to do. She had been practical, no-nonsense. Connie had heard her talk more than once about the unfairness of women's lives hanging in the balance as they waited for the doctors' judgement. A solution was available only for girls who were rich, she had said, and could get themselves to Harley Street. Not that her mother had thought lightly about abortion, but she thought there should be a choice for those in desperate straits.

Was Connie in desperate straits? She wasn't sure. And perhaps she could solve the problem herself. She had heard that moving heavy furniture might bring on a miscarriage, or flinging yourself down the stairs. There were poisons that would flush the baby clean away. Or bleach, or alcohol. She pictured drinking a bottle of gin or tripping deliberately. She felt sick. Imagine doing that on purpose. How much blood would there be?

She stopped, shivering despite the heat. The day Mrs Kolinski lost her baby there'd been so much blood. Connie had been on her way to meet Johnny in the attic when she'd found her neighbour collapsed on the stairs, her daughter Eva, who was only three years old, with her. Connie had raised the alarm, shouting and banging on doors and sprinting to the phone box to call for help. By the time she had got back, Johnny's mother, Dorothy, was there, mopping up the blood. Dorothy had been a midwife once upon a time. According to Johnny she had given it up when he had been born. Now she took in laundry.

Connie carried on walking. Her thoughts were muddled. Her brain foggy with indecision. She reached the High Road and veered into the chemist to pick up her prescription. Afterwards, she walked more slowly until she reached Harrington Gardens. From the end of the street, she could see the bright red leaves of the maple tree marking where she lived, number 24. The door was wide open, but Connie lingered, reluctant to go in. The house had once been full of light and love. Now there were spaces where her mother and Johnny had been, and even her father was an outline of himself.

She ran her fingers over the spiked railings and thought of all the other people who had done the same. Leaning forward she peered down the metal steps that led to the basement. The flat had been empty for months, windows boarded up after kids had broken in. Kenneth had caught them and chased them out of the house, but hadn't involved the police. It was loyalty amongst thieves according to her mother: he was an ex-con, imprisoned for armed robbery, and had bought the house using funds from his life of crime – a stash that the police had missed; a stash which, it was rumoured, had been more than his fair share. Then he'd decided to switch his role from criminal to landlord, dividing the building into six flats for rental: one in the basement, two on the ground floor, two on the first floor and one on the second. The attic had been left as a storeroom.

Connie's mother had hated the fact that the building had been divided. Once upon a time, it would have been a home with walls covered in paintings and rooms crammed with porcelain and crystal. There would have been orchids and ferns, embalmed animals and gilded cages of captured birds. In the attic, there were still crates of discarded items – broken fossils, stuffed and moth-eaten owls and foxes. Her mother would occasionally rifle through them. Once she had found a skeleton – a pair of tiny conjoined monkeys, which she had taken to a museum.

Now Connie stared at the house and the windows met her gaze. Each of them told a story of those inside. Kenneth lived in Flat 1 on the ground floor to the left of the massive front door. The curtains at his bay window were forever closed. People were *nosey bastards*, he said. The young couple in Flat 2, on the other side of the door, didn't seem to care and never closed their curtains. They were actors – Eileen was American and Leonard was from Tooting, and in the evening, you could see them flouncing around with their scripts, gesticulating and pontificating.

Johnny's mother, Dorothy, lived on the first floor in Flat 3, which was above Kenneth. Alone now that Johnny had gone, Dorothy was a stickler for cleanliness and her windows sparkled more brightly than anyone else's. She and Johnny had had furious arguments about being an artist versus working in a trade. Now her life was quiet.

Connie and her father lived in Flat 4, across the landing from Dorothy. Their windows passed for clean and were hung with thick, blue, velvet curtains that were a little patchy and worn. At the top on the second floor, Mrs Kolinski lived with Eva. She had made their curtains herself. They were beautiful, striped in yellow and gold.

Connie let go of the railings, walked along the path and climbed the stone steps to the front door. She tried to contain her thoughts, to stop them rising to the attic. It held too many memories and now was not the time to think of those. Late at night, when the house slept, that's when she gave herself the luxury.

Inside the hall, its familiarity soothed her. The black and white tiles, the smell of dust, the empty sconces, the cobwebs hanging from the light fitting – once a chandelier, now a single bulb – and the wide oak staircase that dominated the space which led to the first landing and then switched direction to the second. A red, patched carpet unfurled along the centre and a bannister, roughened by age, ran all the way up while matching panels lined the lower wall.

Despite the wear and tear, the staircase gave an element of grandeur to the house and normally Connie liked to stand at its foot, imagining a procession of ghosts of all the people who had ever lived in the house. Now, though, she shivered at the idea and tried to think of something else but, despite her best intentions, her mind turned back to Johnny.

That first day she had seen him. He and his mother were moving in. Connie had passed him on the stairs with an easel under his arm. She'd been intrigued by the easel, intrigued by him. Older than her, eighteen or nineteen. Tall and broad-shouldered with those brilliant blue eyes and dark, unruly hair. Like Heathcliff, or Rochester. Or any of those heroes (or anti-heroes) she loved so much in books.

For a while, Connie had tried her best to coincide their exits and their entrances, but Johnny left at dawn and returned at a mysterious hour when she was still at school. Then her mother had become ill and Connie had stopped looking for him.

One day, after her mother had died, and Connie had left school and started working in the bookshop, she was crossing the hall, shoulders heavy with grief, when she heard footsteps behind her and a voice. It was Johnny, saying he was sorry for her loss. She'd been touched by his words. It was a beginning and had grown into an exchange. The two of them had met regularly in a kind of rhythm, seeming to mirror each other's movements in the house.

He had told her he worked at Smithfield, which he hated because he wanted to paint. She had asked if she could see his paintings and he'd invited her to the attic where he had set up his easel in a corner away from the crates. That first time she had emerged from the staircase into the attic, it was like bursting from mist into sunlight. The sunbeams piercing the rooftop windows; the light and shade and texture of his paintings; the slashes of colour, the peacock blue and sunflower yellow. The space

34

smelled of oil and turpentine and something dark and musky which Connie would soon learn was Johnny's scent.

She had looked about her in awe, admiring the beauty of his art, captivated by his talk. He had spoken endlessly about which painters he admired, how he wanted to live like them, study at the Slade like them. He would give anything to go to Paris. That was the place to be, or New York, but he had no chance of affording that. He had little chance of getting to Paris either, not with the amount he earned at the *fucking meat market*.

Connie had listened to him swear. No one had ever sworn like that in front of her: not her mother, nor her father, nor her friends. Nor even Kenneth or Vincent. No one else swore so easily and openly, no one talked about life so darkly. It didn't occur to her that he had never asked her about herself, and it didn't occur to her to tell him that she had a dream too, that she wanted to travel and to be an author.

She had stopped writing. She had stopped dreaming. She had stopped remembering how fervently her mother had told her not to stay still or to get caught out by a man. It had been enough to be with Johnny.

When they were close, she felt her heart hammering in her chest. When he touched her, she felt a pull that started low in her stomach and spread right through her. He had whispered in her ear that it was all right, this was the sixties, everyone was doing it, weren't they? She should see the parties he went to. No one cared and she shouldn't either.

She had known he would leave her and that her love

could never match his dreams, but she had wrapped up her fears and kept them hidden. After all, how could she stop him? He was meeting people all the time, out there, wherever he went: painters, sculptors, a French woman who told him she would introduce him to artists in Paris. It had been so vague: the woman, where Johnny met these people, the rendezvous in cafes and studios in Soho. Connie didn't know what was true and what was not, but she believed in him, and had given him all the money she had saved. She had even taken a necklace that had belonged to her mother and asked Harry to pawn it for her. She had helped to send Johnny away when all she wanted was for him to stay.

'I won't forget you,' he had whispered on their last night together as they lay in each other's arms on the pile of blankets they had brought to the attic for the purpose.

She kissed him and told him that she would wait. Head on his chest, she listened to his excited heartbeat. He would be free, he told her, to live and to create. 'And when I'm established you must come to Paris.'

'I'd like that,' she had replied, smiling and touching his face, although her insides were churning. Would he remember? Would she see him again?

Now, she reached the flat and pushed back her tears. Why hadn't he written to her? She needed him more than she had ever needed anyone.

Breathing deeply, she opened the door. Her heart sank. Kenneth and her father were talking in the living room and the air was thick with smoke. Connie tried not to think about how it would cling to the lace and the tapestries her mother had chosen, or the fact that, of the flowery armchairs the two men sat in, Kenneth had taken her mother's.

He was poised with one leg crossed over the other, in his habitual white shirt, rolled up at the sleeves, and dark trousers. She could see his prison tattoos, a mix of unintelligible numbers and shapes etched on his knuckles and along his arms. He'd been inside for more years of his life than not, although now, according to him at least, he was *on the straight and narrow* and had no intention of going back. No surprise, her father said, considering the enemies he'd made. He was forty, ten years younger than her father, although he looked older. Skinny, with hollow cheeks and furrows around his mouth, he walked with a dark wood cane topped with a silver handle – although most people said the cane was an affectation and there was nothing wrong with his legs.

Her father sat mutely, his expression polite, as Kenneth rattled on about the latest scandal involving Princess Margaret. He was obsessed by the monarchy. His flat, Connie knew, was stuffed with mementos: plates and teapots, biscuit tins and sugar bowls, thimbles and pillboxes, emblazoned with the crown.

She bent to kiss her father and he patted her hand: patience, his touch said; Kenneth would be gone soon. Connie knew he disliked Kenneth and so did she. He reminded her of a reptile, with his thin body and thin-lipped smile, although he'd been generous enough, waiving the rent. She couldn't complain about that. So she smiled at her father and squeezed his arm, but when she straightened, she spotted a green and orange jacket draped across the sofa and her smile dropped.

Victor appeared in the doorway with his shirtsleeves rolled up and three whisky glasses bunched in his hands. His hair was slicked as usual and she caught the cloying smell of his hair cream mixed with aftershave.

'Connie,' he said, grinning. 'Fancy a nip?' He put the glasses on the table, pulled out a hip flask and sploshed a measure into each. 'Puts hairs on your chest.'

She looked at her father.

'We're celebrating,' he said sheepishly. She knew he would be hating every second of this visit but at the same time would consider he had no choice.

'To our new tenant,' said Kenneth, taking and holding up his glass. 'Victor.'

'Tenant?' said Connie. 'Why? Who's leaving?'

'Nobody,' he replied. 'The basement needs filling. The rent will rise if it isn't, and since Victor here has misbehaved and been turfed out of his place . . .'

'I didn't misbehave,' Victor protested, tossing back his whisky and refilling his glass. 'I had a slight disagreement with the landlady.'

'You mean the landlady's daughter,' said Kenneth, grinning.

Connie glanced at her father again who made an apologetic face.

Victor grimaced and shrugged.

'Scarpered then,' said Kenneth, raising his glass. 'Since Victor has scarpered . . . and finds himself without a home, it seems he's the ideal candidate. Here's to getting away with it!'

The men drank while Connie absorbed the news. She had managed to avoid Victor since he had propositioned her in the shop. It wouldn't be as easy if he lived two floors down.

She walked towards the kitchen, feeling the men's eyes on her. Kenneth's stare she didn't mind so much. He watched everyone, storing the details. Victor's gaze, though, made her shudder. Luckily, he was still focusing on Kenneth contradicting him about what had happened with his landlady. The two of them bickered constantly.

Three dirty mugs stood in the sink and the tea strainer had been left on the side. She cleared away, burying her annoyance. The milk had been left out too and when she gave it a sniff her stomach heaved. Was it on the turn, or was it another sign? Opening the window, she took a breath.

'Connie,' her father called, 'come and sit with us.'

'All right, Dad. Just a minute.'

She breathed deeply again and looked out at the shared garden, and beyond to the grey stone church on the next road, and the graveyard that backed onto their garden, where her mother was buried. At the funeral, her heart had broken watching her father throwing a handful of dirt into the grave.

She forced her mind back to the present. To their garden, where weeds throttled the beds. The walls surrounding the lawn were patched and crumbling and smothered in ivy. There was a sprawling magnolia to the side and more trees in one corner, apple and pear, but no one bothered to pick the fruit, and every autumn it was devoured by wasps or left to rot on the ground.

Tea towels were pegged on the line. A pile of rubbish had been left in one corner. At the end, bushes obscured a section of grass. Kenneth had a rose garden and there was an old shed that leaned precariously to one side. An arched doorway had been built into the far wall as access to the churchyard, the door a heavy, studded affair. Connie avoided going that way to her mother's grave. She disliked the shadows and sudden transition from garden to tombstones, the oldest graves broken and lopsided, as if the dead were restlessly shifting beneath the earth.

When she was small, before Kenneth began to grow roses, her mother had a vegetable patch in the rear section of the garden. Connie had helped her look after it, bending to heave out carrots and potatoes. It had amazed her that vegetables could grow in the dark, cold ground. It was a place for dead things, wasn't it, like in the churchyard where bodies rotted and worms feasted? She had woken in the night, gasping with fear, her dreams full of bodies caught under that weight of earth, like the story she had found in the bookshop about the old man stuck beneath the floorboards, his tell-tale heart beating louder and louder.

How cold must her mother be in the ground? Connie wanted to cover the grave with a blanket or lie on top of the stone as if her warmth might permeate the earth. She would do *anything* to have one more day, one more hour, a single moment with her mother. For the chance to touch her face, her hands, to smell her perfume and hear her voice.

Suddenly, hands grabbed her waist and pinned her to the sink. Victor had come in so softly she hadn't heard him.

She brushed away her tears. Turned grief into anger. 'Get off me,' she said, pushing hard against him.

He held her fast, nuzzled his nose into her neck.

'Get off me,' she hissed again, shoving at his hands. 'What's wrong with you?' She jabbed him in the ribs with her elbow and whipped round. 'What do you want?'

'Come on, Connie,' he said, 'are you so innocent you have to ask?'

She resisted the urge to slap him.

'Everything all right?' called her father from the other room.

They stared at each other, Victor smirking, Connie's eyes blazing.

'Fine,' she called out quickly, and to Victor in a lower voice, 'I'll tell him.'

'No, you won't.'

She hated his cockiness especially because he was right. Her fingers itched to grab the chopping board or the rolling pin to bring down on his head.

'You could do worse.'

'I could do better.'

He laughed as she marched past him out into the passage and into her bedroom. Closing the door behind her, she pushed a chair against the handle and sat on the stool at the dressing table. She was trembling with rage more than fear. What right did he have to touch her? She considered her face in the mirror. She looked terrible – features blurred, face puffy. She felt her stomach but it was still flat. Maybe Doctor Franklin was right. She clung once again to the thought. She needed a tonic. Girls missed their periods for all kinds of reasons.

But they weren't sick most mornings.

She leaned her elbows on the table and put her head in her hands. Only today she had vomited in the toilet bowl, turning up the volume of her transistor radio to drown out the sound.

Stifling the sob that was rising inside her, she got up and crossed to the bed. Lying down, she focused on Johnny, imagining him in Paris. She tried to picture his face, but Victor's smirk appeared instead. She could feel the imprint of his hands on her waist. He had bothered her for months, but he was going further and further every time they met. What if next time he touched her he felt the change in her body and guessed?

She shivered even though it wasn't cold.

How could she think straight with a baby growing inside her? She saw it as a seed, throwing out shoots, tiny arms and legs, growing and ripening – and yet she knew nothing about having babies. What if it didn't grow properly? What if it didn't come out? She pictured the fruit rotting in the garden. No one clearing it away.

She had to tell her father. Or else she had to get rid of the baby herself. Doctors were never going to help her. She must find a different way.

From Mrs Kolinski's flat upstairs came the sound of the piano. Chopin, a nocturne. The music soothed her, the notes tumbling, rising, spreading. She lay on her side on the mattress, absorbing the sound, trying to settle, but her mind whirled with contradictions and unsatisfactory solutions. From the other room, the clock chimed five.

*

At last she heard the front door opening as the men exited. She heard their voices too, greeting Dorothy on the landing. An idea struck Connie as the door banged shut. She swung her legs over the bed and onto the floor. Johnny hadn't sent her his address, but he might have sent it to his mother. Despite their furious rows, surely he would be in touch. Maybe Connie should ask her.

She let the possibility simmer before storing it away. It might not come to that – any day her period could arrive. The tonic Doctor Franklin had given her would work. As if to ensure it, she took the bottle from her drawer and measured out a spoonful. It was bright red, like blood, and it tasted as bitter as poison. It occurred to her that the doctor had given her a purge to get rid of the baby because even though she hadn't mentioned being pregnant, he had somehow known.

She shook her head. Not possible. He didn't, couldn't know. Nobody knew but Connie, and apart from her it was only Johnny who *should* know. Soon he would send a letter with his address and she would write back and explain what had happened. She could even turn up in Paris and surprise him. He had said she should come. Her heart danced. Imagine that. Imagine his face. What if she could find the money to pay for a ticket to Paris?

The idea gave Connie energy. She sat at the dressing table and examined her face. It had more colour than before. The rest had done her good. She brushed her hair. When she was little, her mother had teased out the tangles with a comb. Now Connie saw her mother's face in the mirror instead of her own, and there, further away, she imagined another girl with the darkest of hair, and another and another. A whole thread of generations stretching through the years.

Later, she fried lamb chops and boiled potatoes for tea and sat with her father at the kitchen table. Mealtimes were pleasant but quiet. Her mother had been the joyful one, filling the flat with her voice and her laughter.

While Connie dished up, her father sat at the table reading a letter from his sister. Maud lived in Whitby after marrying a policeman from Yorkshire down in London for a visit. The two of them had opened a sweet shop. The policeman had died of coronary disease, but Maud had stayed and Connie and her parents had visited every summer.

'Maud wants us to come.'

Connie stopped her thoughts. 'When?'

'In August – usual time.' He looked at her over the top of his glasses. 'What do you think?'

They hadn't been to Whitby since Connie's mother had died. One summer had gone already and now another one loomed.

'I don't know.' She sat down. 'Would you like to?'

He sighed and took off his glasses, rubbed his eyes. 'I can't.'

'Why not?'

He hesitated. 'The shop.'

There was a silence. They both knew that wasn't the real reason. 'We closed it when we went before,' Connie reminded him gently.

'I know, but business . . .'

'I can stay behind. I can deal with it.'

He shook his head. 'No.'

'Why not? I'm seventeen. I know exactly what to do. You need a holiday. Think of Aunt Maud and all that home cooking.'

He smiled at her fondly and picked up his knife and fork. 'Your cooking is perfect, Connie.'

Not true. The potatoes were over-boiled and the chops tough. She attempted dishes, but she didn't have the knack, not like her mother, or Aunt Maud.

She tried again. 'What about the sea air? You need a holiday, Dad. You need to get away from the city.'

He smiled again, his determination weakening. 'You, my dear, get more and more like your mother every day.'

Connie looked down at her plate. If she was like her mother she wouldn't be in the fix she was.

'Anyway,' he went on, 'we've got a few months to decide. Anything can happen in that time.'

She nodded, her stomach churning. Anything *could* happen. Although some things were inevitable.

After they had eaten and Connie had cleared away, she went to her room pleading tiredness. Unable to sleep, she stood at the window.

A figure skulked in the dark, the tip of a cigarette dancing in the gloom. Kenneth – doing his *yard exercise*, as he called it. He headed away from the house. Connie followed his progress to the end of the garden and then watched as he stepped past the bushes and disappeared.

Clouds covered the moon and the garden dropped

into shadow. It struck Connie how tiny she was in comparison to the vastness of the sky.

How odd to think that life would carry on when she had gone in the same way it had continued without her mother. Someone else would gaze from this same window and the church would still be there, but the graveyard would hold her mother and her father and herself, no doubt.

She got into bed. She could hear her father moving about, rolling back the lid of the bureau. He would be checking the accounts, or writing a letter to Maud, or looking at photos of her mother. She lay with her hands on her belly. A girl, she thought as she drifted into sleep; a girl with dark hair like Eva Kolinski.

5

Marina

January 1992

Marina parks haphazardly, drags suitcases and bags from the car and dumps them at the bottom of the steps. It has been raining, the earth around the trunk of the maple tree is damp and patches of wet concrete glisten in the struggling afternoon light.

She unbuttons her faux-fur coat slowly as she stares upwards at the house, peels off one fingerless glove and rakes at her knotted hair. She feels dishevelled after her journey, and stiff after being hunched at the wheel for so long, beetling on the motorway as fast as the Mini would take her, stopping once at a service station for coffee that tasted like flavoured water and then speeding away again, pushing aside all reservations as she drove.

A tall, thin man, who looks around Marina's age, leaps up the steps from the basement, shoes clanking on the metal. He has light hair, rectangular glasses with thick, black frames, and a cigarette tucked behind one ear. Despite the cold, he wears a short-sleeved shirt, with a battered looking leather jacket hooked on one finger and slung over his shoulder.

He halts at the sight of her. 'Can I help you?'

She smiles brightly back at him. 'I'm moving in.'

He looks at her, incredulous brown eyes blinking behind his lenses. 'Into this house?' He jabs at number 24.

'Well, yes. Flat 2.' She holds out the letter from the estate agent as if to prove it.

'Flat 2,' he parrots. 'But that flat . . .' He stops, scratches his head.

'Yes?'

'Well, it's empty.'

'I should hope so.' A light-hearted approach seems the best way to deal with this man who is looking at her as if she's travelled in time.

'I mean . . . it hasn't been lived in for months. And months.' He stops again, flustered.

'It's all right,' says Marina. 'I've seen the state of it and I also know what happened to the last tenant.'

The estate agent had explained that an old man had lived – and died – in the flat previously, which was another reason it hadn't been easy to let.

'Right.' He looks at her warily.

'And I'm not afraid of ghosts.'

'Ghosts?'

'Seriously. I don't believe in them.'

'Don't you? I mean, that's good.'

'Or just as well.'

A smile curls on his lips at last. He is good-looking in a thin-faced, wolfish way, but there is nothing of the predator about him. He is too self-conscious, and even now he's blushing as he grabs one of her bags and says, 'Let me.' Why not? They walk up the steps together.

In the entrance, Marina pauses. The hall is exactly as it was when she did the tour with the estate agent, but somehow it's still a shock to Marina that she's here, and she gazes about her as if she's never set foot in the place, taking in the single ceiling bulb – its push-button switch on an automatic timer – that illuminates the black and white floor tiles and walls painted ice blue; the bronze sconces, once elegant, now rusted, their sockets empty. The sun struggling through the rectangular stained-glass window above the front door is the only other source of light.

The wide stairway dominates the space. A hundred years ago, it might have been a polished centrepiece. Now the red carpet running along the middle of the stairs is faded and threadbare, the visible treads and the bannister scratched and worn. The first flight hits a blank wall. The second angles away into darkness.

On either side of the staircase are the doors to Flats 1 and 2. Flat 2 is on the right. Marina produces her set of keys and fits first one and then another into the lock until she gets it right. Cautiously, she pushes open the door and steps inside. The flat has a sour smell, a mix of ingrained sweat, mustiness and dirt. She wrinkles her nose and goes straight to the window. Pushing the net curtains aside she heaves up the sash.

The man has followed her in. 'I'm Ron, by the way,' he says, setting her suitcase on a brown rug that looks like a flayed bear.

She hesitates before telling him she is Zoe. In the end, although she'd signed her middle name on the contract, she couldn't hide her first name on the photocopy of her passport. She told them she preferred to go by the name Zoe and nothing much was said. But here in the house, there is still the worry that someone might remember her story – Marina, the baby in blue, and she doesn't want to draw attention to that before she's had a chance to settle.

He extends his hand and she removes her glove to shake it. His palm is as warm as hers is cold.

'If you need anything,' he says, 'just ask.'

'Thank you.'

He scratches his chin. 'And sorry about my reaction out there. I'm not usually that unfriendly – or disbelieving. You took me by surprise. No one told us there was a new tenant and, to be honest, I didn't think anyone would ever take this flat, people are a bit . . . well, you know . . .'

'Superstitious?'

'Exactly.'

'Did you know him?' Marina asks, thinking there's no time like the present to start investigating.

'The guy that died? No. Before my time.'

'How long have you been here?'

'Six months, but I've got something else lined up.'

'So soon?'

'Yeah, well, it's not exactly the Ritz.' He sweeps his arm around the room and grimaces.

Marina grins. 'I've seen worse. I once had rats for flatmates.'

He frowns, not understanding. 'You mean literally?'

'Yes, literally. Rats. Under the stairs. Mind you I've lived with the human kind too.'

She rattles out a story about a boyfriend at university. Three weeks she had lived in his dingy flat listening to the sound of rodents scrabbling behind the walls and beneath the floorboards. One day a larger creature in a fur coat had turned up claiming to be his girlfriend. 'And that was the end of that.'

Ron laughs. 'Then this will seem like a palace.'

'I hope so.'

There's another pause. Ron taps his foot. 'I'll get some more bags.' He is gone before she can stop him.

Alone, she looks around the room. It was two months ago that she met Wayne, the estate agent, a young man in a suit and shoes so pointed they were almost winkle-pickers. His first utterance had been an apology for the state of the decoration; his second, a promise that he could reduce the already low rent still further. They had climbed the steps together, him still talking, her breath caught so hard she couldn't have answered if she had tried. Her head had pounded and his voice had faded into the background until she eventually gave up all hope of following or remembering what he said.

The hallway was imprinted on her memory, but the rest of the visit had been a haze as she simply went through the motions. Still, she must have registered something, because she recognises the black painted fireplace with its chipped pink and blue surround, and she recalls how when she had emerged from the building, she had felt as if a spell had been lifted. How surprised Wayne had been when she'd told him she would take the flat and there was no need to bother the landlord about decorating because she would do it herself. Wayne hadn't even minded when she'd explained she must delay moving in because she couldn't afford double rent.

'That's fine,' he'd said, beaming and pumping her hand, 'and don't worry if anyone else comes forward, I'll tell them the flat's reserved.'

As if either of them thought that would happen.

'Where do you want them?' says Ron, returning with a suitcase in one hand and a rucksack in the other.

'Anywhere, thank you, but you don't need . . .'

Too late: he disappears again, bounding away for the rest of her things, reminding Marina more of a rangy puppy than the wolf she compared him to at first.

The room is dark and claustrophobic after her flat in Wiltshire and she drags back the net curtains again to let in the fading light. There is a chemical smell, but already patches of mould are showing beneath the window.

Ron returns with the final bag and finds her peering at the wall. 'I get that too,' he says. 'Bleach works. You can borrow mine.'

'Thanks,' says Marina, straightening. 'I brought a bottle with me, but by the looks of this I'll need a whole lot more. Don't you complain?'

'No point. Landlord's a lazy bastard.'

'I gathered as much.'

He stands without speaking, scratching his chin. She's busy looking out the window. Apart from the maple tree, the view is parked cars, bricks and mortar. There's a pair of semi-detached houses opposite. One is boarded up, the other has a window box waiting for spring.

'Is it always this quiet?' she says.

'Pretty much, especially at the weekend.'

'No children?'

'It's an old people's road. People come and they stay. Apart from me, I suppose.'

Marina nods absent-mindedly. How long will she be here? In the end, she had told Ruth and David the truth about taking the flat in Harrington Gardens. She couldn't just disappear with no forwarding address. They had questioned and worried but, as always, had supported her and even lent her money. Together with the cheap rent, her earnings from Agata's editing job and a few more projects in the pipeline, it means she'll survive for a while.

'Is there anything you need to know?' Ron ventures. 'Bins, post, communal spaces, fascinating stuff like that?'

She smiles. 'Thanks, but no, the estate agent was thorough. Anyway, weren't you on your way out?'

'Pint at the local. Want to come?'

Marina indicates the mouldy wall. 'I should stay and attack this.'

He shrugs. 'OK. Let me know, though . . . about the bleach, I mean.'

She closes the door behind him and surveys the room. A sense of audacity threatens to overwhelm her and she suddenly laughs out loud. The thought of it . . . moving into the place where she began. *Might have begun.* The correction sobers her. She steadies herself and takes in the reality instead. A grubby, neglected flat. A lonely quest to find her mother. A perfectly loving family left behind.

The bedroom is at the rear of the house. It's stuffy and smells of dust. Marina pulls the net curtains aside and peers out. Ahead of her is a walled garden, edged with fruit trees and shrubs and an overgrown magnolia. It's not well kept, but it's not shocking either. The lawn is mowed; the borders neat. At the far end is a section partially obscured by overgrown bushes.

The grey stone church rises beyond like a spectre. No wonder people were reluctant to rent this place with a graveyard practically in the garden. A man dying in the flat itself and bodies in the backyard is macabre, not to mention the neglected state of the place. Still, she won't let a small issue like dirt and death put her off. She has a mission: to find those who were here in 1964, and who might remember a baby abandoned in a hallway.

The devil is in the detail. The saying comes to her as she unhooks the net curtains and rolls them into a grubby ball. What does it mean exactly? Small clues that make a difference. But do those clues complicate or reveal? She isn't sure.

In the kitchen, she unpacks cleaning materials and scrubs the cupboards that date from the fifties. The lingering scent of disinfectant suggests an effort has been made, but still she unpicks bits of old food from the corners, gathers up dead flies and earwigs, sweeps away the cobwebs.

This is what you get for the sake of a very cheap rent she thinks, grimly regarding the pull-down worktop-cum-breakfast-table. It is scratched and stained and by the look of it entirely forgotten by whoever made the half-hearted effort to clean the flat ahead of her moving in. She uses a knife to scrape away a smear of what could be dried egg or custard or pea soup. The cooker and fridge are ancient but serviceable, though the metal guards around the gas rings are stained. She removes the guards and puts them in the sink to soak. Nothing about this old-fashioned kitchen is quaint and no amount of bleach will get rid of the brown streaks caused by the endlessly dripping tap. At least the old boiler works, after a fashion: the water is scalding, the radiators lukewarm.

Shoving the provisions she brought with her into the fridge, she heads to the bedroom and there, trying not to picture who slept on it last, heaves the mattress over, quickly covering it with her own bedding. She dusts and hoovers, hangs her clothes in the ungainly wardrobe and then moves onto the bathroom where she grimaces again at the chipped bath and stained toilet bowl, the rusty cistern and chain. She won't think of whoever lay in this bath before her. She won't think of them sitting on the toilet seat. She won't think of the man who died, or wonder where or how. It's no wonder that this place is cheap.

The living room gets the same treatment and she cleans the mouldy wall with bleach. Delving into her bags, she drags out a pile of books and sets them on a shelf. There is a telephone directory and, oddly, a copy of the New Testament already there. She finds a framed photo of Ruth and David standing by the White Horse and places it on the mantelpiece. It was taken last summer on her birthday, 7 August. Only that isn't her real birthday. It's the date she was found. A tiny baby, the doctors had said she must have been early. Two or three days old. Nobody was sure.

Marina finishes arranging the room and has a cigarette, standing at the window. She contemplates the street, watching the comings and goings, which as Ron has said are few and far between. While she stands there she sees a man pulled along by a German Shepherd, a young woman riding her bike, an elderly couple walking hand in hand.

Keen to escape the stench of bleach, she steps out of the flat and into the hall. The house is eerily quiet. No clatter of pans or rising smells of onion and garlic or frying meat signifying evening meals, no hungry people rushing home. There is only the musty scent that pervades her flat, and the shifts and groans of the building. She pushes the light-switch. The light is dim. She looks up the stairs and the darkness thickens.

Beside her, the front door is ajar and the detail strikes a chord in her memory: she recalls a clipping she read, an interview with the landlord, Kenneth Quip, who had lived on the premises at the time she was discovered. In the interview, he had mentioned that the door was often left open by neglectful tenants. On that particular morning, when Baby Blue – Marina – was found, he was certain it had been ajar. How easy for a woman to come into the house, to place a bundle on the floor and disappear.

Where would she have left the baby?

Marina's gaze falls on the alcove by the door. Now it's a mess of abandoned boots and brollies. An old bike leans against the wall. But there is space. It's a perfect place: safe and hidden. She crouches and touches the tiles with the flat of her hand. Was it here where she lay? She closes her eyes, searching for answers to her questions. Had she been sleeping, or had she cried for her mother? How long had she been there alone? She shivers, afraid of the answers, and stands slowly, looking about her, sensing a chill like the breath of a ghost. The timer stops and the light goes off.

Marina steps outside; it's a relief to escape the disquiet inside her head, to warm her cold face in a patch of weak sunlight. What a miserable day to have arrived here. She flexes her fingers, fumbles for her gloves in her pocket and pulls them on. Standing there, she rakes over the information she has gleaned through the years. She pictures the plan she once drew of the tenants who had lived here in 1964, at least the ones who had come up in the newspapers: the basement flat, occupied by Victor Wallace; Flat 1, Kenneth Quip, the landlord; Flat 2, Leonard Crisp and Eileen Clarke, who were actors, apparently; Flat 3, Dorothy Light; Flat 4, Thomas Littleton; Flat 5, Natalia Kolinski.

Marina's mind returns to the story of the pregnant woman spotted by a tenant. The tenant was Mrs Kolinski and, according to her, the woman had appeared several times in the months leading up to the abandonment. Who was she? Why hadn't the police tracked her down?

The street lamp in front of the house flickers and comes on. Sickly yellow, it shines on the branches of the maple tree. The tree is spindly and tired-looking, giving the same impression of neglect as the house.

Inside the hall again, she switches on the light then closes the front door, crosses to the far wall and examines a set of five metal letter boxes nailed side by side. She goes through a present-day roll call.

FLAT 1: GIOVANNI GAETTI

Flat 2 is hers, unlabelled.

FLAT 3: HYDE
FLAT 4: MR AND MRS HAMILTON
FLAT 5: KOLINSKI

Kolinski. A connection, the only one, reaching back into the past. Natalia, or a relative?

The silence of the house is broken by a piano. Chopin. The notes drift and, like soft chains, shackle Marina in the hallway. The music stops and she is released, but drawn to its source. The original light has clicked off, but she turns on another – a switch near the stairs this time – and heads up, one hand on the rough bannister, going slowly, taking everything in. The paint is the same cold blue as in the hallway, showing the occasional warm tone of dark green underneath. In places, chunks of plaster have dropped from the ceiling, leaving layers of fine white dust. The house is neglected inside and out, with cracks in the walls and cobwebs in the corners. The landlord should be ashamed, letting the place fall in on itself like this.

The light is weak and barely lasts the climb to the first floor before there is a popping sound. Darkness returns. Fumbling for a switch, Marina discovers another button on a timer, just as in the hall below. She pushes hard and the mechanism whirrs.

The landing is an empty rectangle with bare, dusty boards. Straight ahead is the next flight of stairs. The doors to Flats 3 and 4 sit squarely opposite each other. Marina listens at each one, but there is no sound or movement. She has an odd sensation of having been here before, but knows that she hasn't, not even with Wayne. It's a trick of her imagination, or else she has seen this part of the house in a newspaper clipping and has forgotten.

The music starts again – coming from above. The next flight that leads to the second floor is in darkness. Finding another button, Marina pushes firmly and looks around. Warily, she follows the sound. This stairway is narrower than the first. It's steeper too. Perhaps once upon a time this was the servants' quarters.

She goes slowly and by the time she reaches the second-floor landing, which is much smaller than the one below, the light has clicked off again. However, there's a tiny window set high in the wall on the side of the house, and the late-afternoon sunshine spills weakly through. Marina can see the door of Flat 5 to the right, but there's a door opposite too. She moves across, twists the handle and it swings open. A staircase leads to what must be the attic, high in the eaves. The bare wood steps are stained and splintered and she's about to climb them when the music stops.

On impulse, she turns to Flat 5 and knocks softly. A moment goes by and she raps a little louder. Leaning her head closer, she listens. Nothing. She imagines a woman, although it could be a man, standing a foot away, the two of them separated by the door. Marina plumps for a woman. Is she there, deciding whether to admit this unexpected visitor? Is her hand on the latch? A narrow hand with long fingers and trimmed nails: a pianist's hands. Is she old or is she young? Can Marina hear breathing, in time with her own?

A few more moments pass and the door remains

resolutely shut. Reluctantly Marina leaves. This person, Kolinski, doesn't want to be disturbed.

On the way down, the door to Flat 3 opens abruptly and out steps a short woman in a plain brown coat, a matching hat with a pin, and a handbag hooked over one arm. Seeing Marina, she startles and raises a hand to her mouth. 'Oh,' she says. Her face pales.

'I'm sorry,' says Marina immediately. 'Did I startle you?' She smiles. 'You must be Mrs Hyde. I've just moved into Flat 2 and I saw your name on the post box.'

The woman doesn't answer, only gawks at Marina. In her late sixties, she has a smear of pink across her lips, but she's missed the edges, and her powder accentuates the lines on her face. Her features are sharp, eyes small. Wisps of white hair escape from her hat. Her pose is still, her gaze steady. Marina apologises again for making her jump. Her voice sounds loud in the quiet of the house.

The woman recovers, nods and turns to fiddle with the lock. 'I hope you've settled in,' she says over her shoulder. Her voice is rasping, almost inaudible.

'Thank you,' Marina replies. 'I heard the piano and was curious. The player is very talented.' She hesitates, hoping Mrs Hyde will provide information, but the woman doesn't seem the gossiping type. Quite the contrary, in fact. Ignoring the comment, she opens her handbag, drops the keys inside and closes it with a snap.

Now Marina sees that she has a bible in her hand. 'Off to church?' she says, anxious to be friendly. It isn't Sunday. Perhaps she has a bible class.

Mrs Hyde grimaces and nods and then heads towards the stairs.

'Have you lived here long?' Marina calls after her.

No answer. Maybe she's hard of hearing. There's certainly nothing wrong with her mobility. Marina hurries to keep up as the older woman scuttles down the stairs. In the hall, she asks again.

Mrs Hyde pauses and blinks. 'For a while,' she says, 'and now if you'll excuse me . . .'

She disappears through the front door – leaving it open – and Marina is left with a precarious sensation, as if she's been set adrift. She can still smell the woman's scent, a mix of cold cream and eau de cologne, and she breathes it in like a hunter following a trail.

6

Eva

Eva scrutinises the piano keys. She has made mistake after mistake with this piece. Is she ever going to get it right?

She flexes her fingers, examines her nails. She has been off colour for weeks, ever since she saw the woman in the lamplight, staring at the house. Midnight, awake as usual, she had made hot chocolate and stood at the frosty window warming her hands. How unnerving it had been, seeing the figure standing there like a beautiful statue with the snow settling on her thick, dark hair. Intrigued, Eva had switched off the light and watched.

Two months later and the woman had moved into the building. Eva had recognised the old Mini first and then the woman emerging from the car and hauling out bags. Faux-fur coat and fingerless gloves. *That hair.* There had been no mistaking it was the same person. Ron had helped and Eva had watched him buzzing around with a tinge of jealousy that she had quickly stifled. After all, it had been her fault that she and Ron had broken up. She had rejected him.

She remembers when Ron had moved in. Her mother, Natalia, had met him first, outside on the pavement; had rushed to tell Eva how good-looking he was, how interesting too. He worked in a museum. Natalia had been impressed by that. She liked the kind of people who were interested in history, or the arts – or music, of course. And she had been excited in a way Eva hadn't seen for a while.

A few months later, Natalia had had a heart attack. How difficult Eva had found that to comprehend when her mother had always been so slim, so active. She had walked everywhere, to the shops, to the houses of the ladies she sewed for and of the pupils she taught. And she'd had stamina, staying up late at night to perfect her piano pieces or to finish the clothes or the curtains that she made. It had been a real shock. Her beautiful mother gone – just like that. Some days Eva had hardly been able to get out of bed, and there was no way she could leave the house. It was as if she had drifted back to the dark days when she was a child, suffering from vertigo and panic attacks.

Everyone had been kind. Selena Hamilton, the lady below in Flat 4, had brought her food. Her mother's ex-pupils and their parents had dropped round with flowers and commiserations. There were no relatives alive. Not that Natalia had known about, anyway, and that in itself made Eva feel alone. What would she do? The flat was only rented. Her mother had no money to speak of, which was why they had never moved, and Eva had no qualifications or prospects. She could teach piano, but that was about it. She couldn't even sew.

One day, not long after the funeral, Ron had knocked on Eva's door. He had brought her a box of Turkish Delight. The gesture, along with his shy kindness, had touched her. She had accepted his gift and they had

talked. Their friendship had grown and become something more – until a silly disagreement had separated
them.

She thought about that now. He had criticised her,
said she shuttered her emotions. *Shuttered*. Was that the
word he had used? Either way, he meant that she had a
way of seeming absent even when physically present. She
had taken umbrage, although it was true. And that last
day, when they had planned to go to the common for a
walk, she had still been resentful.

It was the furthest Eva had agreed to go since her
mother's funeral. Until then, she had only been to the hall
to collect her post. She hadn't even ventured to Ron's flat.

Nothing had happened until they stepped onto the
landing. Then the dizziness had come – a teetering sensation as if she were about to fall. She'd heard voices
filtering up from the floor below. A door slamming.
Music playing. It was all in her imagination, of course,
but she had felt fear slinking through her bones, a familiar sense of darkness. She had tried to anchor herself in
the present, the here and now, but it was hard and, ter-
rified of giving herself away, she'd made an excuse to
stay at home. The conversation had turned into an argu-
ment and then she'd sent him away.

It had been an *episode*. Like those she had had as a
child when her mother would find her staring into space,
more in a trance than in a daydream, as if she had
dropped out of the world. It was literally like falling,
although she didn't know whether it was she who was
falling, or the world about her.

Then, she had seen doctors and psychologists, taken

tests, had checks and assessments. The professionals had gathered and discussed and compared notes. But no one had come up with anything other than a vague suggestion of post-traumatic stress, brought on by childhood shock: she'd seen her father knocked down by a bus, and watched her mother have a miscarriage – although she could remember neither event, and no amount of coaxing or cajoling could bring the memories back.

At school, when she had managed to get there, she had been silent and serene, unemotional, a remarkable musical talent. The bullies hadn't understood her so had left her alone. At music college, she had taken on a similar persona, staying in her room at halls and avoiding communal areas like the students' union and bar. She had gone only to the lessons that she had been obliged to go to and spent excessive hours in the practice rooms.

Now, she strikes a chord. She's playing Chopin, Nocturne in E flat major, Op. 9, No. 2. It was her mother's favourite piece and she wants to get it right. Not that she'll ever be able to play as well as her mother used to do. Her mother could have been a concert pianist if her life had turned out differently. If she hadn't experienced the horror of persecution in the Second World War. Even after she had escaped Poland and come to London, life had never been a bed of roses.

Roses. A memory tugs. A face. The curve of a cheek.

Eva shivers and plays more notes. She misses her mother. No one gets over losing their mother. That's the truth. What will she do? Move away? Stay in the flat? She strikes another chord. And then another. She thinks of the woman downstairs. Maybe it was her hair that had unsettled her. Dark like Eva's mother's. Like Eva's. Mind you, the last time she had spoken to a doctor, he had told her if she didn't eat properly, her hair would fall out before she was thirty-five. An exaggeration, of course, but even so.

She plays again, her fingers running lightly across the keys. Better. Standing, she heads to the kitchen to make coffee. She has a rule. One coffee a day. No milk. Late afternoon to pick up her spirits.

There is a light knock on the door. Eva hesitates. She is expecting a pupil, but Toby is young and he hammers on the door. Besides, it's too early. It's not him. She steps forward, her breath rising and falling. She has a second rule that she only opens the door when she knows who is there and a third rule that she never invites people into her flat unless they have a prior appointment. Since that applies only to her pupils or the occasional plumber or electrician, and Ron of course when she was seeing him, she rarely speaks to anyone.

Edging closer, she listens. The person knocks again, a little more loudly. Eva steadies herself, fingers on the doorframe for balance. The footsteps retreat; she can hear a light tread on the stairs.

Moments pass. Gently she opens the door. Voices float upwards from the landing on the floor below and she knows without seeing that one of them belongs to the beautiful woman downstairs.

7

Connie

May 1964

Dorothy Light opened the door swiftly as if she had a place to go. A tiny woman with pointed features and mousy hair scraped into a bun, she wore a drab mustard-coloured dress and a brown apron tied at the waist. Her make-up on the other hand was vivid: bright slabs of blue eyeshadow, daring dabs of rouge, a pink slash of lipstick.

'Yes?' she said. 'Can I help you?'

Connie held out the tea towel she'd retrieved from the line. A souvenir of the coronation, and no doubt Kenneth's, but a good enough excuse to knock. 'I think this might be yours.'

Dorothy shook her head. 'Oh no, speak to Kenneth. It's most likely his.' Then, when Connie stayed, she added, 'Is there anything else?'

Connie cleared her throat. 'I wondered if you had Johnny's address.'

'I'm afraid I don't. Why do you want it?'

Connie lowered her voice. Walls had ears, as her mother used to say, and so did people lurking – and right now she could hear Kenneth's shuffle and the tap of his silver-topped stick. 'There's something I need to tell him.'

'What kind of something?' Dorothy narrowed her gaze. She had small eyes, blue like her son's, but that was the only resemblance. Johnny was tall with broad shoulders. He took up space. Dorothy was compact.

Connie shifted where she stood. She could feel the sweat beneath the waistband of her dress. All morning she had felt stifled in the airless flat. Her father had gone to the bookshop even though it was Sunday. He was waiting for word of an *interesting item* as he called it, a rare book put up for sale by a private collector in York. When the time came, he would travel to York to fetch it and Connie had suggested he tie it in with a visit to Aunt Maud in Whitby.

'It's about an art exhibition,' said Connie, flushing at the untruth and trying to recall what artists were actually showing in London. Dorothy looked blank. 'It's a brilliant exhibition, so if you do hear from him . . .'

Still no response. Connie's shoulders slumped. She hadn't eaten since breakfast and it was two o'clock already. She leaned against the wall and closed her eyes. When she opened them again, Dorothy was looking at her with a curious expression. 'I think you'd better come in.'

Without thinking, Connie stepped forward. She regretted her decision immediately. The flat was even hotter than theirs, with clutter everywhere: baskets of clothes, an ironing board, piles of magazines and papers; while photos of Johnny adorned the mantelpiece, the sideboard, the table and the walls. Connie's stomach churned at the smell, a mix of starch, Windolene and sweet perfume. A bunch of keys attached to a giant ring lay beside the wireless on the sideboard. A prison warder's keys,

Connie thought as she imagined them hanging at Dorothy's waist.

Heaving a basket from the settee, Dorothy gestured for Connie to take its place before sitting in the armchair opposite.

'So,' she said, folding her spindly arms, 'tell me more.'

'Well,' said Connie quickly, 'Johnny promised to write to me and I promised to write back, only I haven't heard from him and . . . well, I'm interested in art and travelling and I'm hoping to visit Paris at some point . . . in the future . . . when my father . . .'

She fell silent. A fat bluebottle buzzed in through the open window. Connie watched its jerky, panicked flight and sudden halt as it landed on a strip of flypaper hanging from the ceiling which was already speckled with dark, dead insects.

Dorothy watched too. And then she sighed. 'I think you need to forget about him.'

'What do you mean?'

'I mean Johnny hasn't contacted me – his own mother – so what makes you believe he's going to contact you?'

'Because . . .'

Connie stopped and looked away. Why *hadn't* Johnny contacted either of them?

'The thing is,' Dorothy said, without taking her eyes from the fly, 'young people think they invented it all, that no one else has ever *been there* or *done that* before.'

Connie was taken aback. This had nothing to do with her request. 'I'm not sure what you mean.'

Dorothy shifted her gaze from the flypaper and fixed

her eyes on Connie again. 'No,' she said quietly, 'I don't suppose you do.'

And then quite abruptly, her manner changed. She became brisk, attentive. 'Listen,' she said. 'I know what's been going on, so there's no need to make excuses about art and whatnot.'

Connie waited, uncertain. Had Johnny told his mother about the two of them? As far as she knew, he had kept their relationship a secret, just as Connie had.

'I've known for a long time,' Dorothy continued. She held up one hand, palm facing outwards. 'And before you ask, no he didn't tell me. Johnny has never confided in me much.'

Connie detected a catch in her voice. When Johnny had spoken about his mother, it had always been with resentment, even contempt. He was misunderstood, he claimed, born into the wrong life. Now she wondered if Dorothy had felt hurt by her son's attitude. Connie glanced at the photos around the room. Whatever Johnny said, these pictures showed devotion.

'However,' she continued, 'I am an observant person. Not that it was hard to miss – all those trips to the attic.'

She raised her eyebrows again and the heat on Connie's face grew stronger. What exactly did Dorothy know?

'The thing is,' she said again, folding her hands neatly on her lap, 'Johnny hasn't contacted you and he hasn't contacted me. Those are the plain facts. We can only hope that he'll come home when he's ready.'

Connie wanted to shout out that she didn't have time to wait. She needed to speak to Johnny now. Instead, she said awkwardly, 'Yes.' She was beginning to feel quite sick again.

A moment passed. Then Dorothy stood up, crossed to the sofa and took Connie's hand. 'Poor girl. It can't be easy without a mother to advise you.'

Dorothy's palm felt rough from hard work. Connie's mother had had skin like that too. Connie pictured her applying cream, kneading it into her hands. She remembered how it had smelled of lavender, but what had the cream been called? And now she felt a panic because she couldn't recall. How many other memories was she losing?

The idea made her feel strangely dizzy. She passed her hand across her damp forehead. Dorothy was still looking at her with that bright, blue stare. She thought of her mother's kind, gentle eyes, of Johnny's distant gaze, always wanting something else. And then she thought of her father and how disappointed his expression would be if he found out about the baby. And there was Dorothy still watching, a small, knowing smile etched on her face. Connie tried to speak but her tongue felt thick. She tried to see clearly but the light was fading and the room was turning.

'Head between your knees,' came Dorothy's distant voice. 'Deep breaths. I'll fetch some water.'

Connie obeyed, leaning forward, breathing steadily, and by the time Dorothy returned, the room had stilled and the light had brightened. Taking the glass, she drank deeply.

'There,' said Dorothy, sitting down and patting Connie's knee. 'Feeling better?'

Connie nodded although the dizziness had left an ache inside her head. She finished drinking and Dorothy took the glass.

'Now then,' she said, setting it down on the carpet. 'Tell me what's wrong.'

Connie massaged her temples. 'I'm sorry. I haven't eaten. I think that's what it is.'

Dorothy sighed. 'Oh dear, do you think I was born yesterday? It all comes back to the idea that the younger generation think they invented it.'

'I don't understand,' said Connie, and she really didn't. The conversation had gone around so many corners she had lost her way.

'Temptation,' said Dorothy. 'I was young once, believe it or not, and I know what men can be like. Even my son. My husband . . . well, he was . . .' She stopped and eyed Connie. 'Let's just say that both his presence and his absence had a bad effect on Johnny. It caused a certain weakness in him. Johnny's not a bad person, but . . . men and boys, well . . . you and I both understand how it is. It's the way of the world.'

'What do you mean?'

'I don't have to spell it out, do I? I know, dear – about your predicament. You're pregnant, aren't you?'

Connie felt herself turn pale. Was it so obvious? And if Dorothy had guessed, had anybody else?

'I was a midwife,' she said, reading Connie's mind, 'so it's easy for me to spot. I doubt very much anyone else has seen it.' She paused before adding, 'Yet.'

Connie hung her head. The pain was subsiding, but the queasiness had returned.

'Now listen, dear. Don't get upset. I know how you feel because . . .' She hesitated. 'I've seen other girls go through this.'

Connie closed her eyes and let out a long breath 'I don't know what to do.' There, she had admitted it. The words had come and now the tears came too, streaming down her face.

Dorothy patted her arm. 'Of course you don't. Why would you?'

She produced a handkerchief from her sleeve and passed it across. Connie took it and mopped at her face. The handkerchief smelled of eau de cologne.

'But what have you considered?'

'I need to tell Johnny,' said Connie, sniffing. 'That's why I want his address.'

There was a silence. On the landing outside she could hear movement, the clunk of Kenneth's stick on the floorboards. She thought of the tea towel that she must have dropped outside the door. She imagined Kenneth poking it with his stick, hooking it up and wondering how it had got there.

'And have you thought about what you'll do if he doesn't send his address?' Dorothy spoke slowly, spacing out her words.

Connie scrubbed at her eyes and shook her head. 'He'll write. He said he would.'

There was another silence between them. A second bluebottle buzzed through the window, circled the room in a busy, zigzag flight.

'Nasty things,' said Dorothy, distracted, 'spreading

germs.' She picked up a magazine from a pile on the floor and rolled it up.

'Look,' she said, half an eye on the fly still, 'Johnny's my son and it pains me to say this, but he isn't the most . . . how shall I put it?' She stopped and lunged ineffectively at the bluebottle as it passed. 'He isn't the most, well, faithful of . . . men.'

Connie felt a growing anger and clamped down her feelings. She clearly knew Johnny better than Dorothy did and she wouldn't listen to this.

'Like I said before,' said Dorothy, 'my husband had a detrimental effect on Johnny's character, and I doubt you'll hear from him again.'

'But he promised,' said Connie, finally.

Dorothy gave her a look as if to say *you poor thing*. Connie clenched her fists.

'There was another girl,' Dorothy went on, 'in the last place we lived. She thought Johnny was the bee's knees. Mooned over him night and day. Always at our door. Pretty little thing, truth be told, but not enough to hold onto Johnny. When we moved, there was no backward glance.'

'But . . .' Connie struggled to understand. 'In my case, it's different, we . . .' She wanted to say they loved each other, but she thought it would sound foolish. 'We care for each other,' she said instead.

Dorothy sat back, hands folded. 'Then why hasn't he written to you?'

'I don't know.'

'How far along are you?'

74

'Three months,' Connie mumbled, her nails digging into her skin.

Dorothy sucked in her breath and shook her head. 'It's a pity you didn't come and see me earlier. Have you tried anything at all?'

Connie stared at her. *Yes* was the answer. She had moved heavy furniture and run fast as if she might dislodge the baby. But she didn't want to admit that, so she shook her head.

'No? Well, it's not too late.'

'But . . .'

'The thing is,' Dorothy continued quietly, 'you're not the first young woman to have made this decision and you certainly won't be the last. When I was a midwife, you wouldn't believe the things I saw. Young girls – younger than you, giving birth.' She shook her head slowly. 'Fourteen, fifteen years old. No fathers to be seen. The babies were passed off as their siblings to avoid the shame or sent for adoption.'

'Adoption?'

'Yes. And frankly that wasn't always what the girls wanted. It was their parents.'

'They were forced?'

'More or less. Of course, the girls had to sign papers, more often than not, but . . . yes. It's the shame, you see. There's no shortage of fingers pointing when society comes across an unmarried mother. There are plenty of young girls with loose morals these days and that's all very well, unless you're caught out.'

Connie hung her head. She knew this was true. She had heard so many stories. A girl at school who had left for a year. On the surface, when she returned, it was as if nothing had happened: the way she looked; the way she had slotted back into lessons. There was a story about her having been ill or some such excuse. But no one had believed it and she had never fitted in again properly. Everyone knew she'd had a baby. Everyone knew too that there was no baby at home. Supposition and rumour had followed. She had murdered her baby, smothered it with a cushion. Her family had thrown the baby into the river. It had been adopted by foreigners and taken off to Russia or Canada or Timbuctoo. Nobody knew the truth, but Connie remembered the sadness in her eyes.

'Then,' said Dorothy, getting into the rhythm, 'there were the girls who were forced into marriage with young men who were marched down the aisle. That wasn't good for either of them.'

'But I'm seventeen,' Connie protested. 'I'm not a child.'

'Of course,' said Dorothy, breezing on, 'there were the lucky ones who got proper abortions by proper doctors, but that's expensive and not easy to do.' She paused, and moistened her lips. 'And if they couldn't afford that route, or left it too late, they could still get it done, quietly –' she dropped her voice – 'but they had to be very careful who they chose.'

'So what should I do?'

'That, my dear, is for you to decide.'

'But Johnny . . .'

Dorothy sighed and crossed her arms. 'Johnny has a career ahead of him. I don't mean painting, of course – that's a silly phase – but once he's got that out of his system, he'll come to his senses. And then . . .' She paused. 'He'll come home.'

Was this what Dorothy was hoping for? For her errant son to return and settle down?

'I need to tell him,' Connie insisted stubbornly.

Dorothy smiled, but it didn't reach her eyes. 'How? When neither you nor I have an address for him? How long do you think you have before other people spot your situation?'

Connie was silent.

'Those are the options,' said Dorothy, spreading her hands. 'It's up to you to decide.'

Connie steadied her breath and glanced at the photos of Johnny. Baby, toddler, child, young man. It was true. He had his whole life ahead of him. And even if he *did* write, time was running out.

Later, Connie made lunch, carving thick slices of ham and cracking eggs into a pan. The ham was sickly pale and the yolks were streaked with red. Blood, she thought, scraping it away with a wooden spoon. The sight of it made her shudder and the smell of the cooking made her stomach heave. She wished she had never gone to see Dorothy.

8

Marina

January 1992

First night. Footsteps cross the ceiling, a door bangs. It's past midnight, but the house is alive.

Marina sits in bed dressed like a Dickens character complete with fingerless gloves, bedsocks and hat. She shivers, hunkers down and tries to sleep. Despite having had the window open since she arrived, the room has a musty, choking smell. The door is propped ajar with the telephone directory, and sounds carry. The front door slams, and the whole house judders. Somewhere, another door opens and closes. A baby is crying.

She switches on the lamp. It highlights the miserable brown wallpaper and she distracts herself considering which colour she'll paint the room: bright yellow perhaps, or rich indigo or burnt orange. She thinks about reading but doubts she'll be able to concentrate and swings her legs out of bed.

In the kitchen, she boils the kettle and makes tea. Cradling the warm mug, she takes it into the living room. Ruth's folder is on the table. Marina has re-read the clippings and notes many times, but she settles in the armchair and leafs through again.

She scans the letter from the nurse who looked after her, Sofía Marques. The tone is warm as she talks of letting her house when her husband died and going to

Ireland to be close to her son. She talks about her son's new job in London too and the whole family returning and the pleasure she gains from her grandchildren. *Children are everything*, she writes. *They help me heal.*

Outside a fox screams. Marina puts aside the letter and looks through the window, but there's no sign of anything. She crosses to her front door and opens it a crack. Despite the hour, beneath the baby's crying, she hears piano music weaving through the house. On impulse, she steps into the hall. There's an eerie stillness among the shadows. Opening the main front door, she stands at the top of the steps breathing the frosty air. The houses opposite are still. Distant sounds of traffic float from the main road, while inside the house, the baby quietens and the music stops. The fox appears, a vixen perhaps, walking nonchalantly along the street, searching for food.

In the morning, Marina wakes to the sound of church bells. She jumps out of bed and braves the icy bathroom before making strong coffee which she laces with sugar. Peering into her sparsely stocked cupboards, she decides to go out for breakfast. Hastily, she pulls on black leggings and a turtleneck jumper, her gloves and coat, and soon she's springing down the steps and into the street.

The sky hangs low and claustrophobic and Marina loosens her collar despite the chill. She has an odd, prickling feeling as if she's being watched, but the houses are as silent as they were last night, their windows shuttered – and when she looks back at number 24, there is no shift in curtains, no one looking out. At least she doesn't think there is. On the top floor, there might be a movement, but the window is open and the wind stirs the curtains. A fat pigeon sits contentedly on the roof. While Marina is watching, it heaves itself into action and flies elegantly away.

Marina galvanises herself too. The public path along-side the house leads – tantalisingly – to St Michael's Road. She puts off her quest for food and gives in to the temptation to seek out Sofía's house. The path is muddy, a well-trodden shortcut, although stone walls enclosing the gardens on either side block out much of the light. Thick shards of glass have been cemented to the top of the wall of number 24.

At the end of the path, Marina halts. Ahead of her, to the left, is the grey church; she can see people spilling out through the entrance and spots the small figure of Mrs Hyde, alone in the crowd. The rest of the road comprises lines of neat-looking Victorian terraces. Marina checks the direction of the numbering and crosses, heading away from the church.

Sofía's house sits in the middle of the street.

Hitching her bag more securely on her shoulder, Marina opens the gate and strides down the path. A firm knock. Nothing. She waits and then knocks again. On impulse, she holds back her hair, leans down and looks through the letter box. She spies a thick, cream carpet in the hall, a tidy line of shoes, adults' and children's. An abandoned truck on the stairs. There is a smell of food, roasting meat. No sign of any movement. Perhaps they've gone out and left their meal to cook: a sign they'll be home soon. She lets the flap of the letter box fall.

Turning back towards the church, she heads down St

Michael's Road, passing the stragglers from the congregation. On Streatham High Road, she waits as the traffic hurtles past. In 1964, the streets would have been quieter, with milk floats and policemen on bikes. Now an ambulance shrieks past and cars and buses pull in to get out of its way. Marina takes her chance and crosses quickly, following the edge of the common before the aroma of fresh baking lures her to a side road.

There is a row of shops including a green-painted bookshop called Crystal's Books, with flowers in the window and spotlighted displays. Next door is an electrical shop with its windows crammed with vacuum cleaners, kettles and heaters. Further along is an old-fashioned looking cafe called Ruby's, a grocer's and a newsagent's.

In the cafe, Marina orders a salmon and cucumber sandwich to take away and a cake soaked in honey and topped with pistachios. Outside, she is tempted to browse the bookshop, but is distracted by a tall man hurrying towards her. Ron. The way he is struggling to put on his leather jacket as he walks, shoving an arm in one sleeve and groping for the other, makes her smile. He waves and she suppresses a laugh watching him turn circles as if he's chasing his tail.

'Need a hand?' she calls.

'You're all right,' he replies, 'I know when I'm beat.' He folds the jacket neatly and hooks it over his arm. 'It's too small. Or I'm too big.'

He asks her which way she's going and she nods vaguely along the street. 'How about you?'

'Meeting a mate.' He indicates the same direction.

'You can join us if you like. We'll probably get something to eat.'

She holds up her food. 'No thanks. I've got mine.'

Still, they set off together. For a while, they are silent, dodging people with bags and buggies. Ron rolls a cigarette with a practised hand and offers it to her. She accepts and borrows his lighter, hooking back her hair, using one gloved hand to cup the flame against the breeze, inhaling quietly while he rolls another.

'So,' he says after a few more moments of quiet. 'What brings you to this godforsaken place?'

'You think it's godforsaken?'

'The house, not the neighbourhood. I like it here.' He glances around appreciatively at the mixture of buildings and the littered street.

'The house has character,' she replies cautiously, 'although I admit it needs work.'

'That's an understatement.'

She shrugs. 'I like a challenge.'

'What do you do?' he asks curiously.

'I teach, usually.'

'What subject?'

'French and German. But I've moved into editing.' She tells him a little about her old teaching job in Bristol and her work with Agata. 'How about you?'

'I work at the Natural History Museum. I'm a curator.' He looks at her sideways and she can tell he's proud of his job.

'Sounds interesting,' she says, smiling at him. 'I'm keen on museums and galleries.'

'Well, you've come to the right place – London, I

mean.' He finishes rolling his cigarette and tucks it behind his ear. 'Anyway, you haven't said . . . What brings you here? Not the tourist attractions, I assume?'

She laughs. 'No. Change.' It's mostly true.

'Fair enough. Change is good.'

They've reached his destination. A block of modern flats.

He presses a buzzer and turns to her. 'Don't forget, let me know if you need anything.'

She hesitates and then says, 'How about a low-down on who's who?'

He raises his eyebrows and adjusts his glasses. 'In the house? Sure. Come round any time.'

A tall, dark-haired woman in a smart, long-sleeved navy dress opens the door on St Michael's Road. 'Can I help you?' she asks in an Irish accent.

Marina shuffles her feet, feeling scruffy in her fake-fur coat and gloves. She gives her name and explains how she's looking for Sofía Marques. Giving her a curious look, the woman asks her to wait.

Marina fidgets, peeling off her gloves and shoving them into her pocket. She crouches to tie her lace and when she stands, sees the face of a little girl at a top window. She smiles and waves as another small head pops up.

The smart woman reappears and invites her in. She is kinder now, her face friendly. One moment of hesitation and Marina steps inside, stopping to take off her boots. The house feels right and she's trusting her instincts. The little girl from the window has appeared and is peeping through the spindles of the bannister. Behind her is the second child, a solemn boy in Spider-Man pyjamas.

The kitchen is warm and smells of the roasting meat. Another woman sits at the table, peeling carrots. She's older, late fifties maybe, with olive skin and black hair. She wears a dark woollen dress and a thick gold necklace, and Marina knows without being told that this is Sofía Marques.

'I hope you don't mind my coming,' says Marina, quickly. 'I wasn't sure if . . .'

Sofia stands up. 'It's wonderful to see you. Ruth telephoned and told me you were coming to London. I was so hoping you'd visit.'

Her voice is rich and her dark eyes moisten even as her face breaks into a smile. She comes across and takes Marina's hands in both her own. 'You're exactly as I imagined you would be.' She turns to the younger woman. 'This is Marina. I had the great privilege to care for her when she was a baby. And Marina, this is my daughter-in-law, Patricia, and those two lovely children hiding in the hall are my grandchildren.'

Patricia smiles pleasantly, takes Marina's coat and moves about the kitchen making tea.

'Come,' says Sofía, leading her to the table like a child, 'tell me about your life.'

They sit together and while Marina talks, her heart swells with the warmth of Sofía's welcome. The children come into the kitchen looking for biscuits and the girl breaks off pieces to feed to her brother. Marina wonders as she often does if she has siblings, living their life with no knowledge of her.

Patricia sets down cups of tea.

'I've been to Harrington Gardens,' says Marina finally.

'Ah.' Sofía nods.

'I went inside.' She baulks at telling the whole truth and is fairly certain Ruth will have left it up to her.

'And has it changed the way you feel?'

It's the question Marina has asked herself a hundred times already. 'I don't know.'

'What are you hoping for?'

Tactfully, Patricia takes the children and leaves the room.

'I suppose I want to know why.' She looks down at her hands.

'Listen,' says Sofía softly. 'Your mother must have felt very alone to have left you. She must have thought she had no choice.'

'I know.'

'She put you in a safe place.'

'That's what Ruth says.'

They are silent again. Quiet laughter floats through the door from the hall.

'Do you think I'm stupid?'

'No, of course I don't.'

'I've always felt connected to the house.'

'Well, you are, that's true.'

Marina fiddles with the teaspoon in the saucer. 'Why do you think,' she says after a moment or two, 'the police didn't find my mother?'

Sofía sighs. 'I suppose it would be impossible to solve every case.'

'But it was all over the news. Surely someone would

85

have come forward – the father, or a member of her family.'

'Perhaps no one knew. Things were different then. Unmarried women hid their pregnancies, especially if they were very young, or if the baby didn't belong to their husband.'

Marina rubs her temples. She knows this is true. She has been through archives and read enough stories about mothers who did exactly that.

'And you have to remember,' Sofía continues, 'there was no automatic access to legal abortion in the early sixties. Vulnerable women were forced to have dangerous and often life-threatening procedures. In the hospital, we saw many women who nearly died that way. They could even be prosecuted – if the police found out.'

Marina thinks about this. 'Is there anything else you can tell me?' she says eventually. 'I've read the articles that Ruth saved for me and I've searched records, but I might have missed something.'

Sofía considers. Then she says, 'I have some articles myself. You're welcome to look at them.'

She leaves the room and Marina waits, head in her hands. She is startled when a small hand touches her arm. The little girl has come in quietly and is contemplating her with solemn eyes. How much has she heard? Children absorb moods and emotions, observe actions without understanding them, or remembering what they've seen. It's the nature of memory, Marina thinks, her mind drawn to Agata's manuscript.

Sofía returns with a folder tied with a blue ribbon. She sets it on the table and takes the girl onto her lap.

'I kept everything that reminds me of you.'

Marina holds back her tears as she listens.

'I would have adopted you if they'd let me, but being single, it wasn't possible. Still, I cared about you very much for those weeks in the hospital – you were so tiny, so vulnerable, they thought you must have come early – and I was glad when Ruth and David came forward. We stayed in touch, you know that, for a while, but . . .' She stops, blinks. 'Well. Lives change. People move on and Ireland is a long way from London – from Wiltshire, but I'm so glad we've reconnected.'

Marina holds the folder close, but she isn't ready to leave. There must be questions Sofía can answer.

'Do you recall a witness who said they'd seen a pregnant woman hanging about the house? Do you think that woman was my mother?'

'I remember the story, but it turned out the woman had a connection with one of the tenants.' She frowns and stirs her tea.

'Was there anyone else? Any other women turning up, or being spotted?'

'Well . . .' She puts down her spoon. 'To be honest, it was something and nothing.'

Marina leans forward eagerly. 'Yes?'

'There was someone else.'

'Who?'

Sofía grimaces. 'It was after you'd been found. A woman came to the baby ward.'

'What happened?'

'A nurse approached her and she left.'

'Did they speak?'

'Briefly. When the nurse questioned her, the woman said that she was lost, but I remember feeling uneasy about it. Security wasn't so good back then, and the nurse said she appeared skittish, which you might put down to embarrassment, but it seemed like a coincidence.'

'Could it have been a journalist?'

Sofía makes a face. 'Unlikely, judging from her behaviour – and in those days, there were few female journalists. We decided in the end it was a curious or misguided member of the public fascinated by the story.'

'Did anyone tell the police?'

'Yes, but there wasn't much they could do and it wasn't reported in the papers or anything.'

She frowns and Marina guesses there is more. She is quiet, waiting.

'On the day that you left the hospital . . .'

'With David and Ruth?'

'No, no. You went with foster carers before that. Anyway, on that day, a group of us went out to the car park to say goodbye – including the same nurse.' She pauses. 'I didn't notice anything at all, but the nurse mentioned later that she had seen the woman again.'

'What was she doing?'

'Watching.'

Marina lets this sink in. 'Why didn't the nurse speak out? Surely she should have alerted somebody.'

'Perhaps, but realistically, if the woman had been visiting a patient the previous time, it made sense that she would come again. We were quite a spectacle, all of us making a fuss of you. A lot of people would have noticed and stopped.' She pauses, smiling fondly at the memory, and shrugs. 'Like I said, it was something and nothing.'

Marina isn't convinced.

9

Connie

May 1964

Dorothy appeared beside Connie as she stood in the hall, staring into the post box.

'How have you been, dear?' she asked in a low voice, stretching up to reach her letters.

'I'm fine,' said Connie, avoiding her gaze.

Dorothy pursed her lips as she shuffled through her post and then she sighed. No letter from Johnny. She wanted one as much as Connie did.

Dorothy looked up, resigned. 'So, have you decided what's best?'

'No,' said Connie truthfully. She had spent the last three days trying to work things out, lying awake at night, tangling the sheets as she tossed and turned, getting up and staring from the window, trying to find an answer in the darkness. To keep the baby or not to keep the baby. To wait and hope that Johnny would contact her, or to go ahead and make the decision alone.

Every morning, she had risen early, pasty-faced, hoping to get the sickness out of the way before her father got up. She had learned that nibbling a biscuit or a piece of dry toast staved off the nausea, so she had taken to keeping a packet of digestives next to her bed.

'Well,' said Dorothy, 'it's your choice, but should you

want to know, I have found a lady. She's very discreet and lives not too far from here.'

'Oh.' Connie swallowed, seized by the urge to cry.

'I could make you an appointment, but only if you'd like me to. It would be a short visit, just to see what's what.'

She gave a faint smile. Connie noticed a smear of lipstick on her front tooth. It amazed her how much make-up Dorothy wore. Her mother had hardly touched it. A little rouge, a touch of power. But then she'd been beautiful, her smooth face marked only by laughter lines, which had enhanced her appearance rather than the opposite. It was only at the end that pain had etched grooves into her skin.

Thinking about her mother made Connie think of her father. His lines had deepened too over this past year. His stature had changed as well. He had lost weight, seemed almost wizened at times, as if grief were eating him inside.

'How about tomorrow?' said Dorothy.

'Tomorrow?' repeated Connie. 'But I . . .' She stopped. What was the point of waiting? If it had to be done, then it should be done quickly. She nodded her consent.

'I'll knock.'

Connie nodded again and looked down at the floor.

'I wish I could ask Johnny.'

'It wouldn't do any good, dear. Men don't take this kind of thing as seriously as women. They don't need to. It isn't them who bear the consequences, who feel the pain.'

The door to Flat 2 opened and Eileen appeared wearing a yellow silk kimono. Black American, in her late twenties, she'd lived in London for the past five years, working in the theatre. Privately, Connie thought she was too good for her actor boyfriend: Leonard had a sallow face, mousy hair and pale eyes. He had a bad temper too judging by his perpetual scowl, and more than once Connie had seen a bruise on Eileen's face.

Yet Eileen had a zest for life. She had a kindness too. When Connie's mother died, Eileen had brought food. Connie recalled her standing in the doorway, clutching a casserole. Barefoot, dressed in white, with her black hair spread about her, she had been like an angel. She had taken the food into the kitchen and set it on the side before putting her arm about Connie and telling her how sorry she was. Most people tiptoed around the situation, barely mentioning Connie's loss. Not Eileen.

Now Eileen grinned as she sailed past in a cloud of perfume and a wreath of smoke. Retrieving her letters, she picked out a slim blue envelope. 'Wouldn't you know it?' she said. 'A letter from America.' She kissed it with a flourish.

'What is it?' asked Connie, eager for an excuse to turn from Dorothy.

'An audition – at least that's what I hope it is. On Broadway.' She winked at Connie. 'How about that?'

Eileen was heading for the horizon. Lucky her.

'What does it say?'

'All in good time.' She glanced at the open door and slipped the envelope into her pocket. 'Don't want his nibs to find me out.'

She disappeared into her flat. A moment later and they heard music. The Beatles. That would be Leonard's choice. Eileen preferred jazz. Once when Connie had been listening on the stairs, Eileen had come out unexpectedly and found her. She had invited her inside and introduced her to Billie Holiday. That voice, a beautiful, sultry sound. Connie liked the Beatles, but Billie Holiday had been something else.

Kenneth appeared, tying the cord of his dressing gown and scowling. He glanced at Dorothy, and not for the first time, Connie sensed a current running between the two of them as their eyes met. It was her mother who had suggested he and Dorothy were more than friends; her father had thought it more likely she was his spy. He said she had keys and snooped inside people's flats when they were out.

Now Kenneth banged on Eileen and Leonard's door, yelling at them to turn the music down. Connie gave one more despairing look at the empty post box and left him and Dorothy to it.

That evening, Connie sat on the edge of the bath with her head in her hands. The running water drowned out the noise of the men talking. Kenneth and Victor had turned up yet again.

It was a relief to relax behind a locked door, even though there was still no blood on the toilet tissue. She laid her hands on her belly. If there was a baby inside her, how big would it be? What would it look like? She imagined translucent skin and tiny fists and eyes screwed shut.

She stood abruptly, dislodging the image, turned off the taps and undressed. Easing herself into the water, she lay facing the window. The hot weather had broken and rain splattered across the frosted glass.

She had spent a miserable day in the bookshop, feigning a headache until her father had given her an aspirin and sent her to rest in the back room. There she had sat, questioning what she was going to do. If only Johnny would write. She felt heavy with longing, as if a lump of lead had fallen to the bottom of her stomach. She could drown with its weight inside her, like a sack of mewling kittens.

They'd had a kitten once. It had arrived on the steps of their house. Black with four white feet – and she and her mother had taken it in and called it Socks. 'No pets allowed,' her father had said, but though he was a stickler for rules, he had given in to the charms of Socks – and Connie's mother. They had kept her, and fed her titbits, and made her a bed in an empty orange crate. If Kenneth noticed, he didn't interfere and even Victor had succumbed, letting the cat sit in his lap when he visited. Mind you, Victor had been a better person then. Her mother had had a knack for bringing out the best in people. It was only after she had died that Victor had shown a different side.

Not that her mother had kept her thoughts to herself. Connie remembered a disagreement she had had with Dorothy. Her ex-husband had turned up out of the blue, drunk and hurling abuse at Mrs Kolinski. Her mother had called the police.

Connie's mind turned back to Socks. One day, the cat had disappeared. Her father had said it was inevitable with a stray, and although her mother had agreed, she had continued to put saucers of milk outside the door, hoping Socks would return.

The water in the bath cooled, but Connie could still hear the drone of the men's voices and catch snatches of their conversation. They were talking about the state of the basement flat.

'I need to employ a cleaner,' Victor was saying, 'unless your Connie wants the job.' He raised his voice, shouting through to her. 'Hey, Connie, fancy earning a bob or two?'

Not on your bloody life. She turned on the hot tap to mask their voices and, for better effect, reached down to the transistor on the floor. She twisted the dial and out came Cilla Black blasting 'Anyone Who Had a Heart'.

Lying back and stretching her toes, Connie listened to the music. She would stay in the bathroom until Victor and Kenneth had gone.

She added bath salts to the water. It made the water green, like a river slick with algae – only it was getting too hot; beads of sweat had broken out on her skin. Still she let the hot tap run because, despite the heat, it was good to be here. Her body felt light, but now her mind was drifting to those women who took boiling baths, drank too much gin and used knitting needles. She shuddered imagining it, even though she had already tried dragging furniture around, rearranging the sitting room. And now this hot bath. Would Dorothy's contact suggest this? What else would Connie have to do? Would she end up like Harry's cousin – or was it his cousin's friend?

Her mind was struggling to focus and she felt horribly

sick, but she stayed in the bath with the hot tap running and the steam rising. A few more minutes and it could all be done. Then she felt a sensation, a tiny quickening. Struggling, she sat up. Was that the baby? Surely it was too soon? Did it know what Connie was doing? In a panic, she leaned forward. The room spun as she groped for the plug and wrenched it out. Clamping both hands on the side of the bath, she hauled herself upwards. Dizzy and stumbling, she reached the toilet, leaned over it, and vomited in painful spasms. Cilla stopped. The Beatles took over. There was a knock on the door.

'Are you all right?' Her father spoke, his voice full of concern. She gulped, chest heaving. 'Connie?'

Turning off the transistor, she swallowed hard. 'I'm fine. Won't be a minute.' Guilt joined forces with nausea as she wiped the spittle from her mouth. If only he knew.

If only she could tell him.

Shivering, she drew her knees to her chest, clasping them tightly to stop the trembling. As she waited for the shaking to subside, she imagined the baby slipping through her in a bloodied mess.

She thought the men had left. In her bedroom, she dressed and brushed her hair, tying it with a band. When she opened the door, she heard voices. Victor had gone, but Kenneth was there.

They were talking about the rent.

'One more month,' she heard her father say, 'and I'll pay off the debt.'

Connie's heart sank. Where would he get that kind of money?

Kenneth sighed. 'I have to say that's very unfortunate. Very unfortunate indeed.'

Connie could imagine his bird-like gaze flickering around the room, his skinny fingers drumming on the edges of the chair.

'I've helped you several times,' he added. 'The sum is growing. Debt is debt and I am meticulous in calling it in.'

Connie gritted her teeth. How was this fair? Kenneth had stolen his money, yet here he was acting holier than thou over an honest loan to her father.

She stepped forward, hoping her presence would shame him, but Kenneth took no notice. Trying not to show her emotions, she sat on the arm of her father's chair. Her heart twisted hearing how politely and respectfully he spoke. She was sure Kenneth must have a whole stash of money hidden somewhere.

After he'd gone, she asked her father why Kenneth wouldn't help.

'He has his own problems.'

'With money? I don't believe it.'

Her father shrugged, reluctant to speak.

'You don't need to protect me, Dad. I know what he's like. Everyone does. He's a crook, a villain. I won't be shocked.'

'I know that, Connie. But you have enough to think about without worrying about this.'

'What do you mean?'

'Working at the bookshop, looking after the flat. Looking after me.'

'You know I don't mind any of that.'

'Well, I do. You should be out there enjoying life like other girls your age, finding yourself a young man.'

She dropped her gaze. 'It doesn't matter. Tell me about Kenneth.'

He shook his head.

'Dad, please. I'm old enough now. We're a team, aren't we?'

He sighed. 'Of course.' He took off his glasses and looked at her fondly.

He was so tired, Connie thought, so fed up with life. She was supposed to lift his mood. It was what she'd tried to do since her mother had gone, but instead of getting happier as time passed, he seemed more miserable than ever.

She regretted pressing him about Kenneth and whatever his problems were, but he told her anyway.

'It's Frank Dennis.'

She frowned. 'Who?' The name was familiar, but she couldn't place where she'd heard it.

'One of Kenneth's old gang members,' said her father, producing a handkerchief and polishing the lenses of his glasses. 'The one who supposedly . . .' He stopped, perched the glasses back on his nose. 'Anyway, he's out of prison.'

Now Connie remembered. Her father was talking about the last job Kenneth had been involved in, an armed robbery in a bank that had ended badly, with one man – a security guard – attacked and left for dead, and Kenneth and his two cronies in prison. Kenneth was already out, of course, and ostensibly on the straight and narrow. Another of the convicted men had died in prison – a suicide, they said. But Frank Dennis was the one accused of assaulting the guard and he'd been given the longest sentence. Only there had recently been an appeal on some technicality or other and he'd finally been released.

'Why's that a problem for Kenneth?' asked Connie.

'I don't know for certain . . . but some of the money from the robbery was never recovered by the police.'

She nodded, remembering.

'And some people think . . .'

He stopped again and Connie made a guess. 'They think that Kenneth stole Frank's share.'

Her father scratched his chin. 'Let's just say, in Kenneth's case, the chickens may be coming home to roost.'

10

Marina

January 1992

Marina unwraps the shawl from its tissue paper, releasing the scent of lavender. Laying the shawl on the bed, she admires the blue. The police would have examined every inch, scrutinised the label, searching for clues, but she can't help thinking there's a secret they might have missed, hidden in the depths of its weave.

Along with the shawl is a white cotton gown, although the material is yellowed and softened with age. Hand-sewn, it's a family heirloom perhaps. Marina imagines deft fingers holding a needle, forming neat stitches.

She places Sofía's folder next to it and tries to quell her anticipation.

A knock disturbs her train of thought and she opens the door to a smiley young woman with short, purple hair and red dungarees, carrying a baby in a sling and holding a plant – a fern in a pot.

'Welcome,' the woman says, holding out the fern. 'I'm Selena Hamilton from Flat 4. That's Bill.' She points to a shy-looking man behind her, who smiles too.

'Pleased to meet you. I'm Marina.' She takes the plant. 'This is very kind.'

'If you need anything, do shout. Or come up and see me! I'm always keen to speak to an adult.' She strokes her baby's head.

Marina thanks her and invites the couple in for coffee, but just as they accept, the baby starts to cry. Selena gives a reluctant sigh and promises to return another time – 'When this one's feeling a bit more sociable.'

As Marina sets the plant in the fireplace, she mentally crosses out any possibility that the young residents of Flat 4 lived in the house when she was born. To be honest, she's relieved not to have to make small talk when all she really wants to do is to read through Sofía's folder.

She opens it. Inside is a sheaf of papers and a bundle of photos. Several of the photos are of Marina in the hospital, lying in a crib or in Sofía's arms. She has a mass of dark hair and is wrapped in the shawl with her eyes screwed shut. Marina examines the corners and the edges, each smudge and spot and grain, and it occurs to her that at the time of this photo, the shawl would have held her mother's scent. Picking up the shawl now, she lifts it to her face. If only Ruth hadn't corrupted the smell with her sprigs of dried lavender. If only she and David hadn't taken her to Wiltshire. What if her mother had intended to return, like a vixen to its cubs or a wild cat to its kittens?

She clenches her jaw. They had no right to take her so far away. Who told them that they could?

Breathing slowly, she shakes her head. It's not fair to blame Ruth and David, the two people who love her more than anyone else. Her mother could have walked into any police station and presented herself at any time. And the scent of the shawl would have faded anyway.

She turns to the clippings Sofía has saved. Most of them she's already seen – in Ruth's collection – but there's one she doesn't recognise, from a local paper. Along with a picture of the house, there's a headshot of the first police-man on the scene. He describes interviewing the ten-ant who, along with the landlord, discovered the baby. The tenant is named as Eileen Clarke, and the landlord Kenneth Quip. Another photo shows the two of them. Kenneth is thin-faced and dressed in a light shirt open at the collar. He gives the impression of having been caught off guard, with one hand raised to his face. Eileen is an attractive black woman, who looks directly at the camera. 'I heard crying,' the paper quotes her as saying. 'And when I opened my door, I found her in the hall, tucked away in the corner and bundled in the shawl. I couldn't believe a baby had been left there. It was very upsetting.' She goes on to say how the front door had been left wide open and how someone must have taken the chance to bring the baby in.

The article is more salacious than those Marina has read before. The focus is on Eileen, describing her as an American model turned actress who performed on stage in the West End and threw parties with her one-time boyfriend, actor Leonard Crisp. There is a quote from a neighbour describing the noise and more specifically a daytime disturbance when Eileen threw Leonard's pos-sessions out of the window. Marina reads in disbelief. There is more speculation about the woman who found the baby than there is about who might have abandoned her and why.

Despite the cold, Marina wants the window open. The air inside the flat is stale. She puts both hands on the edge of the wood and shoves hard. The frame moves upwards by an inch, enough for a thread of air to limbo through the gap.

Someone has pegged out their washing, taking advantage of the frail sunshine: a brown dress, an orange housecoat, a pair of tights. A man appears from the side of the house, feet crunching on the gravel. His overcoat hangs loosely and he wears black leather gloves and a trilby, pulled low. He moves slowly, using his stick, pausing to prod at a clump of weeds, to bat away a stone, to jab at the washing on the line. He pokes the dress as if it's an opponent and his stick is a sword. When he reaches the bushes that partly obscure the end of the garden, he looks back at the house. Instinctively, Marina steps to the side and watches again as he pauses, swivels and swipes at the leaves. Pushing through, he disappears. Marina watches curiously for his return. Perhaps it's Giovanni, the elusive tenant of Flat 1.

The day is changing as the sun drops and the shadows lengthen. A stillness hovers over the garden, and now Mrs Hyde appears too, scuttling along the path around the side of the house, carrying a laundry basket that dwarfs her diminutive body. She grabs the dress, the housecoat, the tights, unpegging, shaking, folding. Her white hair is askew, her skirt long. She finishes her chore and then puts the basket down. For a moment, she just stands there, hands on her hips as if she is thinking, and then she hurries down the path in the direction the man took, leaving her washing behind.

Later, Marina sits at her desk with a blanket around her shoulders. She's been working on Agata's manuscript, following her parents' path into Auschwitz through the barbed wire and the searchlights and the smoke. From time to time she looks out the window, shocked almost to see carefree children passing with their parents, heading for the common.

Distracted, she puts aside the manuscript, finds her coat and her gloves and goes outside. On impulse, she continues down to the basement. There's no bell or knocker, so she bangs on the door. A few minutes later Ron appears. His face lights up. 'Coffee?'

'Are you sure?'

'Putting the kettle on.'

She follows him through a narrow sitting room, noting the blue futon, TV, ornate coffee table, sprawling fern. The kitchen is outdated like hers, but it's larger and warmer. Family portraits and black and white photographs cover the walls – pictures of past London. Books and papers are stacked in piles on a large pine table that dominates the room. Ron gestures for her to sit. Instead of putting the kettle on, he grinds coffee beans, fills the coffee pot and searches for matches to light the stove.

She bends to examine the books. They are mostly historical non-fiction, but there are a few novels too. She spots *Clarissa* and *Tristram Shandy*.

'Have you always been interested in history?' she asks, straightening.

He turns, sugar bowl in hand, and gestures at a photo. 'Mum's influence.'

Marina follows his gaze. In the photo, a younger version of Ron stands beside a tall, elegant, middle-aged woman with grey hair and angular features. Ron has his arm thrown around her shoulders and is looking at her, smiling. The woman stares boldly out at the camera.

'She left school with nothing and had me young. But then she took an archaeology course. I used to go with her on digs. My first memories are of dirt and bones.'

'What about your father?'

He shrugs. 'Never met him. Mum was a single parent.'

'Have you tried to find him?' The question is out before she can stop herself.

'No. I'm not interested. If he wasn't bothered about sticking around, why should I care about finding him?'

She bites her lip to stop herself from asking how he knows it was his father's choice. Families are complicated. She sits down at the table.

The coffee pot splutters. Ron fusses, setting out cups and saucers, a bowl of sugar lumps, a jug of milk, a plate of ginger nuts. Marina watches, eyebrows raised.

Reading her mind, he grins. 'It's the details, don't you think? Makes the coffee taste better.'

She agrees, even though she's the instant, make-it-quick variety of coffee drinker.

'So, how's it been?' he asks, pouring coffee for them both and settling in the seat opposite her. 'Since this morning?'

'Good.' She reaches for the milk.

'Still want a low-down on the tenants?'

She stirs her coffee, adds two sugar lumps and jumps straight in. 'I've already met Mrs Hyde.'

'Mrs Misery.'

'How long has she been here?'

'Forever, I expect.'

'She didn't want to talk to me.'

'She doesn't want to talk to anyone. Except God.'

'God?'

'She's very religious. Goes to bible classes, church every Sunday.'

'That's fair enough. Does she have a husband?'

'If she does, she keeps him hidden away.'

Marina laughs. 'Well, Selena Hamilton was friendlier. She gave me a plant.'

'She gave me one too.' Of course: the fern in the living room. 'Biscuit?' He pushes the plate of ginger nuts towards her.

She takes one. 'I haven't met Giovanni – the guy in the flat opposite me. Although I thought I saw him in the garden. Do you know what he does?'

'Conductor. Not the bus kind. He's in an orchestra, been in the house for about three years, I reckon – longer than the Hamiltons, anyway.'

'So, he's a night bird.'

'I guess.'

Marina nods and sips her coffee. She isn't sure the man she saw with the walking stick fits her idea of a musician, but who knows. She eats her biscuit, reaches for another and chats a little more about plants and not being green-fingered. Keeping her voice casual, she asks about the pianist.

'Ah.' Ron's expression shuts down as he looks at his cup and twists it on its saucer.

'I noticed the name on the post box.' She pauses. 'Kolinski?'

He clears his throat. 'Yeah. That's Eva.'

Marina's skin tingles. Not Natalia, but a relative. She snaps the biscuit in two. 'She's very talented. Is it Chopin I can hear?'

'Yeah,' says Ron. 'You're right. She's good.'

'How old is she?'

'About thirty.'

Natalia's daughter, perhaps. 'Does she live alone?'

'Yeah.'

His voice is flat. He's holding back. Marina dunks one half of her biscuit and speaks carefully. 'So, what's she like?'

He's blushing and now she guesses. 'Oh. I see.' She leans forward, makes sympathetic eye contact, hoping the colour of her cheeks doesn't match his. 'What happened?'

'It's over, although it didn't go far, to be honest.' He stops and frowns. 'She's got one or two . . . issues. Hold on. Why am I telling you this?'

She shrugs, smiles reassuringly. 'I'm easy to confide in.'

He laughs, picks up the pot. 'More coffee?'

'Thanks.'

There's a mewing at the door. Ron stands and lets in a fat black cat that promptly jumps onto the table.

'Meet Sardine,' he says, pushing the cat back down.

'Boy or girl?'

'Boy.' He sets about opening a can, spooning meat into a bowl while Sardine purrs.

Marina senses Ron is controlling his emotions and guesses he's been hurt. She is curious and asks gently about Eva's issues.

Sardine has finished and is licking his paws, wiping

his mouth. Ron reaches across and grabs the cat. 'She doesn't get out much,' he says.

'Why?'

Sardine struggles on his lap. 'She's . . .' He stops again.

'Agoraphobic?'

'Not exactly. She gets anxious and . . . panicky. Her mother died not that long ago, actually.'

'Oh.' Marina feels a ripple of disappointment. He must be talking about Natalia. The only one she thought who might still be in the house and likely to have information. Eva would be too young to remember. Nevertheless, she sounds interesting and Marina would like to know more.

Ron stands to open the door and Sardine darts outside, but by the time he turns around, his face is closed. The conversation is over.

Marina takes another biscuit and changes the subject, asking about Ron's work at the museum. He appears relieved and becomes animated, describing his job. But Marina is hardly concentrating. She's picturing this mysterious woman in her hiding place at the top of the house, playing the piano all through the night. Eva Kolinski. However young or old she is, she's a link to the past, and Marina badly wants to meet her.

11

Connie

May 1964

Dorothy linked arms with Connie as they crossed the main road. Despite her small stature, the older woman walked swiftly and Connie found herself having to half run to keep up.

Dorothy led her along a few more streets and soon they were in a part of Streatham she didn't normally go to. The pavements were narrower here, the houses and gardens scruffier, the dustbins overflowing, and there was a rottenness in the air. A mangy cat sprawled as if exhausted by the heat.

That morning, Connie had woken in a panic, remembering what she had agreed to do. She'd considered telling Dorothy she had changed her mind, that she wanted to wait a little longer – but there was no obligation, and time was of the essence, so what did she have to lose? She'd tried to distract herself by thinking about being in Paris, imagining scenes like paintings with the golden colours and textures of a Van Gogh, or the luminous blue-grey of a Whistler. It would be everything that Harrington Gardens was not.

Now, though, walking with Dorothy, not even thoughts of Johnny's temporary home could offer a diversion. Especially when they stopped at a house with a window box full of pink and yellow pansies. None of the other houses had any sign of care or colour. Maybe the flowers were a secret signal.

A plump woman with silver hair opened the door. She nodded a greeting and, without a smile exchanged or a word spoken, led them into a small room. With its fussy wallpaper, a single armchair, and a vase of lilies on a table, it reminded Connie of a funeral parlour, which in turn made her think about saying goodbye to her mother. The kiss she had planted on her cold forehead and how she had wept, standing in the sunshine, knowing her mother would never feel the heat on her face again.

Connie clasped her hands together and squeezed away her tears.

The woman left and a younger, thinner, fair-haired version replaced her. They could be mother and daughter, a family team. The new woman welcomed them and surveyed Connie, nodding as if in approval.

She explained what would happen: medication, not too unpleasant tasting; a few hours to let the magic do its work; followed by a quick, painless procedure. Bleeding, not too much, a tad more than her usual period, perhaps a little clotting. She addressed Dorothy as much as Connie. Maybe she thought Dorothy was her mother.

Connie sensed her control sliding away. She dragged it back again, asking questions: How long would it take? How much would it hurt? Could she see the place where it would happen?

The woman answered patiently, quietly, until the last question, when her smile faded. Connie felt as if the walls were closing in on her. The cloying scent of the lilies mixed with something else – furniture polish, and another chemical smell. She glanced at Dorothy, who wore even more make-up than usual: a brighter lipstick, a heavier application of rouge, a dark green eyeshadow. It was as if they were going on an outing. Maybe it was to cover up the truth of what they were doing: Dorothy, Connie had concluded, was not a transparent person.

The woman cleared her throat. 'I don't recommend you have too many . . .' She hesitated, searching for the right word. 'Details, for the moment.'

'Why not?' asked Connie.

'We prefer to ease our –' she hesitated again – 'ladies into the right frame of mind. I suggest you go home, take the medicine with you, have a little think, talk it over with a person you trust. And then, when you're ready, settle yourself comfortably and take the medication along with a nice cup of tea. A little extra sugar will sweeten the bitter taste.'

It sounded almost as though she was discussing a treat. 'I'd like to know everything now,' Connie insisted. 'There's no point taking the medication home if I decide not to use it.'

The woman shifted her weight, smoothed her hair with one hand and glanced at the door. 'I wouldn't recommend . . .'

'Oh, but I want to,' Connie interrupted. 'I want to be prepared.'

A second of quiet, a slight nod from Dorothy, and in that instant Connie realised the two women knew each other. Her heartbeat quickened. Who else had Dorothy brought to this place? What about the other girl, the one

Dorothy said had been mooning over Johnny? No. Connie swept the possibility away. Dorothy had been a midwife once. That must be the connection.

'All right,' said the woman, sighing heavily. She led the way to the rear of the house.

Connie hardly expected to see a room similar to a doctor's surgery: a narrow bed with clean, white sheets; a sparkling sink; sets of shining metal instruments; the smell of disinfectant. Still, she was taken aback when she stepped into an untidy kitchen.

'Where?' she said, looking around, hoping to spot a secret door.

The woman coughed and waved her arm vaguely.

There was a table pushed against one wall and above it a cupboard. The door had been left half open and Connie could see that it was stacked with a jumble of misshapen bottles, all filled with a murky liquid. She spotted a red contraption made of rubber – a syringe with a bulb in the centre of the hose – and, beside that, a basket of sharp metal objects. Noticing, the woman discreetly pushed the door closed.

A child's trike stood in the corner, wheels muddied from recent play. There were remnants of a meal left on the side too, dirty crockery, pots and pans.

Stepping away awkwardly, Connie collided with the edge of the table.

'It's all right,' said the woman. 'Everyone reacts like this at first, but the alternative is far worse.'

She told the story of a girl as young as Connie, who'd been refused the *procedure* by doctors, but hadn't been lucky enough to find someone like herself. 'You can imagine what happened next,' she said. Her voice was soothing, as if she was telling a bedtime story – a fable with a message to be learned.

Connie put her hand to her mouth. She didn't want to imagine what had happened to the girl. It was all she could do to envisage swallowing that medication. She saw herself lying on the table while the woman inserted one of the sharp metal objects inside her or squirted a strange liquid from the pump.

From somewhere in the house, a baby cried. The woman glanced at the ceiling. Connie looked up too, feeling the irony, wondering about the woman's motivation. Was it to help young women or was it simply for the money? Somehow, she didn't seem the type to care about a girl's plight. And what about Dorothy? Whose interests did she have at heart – Connie's or her own? All those photos of Johnny on her walls, yet none of his art. Maybe Dorothy didn't want anything – or anyone – to come between herself and her son. His obsession with art, his baby inside Connie.

'No,' she said with sudden clarity. 'I've changed my mind.'

She turned, pushed past Dorothy and ran.

12

Marina

January 1992

Marina sails about London as if she is mapping it out. She takes long bus rides with no sense of her destination, getting off at the city's edges and returning the way she has come.

She walks purposefully through streets and squares and alleyways, never using her A–Z. When she is lost or tired, she hops onto the Tube and travels beneath the capital instead. She crosses bridges and parks and climbs high buildings, examining her world from every which way. Spiralling away from the centre, she visits markets and sits in cafes or wanders amongst stalls. From time to time she wonders if a voice she hears in the crowd might belong to her birth mother, or if a place she goes to is somewhere her mother might have been.

In Streatham, she wanders the common and sits on a bench. A tired-looking woman rocking a pram occupies the other end. Marina smiles, but the woman doesn't notice.

Marina thinks of an article she read about a newborn, a girl, wrapped in a blanket and left in a park. She would have been warm, only there had been a storm that night. A homeless man had come across the bundle and taken her to the hospital and miraculously she had survived. Marina has read other stories too, about newborns abandoned outside churches, hospitals and houses; in fields, forests and rubbish dumps. She puts the stories into two camps: mothers wanting them to be found by priests, doctors or well-meaning people; and those who abandoned them to the elements. She thinks about motives: too young, too poor, too alone, too frightened. She imagines the secrecy of giving birth in a bath, an alleyway or a public toilet. She imagines the fear, the stifling of screams and crying in silence. She doesn't judge.

The woman stills the pram. The baby wails. Marina tenses and glances across. There is an expression of despair on the woman's face, but when Marina smiles this time, her face clears and she smiles back. Reaching inside the pram, she lifts out her baby to feed.

One day, Marina drives to the hospital. How strange, walking through the entrance – the buzz, the disinfectant, the slow-walking patients attached to their drips, the fast-running staff responding to calls.

She tries to imagine how it would have been nearly thirty years before. How much has changed? Different decor, uniforms, treatments and equipment. The nurses might have worn hats and capes. The doctors might all have been male. She sets the scene for the day she arrived: staff making a fuss of her, poking and prodding, checking her health, looking for clues. Interested parties: journalists and photographers. A whirl and a fuss for the baby in blue.

In the car park, she wanders, hands in her pockets. She visualises the foster parents, perhaps a social worker, Sofía and other nurses crowding round to say goodbye.

She thinks about the unexplained woman. Did Ruth know that story? Had she thought it mysterious too?

Marina takes her thoughts to a nearby cafe – a dreary place with grey-looking walls and sticky tables. She orders coffee and then uses the payphone at the counter. She calls Ruth, who answers quickly.

'Marina,' she exclaims. 'I've just this minute put down the phone to Aunt Lydia. Tell me your ears were burning.'

'My ears were burning. What did you say about me?'

'I said you were finding your fortune in London.'

'Like Dick Whittington.'

'Exactly.' There is a pause. She speaks more seriously. 'So, how are things?'

'They're good.' Marina transfers the receiver to the other ear. 'How's Aunt Lydia?'

'Fine. She's thinking of going on a cruise. How odd is that?'

'Did you say that to her?'

'Yes, I did. I said organised holidays are for lazy people.'

Marina laughs. Lydia is Ruth's sister and the two of them are like chalk and cheese.

'How's the house?'

'It's . . .' Marina stops. Disturbing, uncomfortable? Oddly like home?

'It must be strange,' says Ruth carefully.

'I suppose it is.'

There is a silence. Marina can hear Ruth breathing on the end of the line. 'Have you seen Sofía?'

'Yes, actually.' Pause. 'That's why I'm calling. I wanted to ask you about something she said.'

'Right.' Again, that cautious note.

'She mentioned a woman who turned up unannounced at the ward they put me in. She said the incident was noted, but never followed up. The thing is this woman was there again on the day that my foster parents took me away.'

Ruth clears her throat. She speaks slowly, spacing out her words. 'Sofía never mentioned it.'

Marina senses a *but* coming. She leans with her back against the counter. A couple are seated by the window. The woman is heavily pregnant. Marina pushes the receiver against her ear and looks away.

'But . . .' Ruth stops and Marina pictures her, fiddling with the beads around her neck. 'There was an occasion when something similar happened.'

Marina straightens. 'What was that?'

'I never mentioned it before because I thought it was a flight of fancy. I was nervous, jumpy. We'd only had you for a few months . . .'

'Yeah. Go on.'

'It was at your christening. I hadn't wanted one, as you know. Your dad persuaded me and I agreed on condition we also had a naming ceremony.'

Marina has photos of both occasions. A vicar, a church, a font. A marquee in a field near Stonehenge.

'Like I said, I was nervous.'

'But why?'

'I suppose I thought that someone would suddenly appear and accuse us of kidnap.' Ruth gives a laugh.

'Silly, I know. We'd done everything correctly, gone through all the checks, signed the right papers, but still, it was early days.'

Marina is quiet, listening.

'We had guests. Friends, family, neighbours. It was a private affair. Right at the end of the service, as we were walking out, I noticed a woman sitting at the back of the church. She was . . . different somehow.'

'What do you mean?'

'I can't properly explain. It was the way she was looking and not looking.'

'I don't understand.'

'Neither do I, really. I mentioned it to your dad, but you know what he's like. He thought I was being whimsical.'

'What was she like?'

'It was a bit of a blur. I remember she wore a coat and hat. I guess it covered her up. Maybe that's what I meant about looking and not looking. She was obviously there for a reason, and perhaps she'd just got the wrong time or place – but it seemed as though she didn't want to be seen, or something. But I didn't really think anything of it at the time. I was preoccupied with you, and making sure I thanked people for coming.'

'Right,' says Marina slowly. 'And nothing else happened?'

'Well.' Ruth pauses. 'The thing is, I thought I saw her again. Or should I say something similar happened. It was twenty years later, so I couldn't be sure it was the same woman.'

Marina feels a sliding sensation. 'When was it exactly?'

'At your graduation ceremony.' Ruth gives a short laugh. 'I know what you're thinking. It's stupid, isn't it?'

Marina rubs her forehead. 'Did you speak to her?'

'No. It was a crowded room. By the time I decided to approach her, she'd gone.'

Marina closes her eyes. Why hadn't Ruth told her this before? 'Did you talk about it to Dad that time?'

'No. It was silly. Honestly, Marina, I decided it was a coincidence and that it couldn't possibly have been the same woman. I put it out of my head. At least I tried to. Your saying what you said about Sofía . . . Well, I suppose it brought it back.'

A week passes. Marina stops exploring London and focuses on the house. She paces the dusty hall gauging its length and width as if long forgotten secrets will be revealed through mathematics. She examines the alcove on her hands and knees, considering the angle of the door, calculating how many seconds it would have taken to come in and leave the baby. It would have been risky, she thinks. Either of the tenants in Flat 2, Eileen or Leonard, could have come out and discovered her – or the landlord for that matter, Kenneth Quip. She peers at the post boxes as if they might hold the key to the past. None of them have locks. The box belonging to Giovanni Gaetti in Flat 1 is so full the flap hangs open.

She climbs the stairs, holding the bannister, imagining the people who have touched it before. Sometimes regret stirs and sweeps through her like the breath of a ghost. Mostly, though, the atmosphere is still, the stairway dark and claustrophobic. The air is musty with an underlying rottenness, the scent of damp and decaying wood.

From Mrs Hyde's flat on the first floor, she hears a rhythmic thumping – the sound of an iron on an ironing board. Marina has noticed people coming and going, carrying bags of laundry. The radio plays, or perhaps it's the TV. Songs of praise or evening services, hymns and chants and sermons in low voices.

On Eva's floor, she stands on the small square of landing. The dark wood floorboards creak; there's the sound of the piano, followed by light footsteps. She cannot resist the urge and knocks again. There's no answer although Marina is certain Eva is inside.

She ventures through the door that leads to the attic. The stairway is narrow and dusty and she moves slowly, brushing her fingers against the cobwebbed walls, emerging into unexpected light. The room has a neglected smell like the rest of the house, and bare, splintered floorboards, but large windows are set into the roof and, despite the clutter, there is space. According to the estate agent, the loft is communal. It's a place where tenants can store whatever they like. Marina suspects it hasn't been cleared for years.

Boxes are piled high. She opens some of them and finds rubbish: damaged kitchen utensils, broken toys. There are other discarded items scattered around too: a vacuum cleaner, a faded footstool, a portable TV, trunks of old books. Marina roots through and finds a mixture of the classics, volumes of poetry and detective novels.

The books are second-hand with names and dates written at the front. Some have a note written in pencil:

Not to be sold. She flicks through a book about the suffragettes and recalls one of the articles she read that mentioned Thomas Littleton being a bookseller. Maybe he'd owned a shop locally.

Battered orange crates are stacked against one wall and there's an old chest of drawers that contains dried-up paintbrushes. She takes a crate, turns it over and sits. From this angle, she notices that several paintings have been slotted behind the chest. Curious, she pulls them out. Sunflowers and sunsets, a Van Gogh-style depiction of a starry night, an unfinished sketch of a woman in a cloak with hands clasped in prayer. She stares at these, her mind fizzing, wondering who painted them. They are good, she thinks, examining the details, the bright yellows and blues.

There's a tapping sound above and she glances up to see birds on the roof. Clouds scoot past and she has a sense of time hurtling by at great speed. Dizzily she steadies herself, looks down, touches the daubs of paint on the floorboards, their colours muted by the years. The artist worked here, she realises.

Her gaze falls again on the boxes of books and she remembers the bookshop she spotted. What was it called? Crystal's Books. Is it worth checking out? Marina stands and as she does, a bird lifts from the roof and wheels through the sky.

Crystal's Books is bright and modern. It's a narrow space, seeming larger thanks to a combination of mirrors, lamps and light-coloured walls. Incense burns. The pale wood shelves are packed neatly. There are nods to the past: a display of old-fashioned signs and a line of black and white photos on one wall. A grandfather clock stands silently at the far end. Through a low doorway she can see stairs up to a second floor. A slim woman in jeans, with curly red hair, stands at the top of a stepladder, slotting books into spaces.

'Two ticks,' she calls when she spots Marina.

'No hurry.' Marina is a little disappointed. She would have liked to have been greeted by a Dickens character: a hunched old man who might or might not be Thomas Littleton. She wanders to the far end of the shop to a shelf labelled *Myths and Legends*.

'Looking for anything in particular?' asks the woman, climbing down from the ladder.

'Not especially.'

'Shout if you need me.' She brushes down her jeans. In her fifties, perhaps, she wears a russet shirt that sets off the flames of her hair.

Marina picks out a book on burial grounds and stone circles which is perfect for Ruth. She browses the rest of the shop contemplating a gift for David and settles on a biography of Jacqueline du Pré.

At the counter, the woman is reading what appears to be a manuscript.

'It's a sideline,' she says when she sees Marina looking. 'I teach creative writing.' She gestures to the floor above. 'We give lessons in the upstairs room, literacy classes too.'

'You sound busy.'

'Not enough money in books alone, unfortunately. Mind you, the literacy is a community project. We're always looking for volunteers if you're interested. Free tea and biscuits.'

Marina smiles at her warmth.

'I'm Crystal by the way, in case you haven't guessed.'

'Marina.' No need to hide her name here.

Crystal rings up the books on the till, pausing to examine the cover of the one Marina picked out for Ruth. 'This looks interesting.'

'It's for my mother.'

'Lucky her. There's more like this. I can search them out if you want. Are you local?'

'Yes.'

'Wonderful. New to the area?'

'Yes, I've just moved into a shared house. I used to be a teacher actually – French and German.'

'Is that right? I've been thinking about providing language classes. Interested?'

'Sorry. I've got no plans to teach again. I'm editing.'

'Editing?' Crystal waves the manuscript at her. 'Perfect.'

Marina laughs. Crystal reminds her of Ruth. They're both persistent. Ruth used to convince her to do things – swimming in the sea, making a cake, abseiling – from the simple to the daring, persuading by stealth, dropping advice, building Marina's confidence.

She agrees to at least consider Crystal's teaching proposition. Then, on the way out, she glances at the wall display. Next to the black and white photos, there's a montage of postcards arranged in a glass frame. The photos show south London through the decades. There's a picture of Streatham High Road complete with buses and shops and an advert for John Bull. And another with a group of young people in suits and short skirts dancing in a club.

An old-fashioned sign hangs alongside. Marina reads:
THOMAS LITTLETON BOOKSELLER
BOOKS BOUGHT AND SOLD
RARE AND SECOND HAND

Her stomach flips. Her instincts were right. The tenant from Flat 4 once owned this shop. She glances at Crystal who is absorbed in the manuscript, her lips moving as she reads. Marina hesitates before she calls across. 'How long have you owned the shop?'

Crystal frowns, thinking. 'Let's see, we bought it in the early seventies – that's my ex-husband and me. Cheap as chips, which was great for us, not so much for the owner.' She nods across at the sign.

'What happened to him?'

'He died.' She picks up a paperweight and balances it on the palm of her hand. 'We got everything – every book, pen and trinket. Some things we hung onto, like those photos, for authenticity, you know, a homage to the past, but generally it took a lot of work to get rid of it all.'

'Why did that happen?'

'It was a complicated situation. No one to inherit or something.' She puts her head on one side. 'Although there was a sister, I recall. I think she kept the shop shut up for several years. I can't remember exactly what happened. Something to do with the will. My ex dealt with that side of things. I wasn't financially adept, not then. I had to learn after he ran off with our savings, though. So many years ago. God, time goes quickly.'

Marina agrees. The present becomes the past in a moment.

13

Eva

January 1992

Eva remembers many things about her childhood.

She remembers birthdays – her mother icing a cake, wrapping her presents in gold paper, which she reused every year. They went to the pictures, or to the ice rink, or for a picnic on the common. They sat on a blanket and ate sandwiches and Eva would listen to her mother talk.

She said it was important to remember the past in case people forgot – and then she would tell Eva the story of how her family had been rounded up and taken to a concentration camp, but how she had been smuggled out of the country and sent to England on her own. She would describe the Jewish orphanage where she had stayed before a family had taken her in, and the happy times she had had with them, growing up an only child, but loved by her adoptive parents. She would say how she had met Eva's father, her beautiful face lighting up at the memory of that moment, at a wedding, when their eyes had met across a crowded room. How awkward they both had been. How tentatively they had danced. How quickly they had fallen in love. Two people finding a connection through bleak memories and hopefulness.

Recalling her own past now, Eva remembers scraps and leftovers. She remembers her mother watching her eat and then scraping the saucepan or Eva's plate. She remembers carbolic soap and cold water, mended clothes and blackened shoes, men calling them names, boys throwing stones.

Her mother had a strong, beautiful face. She played a piano which Eva's father had bought second-hand and then restored. She gave music lessons to children. She was a dressmaker too, making clothes for wealthy women who would sweep up the stairs to their door. Eva remembers these women standing in their underwear, while her mother, with pins in her mouth, knelt at their feet.

Eva remembers many things.

What she can't remember is her father – at least, not beyond a soft face and a kind voice. Or her mother's miscarriage, even though she knows she witnessed it.

What she can't remember with any clarity is anything before the age of about three or four. Although there are blurs. Images that dance about in time. Impressions. Faceless people. When she tries to recall the details, all she gets is the same precarious sensation as if she's teetering at the top of a great height. Sometimes, she stands at the window, like she does now, touching the glass. What would it be like to fall, to open the window and lean until she drops and the decision has been taken from her? Perhaps in those split seconds before she hit the ground, the blanks in her head would be filled.

The new tenant is walking towards the house. She is hunched inside her furry coat with her hair loose about her shoulders. Head bent, one hand is in a pocket, the other swinging her bag. She reaches the house and disappears inside.

The door of the house opposite opens and a man and

his son appear. The boy is small, five or six. They are holding hands and the boy sets off, feet together, jumping down the steps. Eva leans forward, watching them as they reach the bottom laughing. She eases the window open so that she can hear their voices. A wind has come up. It runs through the maple tree below and slips through the gap of the window and into Eva's room. Chilled, she wraps her thin arms around her body.

Eva closes her eyes. A memory is coming.

She is Little Eva. A piano is playing. Her mother is performing Chopin, but she is weeping as she plays, all the sadness of her life pouring through her fingers. Little Eva cannot bear her mother's sorrow so she slips out of the flat and down the stairs.

What next?

She sits on a step with her chin in her hands. She has bare feet and a purple dress that swirls around her legs when she runs.

A woman appears and takes her hand. Together they climb back up the stairs all the way to the top. Little Eva is jumping, two feet together, in the way that children do. Who is the woman? Is it her mother come down to fetch her? What next?

The scent of roses.

Eva blinks and the memory disappears.

14

Marina

January 1992

The estate agent is close to the Tube station. Marina enters and Wayne jumps up from his desk and hurries to greet her.

'Is everything all right?' he asks, running his hand through slicked-back hair.

'It's the boiler,' she says, and explains the problem of the scalding water and lukewarm radiators. 'Can you contact the landlord?'

He shuffles his feet. 'I can try.'

'Try?' Marina is taken aback. She knows the rent is low and that she agreed to accept the place as it is, but even so, she has rights.

'I mean, I'll ask him to OK repairs.'

'Ask him?'

'Tell him. Yes. Tell him.'

Marina is unconvinced. 'Why don't you give me his number?'

'I can't do that.'

'Cut out the middle man.'

He looks around helplessly. He is a good five years younger than Marina and a lot less self-assured. An older woman stares across disapprovingly from her desk.

Marina lowers her voice. 'Listen. I understand that you can get into trouble. But it's freezing in the flat.'

She holds out her hands and wiggles her numb fingers. He peers at them and grimaces.

'Give me his number, or his address, if you like. I can say I found it myself . . . No one needs to know.'

He sighs. 'It's very unorthodox. And the landlord is quite particular.'

'What do you mean?'

'He prefers to be anonymous.'

Marina resists the urge to roll her eyes. Instead, she lays her hand on his sleeve. He blushes. 'I understand. But he doesn't need to find out. Why don't you tell me his name?'

He opens his mouth. The woman clears her throat. Wayne shakes his head. 'I'll call him today, I promise.'

She frowns and gives up. 'Fine. But please tell him it's an emergency.'

'An emergency,' he parrots. 'Yes, of course. In the meantime, there's an electrical shop not far from here where you can buy . . .'

He doesn't finish his sentence, because Marina has left. She is marching to buy an electric heater that she will charge to the negligent landlord.

When she gets home in possession of the heater, there is a decorator's van parked in the street and migraine-inducing hammering coming from above. Marina mutters as she steps inside her flat, heaves the heater from its box, crouches on the carpet and fiddles with the dials. A piece of plaster drops beside her.

'And now the sky is falling in.'

She smiles thinking of David reading her the story of

Chicken Licken. It was always David who performed those quiet tasks, the tea parties for her dolls, the animals on her farm, the Lego and the games. Ruth was a force of nature, ferrying her from one adventure to the next.

She plugs in the heater and warms her hands over its pathetic seep of air.

'Hey!' Ron pokes his head into the room. 'You left the door open.'

'Did I? Must be the noise interfering with my sense.'

He saunters in – yellow shirt and khaki shorts – and waves a bottle of wine in her direction. 'Fancy a drink?'

'Aren't you cold?'

He chuckles. 'Never feel it.'

'Lucky you. Shouldn't you be at work?'

'Day off.'

'Double lucky you.'

She disappears into the kitchen to open the wine and fetch glasses. When she returns, he is examining the photo of Ruth and David. 'You look more like your dad than your mum,' he says, taking his drink.

She suppresses a smile. People see what they believe they should see.

He raises his glass. 'Cheers.'

'Cheers.'

They sit in armchairs facing each other. Ron lounges easily, long legs sprawled. Above them, the hammering transforms into thumping.

'You'd think the landlord would mind – at least a bit,' says Marina.

'Makes his life easy.'

'I suppose. I'm planning to paint. So far, I've managed that.' She points at a trio of samples on the walls – burgundy, dark blue and bronze green. 'What do you reckon?'

'I like the blue.'

More loud noises above them. They look up in unison.

'Maybe they've discovered a body,' suggests Ron, 'underneath the floorboards.'

'God, I hope not.' Marina takes a large drink of her wine. The heater sputters. She leans across and alters the setting. 'I've told the estate agent that the landlord has to fix my boiler.'

'Good luck with that.'

'I wanted to call him myself, but they won't give me his number.'

'You could always intercept him.'

'Where?'

'He sometimes wanders about in the garden. Old guy with white hair.'

'Oh, I think I've seen him. Does he have a cane?'

'That's him.'

'I thought he was Giovanni.'

Ron laughs. 'Giovanni's thirty years younger than our lovely landlord.'

'I don't believe he exists.'

'Giovanni? He does, I promise you. He's an interesting guy.'

There's another crash above them. Marina makes a face. 'How am I supposed to get any work done?'

She tells him about Agata's memoirs and he listens, interested.

'Not an easy read,' he remarks.

'Not an easy life. An orphan, alone in another country.'

He nods, agreeing. 'Do you do much research? Must be difficult.'

'I trust Agata to get her facts right, though I do check dates and main events. I lived in Poland for a bit.' She hesitates before she says, 'I visited Auschwitz.'

'Shit. How was that?'

She shrugs. 'I told myself that my feelings were irrelevant in comparison to the suffering that had happened there.' She shuts her eyes, remembering the visit that no words can really describe.

When she glances at Ron again, he is looking at her thoughtfully. 'Eva's parents had a similar experience. I mean they both had to flee Poland.'

'Did they? You said her mother died not long ago. What about her father?'

'He died too, when Eva was very small – had an accident I think.'

Ron swirls his wine, stares into the glass and adds, 'She doesn't talk about it much, or anything about her past for that matter.'

Marina frowns, sensing the disappointment in his voice.

He continues. 'Of course, she might talk to you since you're editing articles about the war.'

'Not articles,' she says. 'It's a memoir. Although . . .' She stops and plays with the stem of her glass. She is almost tempted to tell Ron the truth, but resists because a new idea is forming. 'I've been thinking about branching out, you know, from publishing into journalism. I worked in local radio for a while . . . a long time ago.'

'Impressive.'

It isn't really. She's exaggerating. Ruth had known one of the producers and had wangled some work experience for Marina when she'd been at school. It had amounted to making tea and running messages.

'Anyway, I've been looking around for a story to write about.'

'And you're thinking about Eva's? I don't . . .'

'No, no. Not that,' Marina says quickly. 'A local story, a case that has never been solved, which I could find a new angle on, and take to a local newspaper.'

'Sounds interesting. Do you have anything in mind?'

'Well,' she speaks slowly. 'I did hear that a baby was abandoned in this house.'

He raises his eyebrows, surprised. 'Yes, I heard that too.' He frowns. 'I'm trying to remember who told me. Selena, I think. You know, the woman upstairs.' He jabs his finger at the ceiling where there is still the sound of heavy hammering.

Marina shifts in her seat. 'Do you know the details – of the baby, I mean?'

He shakes his head. 'Not really. You should talk to Selena, or you could go to the library or something, go through the newspaper archives.'

'That's a good idea.' She sips her wine, slowly. 'I've been thinking about tracking down some of the tenants who lived in the house at the time. I think there's only Eva still here.'

He looks at her, surprised. 'You've already started researching?'

'Only a bit,' she replies hastily.

'Well, what year did it happen?'

'I think . . . early sixties.' She keeps her voice vague.

'In that case, I doubt Eva would have much to say. She'd be too young.'

'Yes, but she might remember what people said.'

'Well, if you're serious, I could ask if she would speak to you.'

Marina's heart beats harder. She moistens her lips. 'Would you?'

'I can't promise she'll say yes. Like I told you, she's a bit . . . ' – he makes a wry face – '. . . unsociable.'

He drinks the rest of his wine. The hammering stops and drilling begins.

'In the meantime,' Ron says, holding out his empty glass to be filled. 'I think you should complain.'

Later, after Ron has gone, Marina knocks on the door of Flat 4. The noise inside is so loud, it takes a while before Selena answers, but when she does, with the baby in its sling on her chest, she's beaming. She must have a permanent smile etched on her face. It's infectious. Marina grins stupidly back.

'I'm so sorry.' Selena gestures to the drilling behind her and then runs her fingers through her hair, which has changed from purple to green. 'I'll tell Pete – that's our decorator – to keep down the noise.'

'It's not a problem,' Marina replies, almost guiltily, before politely mentioning the damaged ceiling. 'I just thought you should know.'

'Oh God. Sorry. I'll ask Pete to do something about it. In the meantime, do you fancy a cup of tea?'

Marina hesitates, but curiosity takes hold and she agrees.

Selena disappears to find Pete and the drilling stops. They go into the kitchen. It is the same narrow shape as Marina's, only the table and worktops are covered with baby paraphernalia – teething toys, dummies, bibs – alongside unwashed mugs and breakfast bowls.

Selena looks ruefully at the clutter and shifts the baby higher on her chest.

'Shall I make the tea?' Marina offers.

'No, it's fine. Maybe you could have Lottie?'

Marina takes the baby awkwardly, holding the fragile body lightly as Selena piles dirty crockery into the sink and wipes the surfaces, quickly and efficiently, taking advantage of her freedom. She puts on the kettle and assembles mugs, teabags and biscuits. Her face looks tired and there are lines around her eyes.

'Do you like children?' she asks as she works. 'Milk, sugar?'

'Yes, although I don't have much to do with them to be honest, and yes please, milk and two sugars.'

'Any nephews or nieces?' The kettle is boiling. She pours it onto the tea.

Marina shakes her head, breathes in the scent of the baby's hair. She has fallen asleep in her arms.

In the living room, Selena sets the mugs on the glass coffee table and clears a bundle of clothes from an armchair for Marina to sit. She lowers herself gingerly, but the movement wakes the baby and Selena takes over. They settle, Lottie in her mother's arms now. She has a slick of black hair and a bald spot on the crown.

'She was born with a shock of hair,' says Selena, shaking her own short crop. 'Now it's fallen out and she's like a little monk.' She gives a laugh. 'I was the same, according to my mother.'

Marina makes suitable noises, while surreptitiously looking around the room. According to her notes this is Thomas Littleton's flat. Post-decoration, the room is bright. Modern. There is a sense of calm. Perhaps it's the tangerine walls, the gauzy yellow curtains, the paintings of poppies on the walls, the light-coloured, angular furniture. She asks if the landlord minds them working on the flat.

'He's fine with it,' says Selena. 'We did the bathroom last year and had no complaints. Mind you, we don't spend a lot; no point as we're renting. It's only the paint really.'

'Oh?'

'My husband has a gardening business. His friend, Pete, is a painter and decorator. They exchange skills.'

'Sounds like a good arrangement.'

'Are you thinking of decorating too?'

'Yes, but I can't decide on the colour.'

'It isn't easy, is it?'

'How did you decide?'

'I wanted a contrast. The place was empty for years before we moved in. Dark, no carpet, tatty velvet curtains, peeling wallpaper. It was cheap of course, which is why we took it. The previous tenant died some time before, I believe. Not sure why it wasn't rented out for so long.'

Marina nods, thinking about this. Thomas Littleton,

she supposes, although there could have been a different tenant in between him and the Hamiltons. Yet the story chimes with what Crystal said. The death of the owner, the delay in sorting things out. Should she ask Selena for his name, or would that be strange? She decides against it. 'How long have you lived here?' she says instead.

'Too many years,' says Selena, shifting Lottie from one shoulder to the other. 'It would be good to move on, but we can't afford it. Bill's gardening business earns enough to keep us going. I should work, but it'll be hard to find care for Lottie, and besides, we waited so long for her to arrive, I don't want to leave her. Not yet.' She kisses the top of the baby's head. 'I used to teach yoga; maybe I'll give private lessons. It works for the woman upstairs.'

Marina takes the chance to talk about Eva. 'She teaches piano? I've heard her playing. She's very talented, but does she always play in the middle of the night?'

Selena laughs. 'Yes, and I would complain, but I'm usually awake at that time anyway, with this one, and I find it soothing.'

The baby is stirring, her face puckering. Selena prepares to feed her and Marina looks away politely. Her gaze fixes on the bookcase.

Selena notices. 'Feel free.'

The books are mostly non-fiction coffee-table books about art and Scandinavian furniture and places to visit. There's one about interior design which Marina is about to investigate further, when she notices a hardback. The spine is battered and worn. Pulling it out, she discovers a volume of poetry: Donne, Fletcher, Jonson. The book is covered in a fine brown dust; the cover is detached and frayed at one end. She turns it over carefully and examines the first page. The writing is difficult to decipher, but she makes out the names of previous owners. Mr R. Morfitt 1884; Joyce Davidson 1945; Timothy something or other; and a note in faint pencil saying *Not to be sold.* She frowns and then smiles, remembering. The same words were written in some of the books she found in the attic. Maybe Selena had retrieved this one from there.

The paper wears the ghostly imprint of fingerprints. The breath of book lovers is caught inside its pages. She turns the stiff, yellowing pages and experiences an emotion akin to when she's close to old art and ancient places. Marina picks out memories of poetry lessons at school and remembers a few lines of Donne:

> Though I must go, endure not yet
> A breach, but an expansion,
> Like gold to airy thinness beat.

She glances at Selena to ask about the book, but she is feeding her baby, absorbed in the moment. It seems intensely private and Marina looks away, but the image is fixed. Mother and child. Tears prick her eyes as she returns the book to its place and brushes the dust from her fingers. She takes out the one on interior design and opens it randomly at a page about choosing the colour of the walls to suit your personality.

'You can borrow that if you like,' says Selena, looking up.

Marina thanks her and takes the book to her seat. Her mood settles as she reads about the calming effect of blues and greens. The wind stirs at the window and the gauzy curtains flutter in the breeze, moving formlessly like a couple of ghosts.

15

Connie

May 1964

As Connie ran from the house, a young woman was approaching, emerald coat buttoned tightly. The woman checked her watch as she drew close and Connie wanted to say, 'Don't go inside!' Not that she knew the woman was intending to, of course, but there was something about her – a slight uncertainty, a kind of nervousness – that made Connie suspect they were in the same predicament.

She didn't speak, however; didn't even pause. She had to get away, as far and as fast as she could. So instead, she chased along the roads and through the common before finally stopping to rest, breathing deeply, letting the sunshine warm her face as she took in the grassy scent and the sweetness of the blossom that frothed amongst the trees. Yet nothing could obliterate the smell of that dreadful house – its chemical tang laced with rottenness. It was as if she could taste it.

A passing woman, pushing a pram with silver wheels that flashed in the sunlight, glanced at her with disdain. Connie looked down at herself. She was a sight, with her dress awry and her make-up smudged from crying.

Straightening her dress, she thought back to her predicament. She should choose what to do with her body – and her baby – but did she really have a choice?

She would never be granted a proper, clean operation by Doctor Franklin, or any other doctor for that matter. At the same time, she couldn't, wouldn't be subjected to a backstreet abortion. The memory of the spikes and the pump brought a fresh wave of nausea and she took deep breaths, forcing back the bile. How did those things work? How much would it hurt? She put her hand to her belly and blinked. Tears rising, she galvanised herself and headed for home.

A man with ears like handles and sandy-coloured hair stood at the end of the path alongside the house. He was smoking, cigarette pinched between thumb and first finger, taking fierce drags. He stared at Connie, rising on the balls of his feet like a boxer. She lifted her chin and tightened her fists, scowled and then regretted it. He seemed like what her mother would have called a ne'er-do-well, in scruffy jeans and a zipped-up dark blue Harrington jacket despite the heat, his wiry body tensed for a fight.

Disconcerted, Connie turned in at number 24. Reluctant to shut herself away in the flat, she followed the path around the side of the house and, using the key Kenneth had recently given her, unlocked the padlock on the gate. Another one of his security measures. Last week, she'd heard him yelling at Mrs Kolinski for leaving the front door open. Mrs Kolinski hadn't reacted, only closed the door quietly in that calm way she had and continued up the stairs with Eva.

Dorothy's housecoats and aprons were pegged out on the line. Connie glared at them and then forced herself to calm down. Dorothy wasn't to blame for her son's absence or for the trip to that awful house. It was Connie's fault for making the decision to sleep with Johnny in the first place, for believing him when he told her how unlikely it was she'd get pregnant.

How stupid she'd been, listening to him. It wasn't as if she was naive and didn't know about sex. There had been enough conversations at school, and her mother had always been careful to explain things. Not like some of the other mothers. She remembered one of the girls in her class, Eliza Langtry, who'd screamed blue murder in the toilets when she'd started her period. She'd thought she was dying, literally bleeding to death. The other girls had laughed, but Connie had felt sorry for her.

Before. That was how Connie saw it. Two halves of her life. Before her mother had died and after. Not that she could live by that rule now. Her life had changed again. This pregnancy had become a new before and after.

The end section of the garden was cut off by an overgrown curtain of bushes, plants and leaves. Behind the curtain was a patch of earth and Kenneth's roses, of all kinds and colours. He had given Connie a tour once, described spraying and deadheading and mulching and knowing your roots. She'd been surprised by his passion. Beyond the roses, next to the old shed and set into the wall, there was an arched doorway that led straight into the graveyard, though it was never used and was blocked by weeds. Connie usually visited her mother's grave via the lychgate on St Michael's Road, but now she was here, she decided to take the shortcut, even though she had no flowers as she usually did. On impulse, she seized a pair of secateurs from the shed and snipped the stem of an early, errant rose.

The door was studded wood, dark and gnarly. Connie cut wildly at the weeds covering it, hacking and slashing until she managed to clear them. Dropping the secateurs, she rested one hand against the door and, with the other, reached for the rusting metal ring and twisted hard. The door resisted. She pushed her shoulder against the wood. It didn't budge. Kenneth. She rolled her eyes and looked about for a key. How did he think anyone could possibly get through this door?

She reached up, fingers fumbling among the dips and crevices in the bricks, searching for a hiding place. As she did so, she heard male voices in the main part of the garden. Her skin prickled and she thrust the rose behind her back. Kenneth didn't take kindly to theft. He was a born-again honest person, her father joked.

The voices grew louder, and the smell of cigarette smoke drifted on the air. Tiny flies buzzed around Connie's face. Brushing them aside, she strained to hear the conversation.

'Don't be so fucking stupid. Why the hell would I do that?'

Connie froze. She'd never heard Kenneth swear. On the contrary, he considered it lazy and demeaning, a sign of poor intellect. 'I may not have had the benefit of a good education,' he would say, 'but what I've taught myself is worth more than schooling ever could have done, and that's dignity and self-respect.'

Well, he wasn't being dignified now.

The man responded in a low, tense tone, too quiet to hear.

'What are you saying, Frank? I'm loyal. You know that.'

More muttering. Connie leaned closer.

'We agreed, didn't we? No contact. What did you do, hire a bloody detective to find me?' The voices faded as the men moved away.

Connie peered through the branches and caught a flash of navy blue as the stranger rounded the house. It was the man she'd just seen in the street. An acquaintance of Kenneth's. No surprise judging from the look of him. An ex-con? She shivered remembering what her father had said about the gang member who'd been released from prison. Hadn't his name been Frank?

Stepping from her hiding place and still grasping the rose, she walked quickly to the front of the house, planning to take her usual route to the church as she couldn't unlock the arched door. But the men were talking on the pavement, which meant visiting her mother's grave would have to wait. Hiding the rose, she nipped up the steps and into the sanctuary of the hall.

Music blared from Flat 2. She paused to listen to the Beatles singing about money and love. She would miss Eileen if she went back to America to star in a show. Even though they didn't speak much, she felt like an ally.

The music stopped and shouting took its place. Connie pressed her ear to the door. Leonard was yelling about Eileen not being good enough. Connie's blood boiled. Eileen might not have been caught out by a baby like Connie had, but she was trapped by Leonard. No wonder she wanted to leave. There was a crashing sound and then silence. Johnny had been fiery, but he had never hurt her, and her father would never have harmed her mother either. But had her mother been happy? Was Connie? There were different ways to be ensnared.

A creak on the stairs. Connie spied little Eva in her purple dress. Barefoot, with sharp elbows and bony knees, she was as wispy as a willow. Connie pushed away her self-pity. It was worse for Eva, with no father and a mother who cried all the time, and hardly any money.

'Hey,' she said now, running up the stairs and crouching beside the little girl. 'What are you doing here all alone?'

Eva looked at her with wide eyes. In the past, Connie's mother had given Eva treats – a sugar mouse, a slab of toffee, or else she had passed on an item of clothing like the dress she wore now or a toy that had belonged to Connie. Once it had been a jack-in-the-box with a harlequin clown, another time a red and yellow spinning top. Connie's mother had said that it was a disgrace how people treated the Kolinski family. She said they had suffered too much already and that if she could help in any small way she would. She'd invited them for tea and Connie had taught Eva how to press flowers.

She ran to the flat. Rooting through her wardrobe, she pulled out a rag doll with plaited hair. She felt the softness of its body and the tug of a memory – her mother tucking the doll in beside her at night, kissing both of their foreheads, leaving behind the scent of lavender oil as she softly closed the door.

'She's called Sarah,' she said, back on the stairs, giving the doll to Eva. 'After my mother.'

Eva smiled and Connie felt rewarded. She took the child's hand and led her home. In her delight, Eva clung fast, jumping onto each step with both feet together.

The door to the top-floor flat was open and the sound of Mrs Kolinski's playing spilled through. Connie gave Eva a kiss goodbye, and then, noticing how the child's eyes were fixed on the rose, she gave that to her too.

'Watch out for the thorns,' she said, 'and don't tell anyone. Especially that old misery guts, Kenneth. Not a word. It's our secret.'

Eva nodded. Such a silent, solemn child. Connie doubted she ever said much at all.

Later, Connie stood at the front window. Kenneth had gone, but the man with the blue jacket stood in the street, smoking, taking those sharp drags before flinging down the dog end and grinding it with his heel. One quick, aggressive look at the house and he stalked off in the direction of the main road, hands shoved into his jacket pockets.

16

Marina

January 1992

It's early morning. The house is quiet, but Marina cannot sleep. She sits up in bed, studying her notes. She has made a spidergram, circles with the names of tenants inside, lines spiking outwards from each one. Eva and Natalia. Dorothy Light. Thomas Littleton. Kenneth Quip. Eileen and Leonard. Victor.

She taps her pencil on her teeth. She needs facts about these people. She could go to Somerset House or maybe a library as Ron mentioned. Her eyes light on the phone book propping open the door. It's not surprising that there is only one tenant left after all this time, but people often stay in or return to an area. Take Ruth, for example: born in Westbury, studied in Bristol, travelled around India, then moved back to Westbury.

She jumps out of bed, grabs the phone book and replaces it with a dictionary. Back under the duvet, she flicks through the pages, stops at Littleton and looks for Thomas. She finds addresses with the wrong initials and others with the wrong spelling, a *y* instead of an *i*. She tries Kolinski, but there is only N. Kolinski at Harrington Gardens. Flipping to the end of the book, she moves backwards and stops at Wallace. There are several more options here. There's V. Wallace and then another

V. W. Wallace, both in SW16. Could one of these be Victor? It's worth a try.

It's too early to call, so Marina gets up. She stands at the front window drinking coffee. It's a boring street. Blank houses with closed curtains like shuttered eyes. Empty trees with spindly branches. A boy appears at the window of the house opposite. Marina gives a tentative wave. The child stares, but doesn't react.

At ten o'clock, Marina picks up the phone. She hopes her nerve will hold as she taps in the first number. A woman answers on the second ring.

'Yes?'

'Oh,' says Marina, unprepared. 'Is that . . . Is that . . . Mrs Wallace?'

'Yes.' There is a pause. 'Who's speaking?'

'My name is Zoe Alexander.'

'Who?'

'I'm writing an article . . .' She flounders. 'I'm trying to track someone down.'

'Track someone down?' The voice is disbelieving. Impatient. 'Look, I'm in a hurry. Who are you?'

'I'm writing an article,' she says, speaking in a rush. 'And I'm trying to find Victor Wallace. He used to live in Harrington Gardens.'

'Never heard of him.'

The line goes dead. Marina sighs and then quickly taps in the next number. No answer.

To pass the time, she takes a shower. There are two settings she has now discovered that actually work – boiling or lukewarm. She chooses the second and tries not to think about the previous person who stood where she stands now. She vows to chase Wayne as she emerges, shivering, and then hauls on her dressing gown and thick socks before bundling her hair up in a turban.

It's an effort to take care of her hair. Maybe she should cut it off. A short, sharp pixie cut. Would it suit her? She stares grimly into the mirror. Since she's been in London, she's lost weight. Her face is thinner. There are dark smudges beneath her eyes. If Ruth were here, the roast would be in the oven, the crumble made in moments. She'd be piling up Marina's plate, talking with studied nonchalance about anything that came into her head, pretending she wasn't worried.

She's always been like that, fussing in a bid to hide concern. Yet Marina never had typical teenage issues – was never prone to angst about appearance, eating disorders, emotional outbursts or even frequent tears. On the contrary, she'd been the sensible girl at school, the one who listened and gave advice.

Maybe, Marina thinks now, it was because she'd had other things to worry about. Like who she had actually inherited her looks from.

She does her make-up, piling on black eyeliner and mascara, painting her lips red. By the time she's dried her hair and pulled on a pair of trousers and a thick, black turtleneck jumper to keep her warm, an hour has passed.

She settles in the armchair and calls the second number once again. This time, a man answers. 'Hello?'

'Hello.' She gets to the point. 'I wonder if I could speak to Victor Wallace.'

There is a long pause. Marina's shoulders slump. Another wrong number.

Then he says, 'Yes. That's me. Who am I speaking to?'

Her heart accelerates. 'My name is Zoe . . . Zoe Alexander, and I'm writing an article.' She stops.

The man's loud breathing travels down the line.

'It's about an incident that happened in the 1960s.'

'Are you the police?'

'Oh no, nothing like that.'

'A journalist?'

'No. I mean, I work freelance.'

'So, what has this to do with me?'

'Well.' She transfers the receiver to her other ear. Despite the cold, her skin feels hot. 'The article is about an abandoned baby.' She pauses again before saying, 'The baby was abandoned in the house you used to live in.'

More loud breathing.

Marina shifts in her seat. 'It was 24 Harrington Gardens. I don't know if you remember . . .'

'Yes,' Victor says, 'of course I remember. What exactly do you want?'

She swallows, moves the receiver back again. 'I was wondering, if it would be possible to meet you. I'm looking for people to interview, tenants I mean, connected with the house.'

'How did you find me?'

'In the phone book.'

'Have you interviewed anyone else?'

'No,' she admits. 'Not yet. I thought . . . I thought I would try to find *you* first.' She injects a smile into her voice, a hint of flattery. 'I'm guessing as you still live in the area, you know it very well.'

'Well, yes, I do.'

There. It has worked. She can hear his satisfaction.

'So . . . would you agree to meet?'

There is another long pause. Then he says, 'All right. Since you tracked me down you'll know my address. You can come tomorrow.'

'Actually, I wondered if we could we meet in a cafe. I'll buy you a coffee to say thank you.'

'All right.' There is a hint of amusement in his voice. He goes on, 'I'll meet you in the greasy spoon on the corner of my road. The Golden Egg. Midday.'

She agrees and they finish their call. She considers his voice and wonders what he looks like. She can't remember having seen his photo. Jumping up, she grabs the folder. Sorting through the cuttings, she finds the quote that originally gave her his name.

Victor Wallace, who lives in the basement flat, said, 'I was with my girlfriend at the time. When I arrived that afternoon, the baby had gone.'

Sounds like an alibi, Marina thinks cynically. She searches again in case she has missed a photo. There are photos of Kenneth Quip, Natalia Kolinski, Eileen Clarke and Leonard Crisp but none of Victor Wallace.

Neither, now she comes to think of it, is there a photo of Thomas Littleton. No quotes either. Only a reference from Kenneth Quip, the landlord, who describes the layout of the house and mentions that the residents of Flat 4 had been away. Marina frowns at the use of the plural. She has only ever come across one name for that flat – Thomas Littleton. Who else lived there?

*

The next day, Marina arrives early at The Golden Egg. The place is almost full, the atmosphere lively. She scans the men at the Formica-topped tables. Many are young builders in hi-vis jackets and none are candidates for Victor, who Marina guesses must be at least fifty.

She orders coffee and settles by the window. Outside, drizzle turns to rain and drops of water trickle down the glass. A man opens the door and steps inside. He is middle-aged, tall and broad, in a green jacket and black trousers. His hair, which is mostly grey, is thick and swept away from his forehead. He is unnervingly good-looking. Their eyes meet and he smiles, lifting one corner of his mouth. There is a fleck of shaving foam on his chin and when he comes closer she catches the scent of spicy aftershave.

'You must be Victor,' she says, standing and holding out her hand. 'I'm Zoe. Thank you for agreeing to meet me.'

He stares with unashamed admiration, holding her hand for a fraction too long, pulling her towards him as if to see her better. Marina stares coolly back, keeping it clinical. She is used to men's – unwanted – appreciation and today she has adopted an efficient, need-to-get-the-job-done image. Her hair is twisted into a tight bun, her make-up minimal, and she wears no jewellery.

Victor insists on buying her another coffee and offers her something to eat, which she declines. At the counter, he orders an all-day breakfast and flirts with the young woman who is serving.

At the table, he sets down her coffee and his tea and then leans back in his chair and stares again. If he had a moustache, Marina thinks, he would give the ends a twirl.

'So, Zoe,' he says, 'how can I help?'

She blinks, disconcerted by the use of her middle name, despite the fact she gave it to him. 'First let me say how grateful I am for your time.' He nods, appraising her still. She clears her throat. 'As I mentioned, I'm writing an article. It's about the baby that was abandoned in Harrington Gardens. In 1964.'

He frowns and scratches his face.

She tries to speak casually. 'It was a girl. The media nicknamed her Baby Blue.'

'Yes. I remember.' He fumbles in his pocket and draws out a packet of Marlboro. Shaking out a cigarette, he lifts it to his lips, flips his silver Zippo and the flame catches. He inhales. As an afterthought he offers her a cigarette too.

'No thank you.'

He leans forward. 'Why?'

'I'm trying to cut down.'

'No. Why are you writing this article?'

'Oh.' She looks away and then back at him again. 'Because I'm hoping to move into journalism. I work in publishing and . . .'

'No.' He flicks his ash into his saucer, his voice patient. 'I mean why do you want to write about an abandoned baby?'

She glances at her notepad, gathers herself. 'Because it's an interesting case. I'm trying to find a new angle.'

'You mean you want to solve the case? Like a regular Miss Marple.' He laughs.

'I don't expect to do that.' She speaks firmly now. 'I'm planning to take a broader look at the effects on the community and specifically on the people in the house.'

Victor seems unconvinced, but then he shrugs. 'Fire away.'

'So, when did you live in the house?'

'In sixty-four.'

'Where were you before?'

A smile plays on his lips. 'In digs.'

'In the same area?'

'Tooting Common.'

'Why did you move to Harrington Gardens?'

He taps his cigarette again. 'I'm not sure that's your business.'

Has she overstepped the mark? Flustered, she turns a page.

He narrows his eyes and then changes his mind. 'I fell out with the landlady.'

She waits, hoping he'll continue, and he obliges. 'She didn't like the relationship I had with her daughter who, in fact, became my wife. Not that we're married anymore. Are you?'

'No.' She shifts uncomfortably and moves on by asking him about his work.

'Think Arthur Daley,' he replies, 'or Del Boy. Wheeling and dealing.'

'Really?'

He laughs. 'Actually, I was a supplier of goods to businesses.'

'Local businesses?'

'Yes, mainly. Second-hand dealerships, bookshops, that type of thing.'

She lets this information sink in and makes a guess. 'Did you supply books to Thomas Littleton?'

He looks surprised. 'Yes, I did.'

'How long did you live at number 24?'

'Not long. I moved there in the summer, got married three or four months after that and we went to live with the mother-in-law – the aforesaid landlady.' He makes a face, rolling his eyes, which Marina pretends not to notice.

He looks at her curiously. 'Why do you need to know this?'

'Background information.' She smiles sweetly, feeling only vaguely guilty at the lie. 'I want to get the story right and it sounds as if you have an excellent memory.'

Her flattery works. He puffs himself up.

The waitress comes and sets down his food. While he eats, Marina warms her hands on the second mug of coffee and makes small talk. She has a list of questions in her head, but she doesn't want to spook Victor, so when he finishes and is smoking again, she skips most of them and gets to the point.

'Eileen Clarke who lived in Flat 2 found the baby. Did you know her?'

'Oh yes. Wild as they come.'

She ignores his comment. 'Do you know where she is now?'

'No idea. Like I said, I only lived in the flat for a few months – but she was American so I suppose she might have gone home.'

'Were you in the house when they found the baby?'

He gives a surreptitious glance at the counter and then takes a silver hip flask from his pocket and pours liquid into his tea. 'No. I was staying the night at my old digs – with my girlfriend – the aforesaid.' He winks.

She leaves the topic alone. 'What do you remember about the other tenants?' She glances at her notes. 'How about Dorothy Light?'

He pulls a face. 'Vinegary woman. Always snooping about, far too close to the landlord.' He raises his eyebrows. 'If you know what I mean.'

'They were having an affair?'

'Most people thought so.'

If Marina was worried about Victor not wanting to talk, she isn't now. He is a man who likes the sound of his own voice. She presses ahead. 'So, she wasn't married.'

'Separated.'

'She lived alone?'

'No, she had a son, Johnny. Always arguing from what I recall and then he ran off. I think actually that upset Dorothy more than she admitted.'

'Where did he go?'

'Paris.'

'Paris? Why?'

'He fancied himself as an artist.'

An artist. Her mind flies to the attic, to the paintings and the brushes. 'Was he any good?'

'How should I know? He was a time-waster.' A look of dislike crosses Victor's face.

No love lost there then.

'Where is she now?'

'The mother? Probably still in the house.'

'No, she was in Flat 3, wasn't she? There's a Mrs Hyde there now.'

'That's her,' says Victor waving his cigarette around. 'Married again.'

'Ah.' Marina hadn't thought of that. Dorothy Light had become Dorothy Hyde. 'What happened to Mr Hyde?'

'Did a runner from what I remember. A wastrel, living off her and the social.'

'What about the first husband?'

'Left her too – at least he wasn't living in the house in 1964 if that's your question. He did visit though. Now *he* was a nasty piece of work, as well as a wastrel. Older than her, he marched at Cable Street, on the wrong side – a Blackshirt.'

Marina had learned about Cable Street at school. Fascists marching through the East End, but ultimately stopped by local people. Victor goes up in her estimation for condemning the Blackshirts.

'You said that she and Kenneth were close.'

He laughs again. 'I'm pretty sure she was his paramour.'

Strange choice of words. In fact, he has an archaic way of speaking. Maybe it's an attempt to make himself seem clever.

'And his spy of course. I swear she used to snoop in people's flats.'

'She had keys?'

'That's what I thought.'

'So why do you think she's stayed in the house for so long?'

'I told you, she was pretty cut up about her son's disappearing trick. I suspect she's still waiting for him to come home. Maybe she reckons he won't find her if she moves.' He gives a hollow laugh. 'I can't see him turning up though, not after all these years.'

'So, they're still estranged?'

'I guess so.' He stubs out his cigarette and looks at his watch. 'No offence, but time and tide and all that.'

Marina quickly asks him about Mrs Kolinski, but he doesn't recall much about her. 'She was foreign,' is all he can say.

'And the landlord, Kenneth, was next on the scene. Is that right?'

'I think so, but like I said I was absent on the day.'

'What was Kenneth like?'

'Tough as an old goat. Spent most of his youth inside.'

'Prison?'

'Yes.'

'What for?'

'Robbery.' He lights another cigarette, takes a drag and blows out a smoke ring. 'The thing is, he had a reputation.'

'What for?'

'Double-crossing his mates.'

'How?'

Victor coughs and taps his finger to his nose. 'Loose lips and all that.'

She tries not to show her eagerness. 'It would be interesting to know more about him.'

He raises his eyebrows cynically. 'More background information?'

'Exactly.'

'Why don't you ask him yourself?'

She frowns. 'Do you know where he is?'

He shakes his head. 'The old dog keeps his where-abouts close, but wherever he is, the house will be as secure as Fort Knox.'

'Why?'

Victor laughs. 'Kenneth was paranoid. Although I must say, with the number of people who were after him, I'm not surprised.'

'Why were they after him?'

He taps the side of his nose again. 'Honour amongst thieves.' Marina is getting fed up of his clichés. 'Or lack of it. He stole from his mates. Common knowledge.'

'What happened?'

'Kenneth and his gang went to prison for armed rob-bery. A lot of the money they stole wasn't recovered by the police and it's unclear what happened to it. However, when Kenneth came out, he was a lot richer than when he went in.'

'Why didn't the police go after him again?'

'I guess he covered himself. He was *meticulous*,' Victor adds. 'He loved to tell us that. Never stopped, in fact.'

'What about the rest of the gang? Didn't they try and claim it?'

'One of them died in prison,' says Victor, 'and the third – Frank – had a longer sentence because he injured a guard.'

'Really?'

'Allegedly. The accusation got overturned, they let him out and then he died.' Victor stubs out his cigarette and grimaces. 'Conveniently.'

There is a silence while Marina processes this tale of dishonour amongst thieves. 'So, if they're all dead,' she says slowly, 'why is Kenneth still paranoid?'

'Aye, there's the rub.'

Marina raises her eyebrows at Victor's unexpected Shakespeare.

'The fact is, Kenneth has always been stupid. Always looked in the wrong direction, never noticed what was going on.'

'And you're sure you don't know his address?'

'No, but it shouldn't be too hard to find out. He's still the landlord at Harrington Gardens.'

'I didn't know that.'

'Well now you do.'

He grins at her and an image of the old man shuffling with his stick in the garden comes to Marina's mind. Now she has all the more reason to talk to him. The boiler is the perfect excuse. She will call Wayne and hurry him along.

Outside the house, she collides with a teenage boy wearing owl glasses who mumbles an apology and avoids eye contact as he lollops up the steps, taking them two at a time.

As soon as she steps inside her flat she knows that someone has been there. There is a scent. A faint sour smell like sweat with a sweetness underneath.

Leaving the door open, she stands in the middle of the room, heart banging. Are the curtains wider? Are the papers on the desk disturbed? She walks slowly into the kitchen and examines the window, looking for signs of a break-in. The scent is here too. She scans the cupboards and the worktops. The flap on the boiler is hanging down. Did she leave it like that? Her mind whirrs. She can't remember. Then it clicks. It must have been the landlord letting himself in with a key, checking the heating as Wayne requested.

'How dare he,' she mutters as she stalks about the house trying to find evidence of intrusion. It's all very well her wanting him to come but to enter the flat without her knowledge is different altogether. She is fuming, opening drawers and cupboards. The box with the shawl lies on her bed. What if he looked inside? She grows angry imagining Kenneth Quip rooting around. Would he have recognised the shawl? Would he have guessed who she is?

She steps back out into the hall. The stairway is dark. The house still. No baby crying. No music playing. No creaks or groans. Yet she is sure there is something. A sound creeping beneath the silence. What is it? Breathing. A heart beating. Blood creeping through veins. Impossible. She's being foolish. Click. A door closes. She breathes heavily and the piano music begins. Not Chopin. This music is more robust. After a moment, she goes inside her flat and double-locks the door.

17

Eva

January 1992

Eva has a pupil. He is by far her most talented. His name is Toby and he plays Rachmaninov with panache.

She hears his clumsy tread on the stairs followed by a pounding on her door. As soon as she lets him in, he hangs his head and blushes furiously.

They talk about music and he speaks quickly and quietly. When their eyes meet, he blinks behind his glasses and blushes again. When he touches the piano keys, he throws back his head and performs.

He is playing now, nearing the end of the lesson. Eva stands beside him, her eyes closed. She is focused and not focused. Part of her mind is caught up with Ron – the telephone call and the request to see her. She had agreed and he had come, bearing gifts of Turkish Delight and a red rose wrapped in cellophane.

They had drunk tea, made small talk, while he had sat in his short-sleeved shirt and jeans, arms crossed and shoulders hunched. Instinctively she knew that if she gave him the signal, their relationship would start again.

Eventually, he had told her about the woman downstairs. Her name was Zoe and she had moved into Flat 2. She was from Wiltshire, had come to London for a change of scene, worked in publishing and wanted to move into journalism. Eva was still, listening to each drop of information, collecting it like rainwater in a tin. When Ron explained what the woman wanted, Eva had surprised Ron and herself by agreeing to see her.

Now, as she listens to Toby, Eva considers more carefully what to expect and what food and drink she will prepare and where the two of them will sit. She looks around the flat, placing the woman first in one chair and then in another. Her gaze is restless. It travels from the armchairs in the room, to Toby's fingers skittering across the keys, to the table where she has placed Ron's rose in a vase. It lingers and her mind returns to the memory she had before.

Little Eva. She is jumping up the stairs, holding tight to a woman's hand. It must be her mother. Who else could it be? In her other hand, she holds a rag doll that has the softest hair and the prettiest smiling face. At the top of the stairs, on the second floor, they step onto the landing. Her mother crouches and presents her with a red rose. Her lips are moving. What is she saying? Her voice is like an echo.

Toby finishes Rachmaninoff and segues seamlessly into Chopin. Suddenly, Eva recalls that it isn't her mother in the scenario she has been painting. There is music accompanying this memory. Her mother is playing the piano which means she can't possibly be standing on the landing giving her a rose.

She closes her eyes trying to recall. The soft palm, the scent of the rose and something else. Perfume. It's sweet and gentle and reminds her of the stars.

Eva's eyes snap open. That's not possible. She is muddling memories and mixing up senses. Her head is aching. She touches her temple with her index and middle finger, wills herself to focus until she is back in the role of Little Eva taking the rose. Now she sees that it's a young woman who is looking at her, and smiling in that lovely way she has, pushing back her thick, dark hair. Her eyes are warm and her expression is kind, though Little Eva knows she is sad because she has seen the same look in her mother.

The memory leaps forward like an old cine film. Now Little Eva is standing again at the top of the stairs, alone this time. The image is strong as if a spotlight is on her and she is about to perform on stage. She is wearing a purple dress that is way too big for her. When she twists, the material swirls and caresses her legs like butterfly wings or feathers. The spotlight shifts until she is slightly off centre. And now there are sounds in the dreamy sequence. The piano behind her and voices below. The voices are arguing and she doesn't like it so she covers her ears. There is warmth running down her legs and she realises she has wet herself and she is ashamed because her lovely dress is ruined. Tears well in her eyes and she squeezes them away with the palms of her hands. When she looks again, there is a space at the bottom of the stairs. The voices and people have gone.

In the present, Eva concentrates. Chopin is fading. Toby is finishing. He plays the last note. They talk about what he can do to improve. She explains how he can put more expression into his playing, how he can lift his hands more delicately and place them more correctly. She tells him what to practise and they arrange their next lesson.

When he leaves, she closes the door behind him and listens to his clattering tread on the stairs. She smiles, thinking of the contrast between his clumsy feet and his delicate hands. She can identify with such a disconnect, but in her case the disconnect is inside her head.

She crosses the room and touches the rose. A petal falls and she draws back her hand. Her head still aches. She should take an aspirin. Maybe she should call Ron and tell him she has changed her mind about seeing this woman. The prospect has clearly disturbed her. She walks to the window and opens it a crack. A wind is picking up. It stirs the branches of the maple tree and swirls dead leaves across the road. She touches the glass, feels the familiar precariousness as she listens to the call of a lost gull overhead, the sound like an abandoned animal, or a baby crying for its mother.

18

Connie

May 1964

The next morning, Connie came out of her flat and almost immediately Dorothy appeared from hers.

'There you are, my dear. I've been worried about you.' She clicked on the light.

'No need,' replied Connie, but her hands were shaking as she turned her back and closed the door. She'd had a terrible night and spent hours awake, staring into the darkness, thinking about that house, that kitchen, those awful implements.

'What made you run away?' said Dorothy. 'You needn't have done that, you know. You could have told me how you felt and I would have come with you.'

Her voice was full of reproach. Connie turned to look at her. Such a diminutive figure, in her brown coat, with a funny matching hat like a tea cosy perched on her head. Connie wondered how old she was. Forty, perhaps, which would make her a similar age to her mother when she died, although the two of them couldn't have been more different in looks, or personality.

'I changed my mind,' Connie said.

'It's natural to have second thoughts, but Barbara . . .'

'Barbara?'

'The lady you spoke to. I explained your situation and

she agreed to give you another appointment. We can't leave the decision for too long, you see.'

Connie did see.

'Why don't you give it another chance? We could sit down and thrash out the details. And . . .' Dorothy paused. 'There are always the other options.'

'I don't want any of them,' Connie said quietly. As soon as the words escaped her, Connie realised they were true. She hadn't known she would say them. She hadn't even known they were inside her head.

Neither of them spoke. It was quiet. Downstairs, Connie could hear the deep rhythm of jazz. Leonard must be out.

The light clicked off. 'And what about Johnny?' said Dorothy, making no move to switch it back on.

'He'll be in touch.'

'And if he isn't?'

Was it Connie's imagination, or had Dorothy's voice hardened?

'Then I'll deal with the consequences.'

'Yes, of course.' Another pause, and then: 'But you still need to think about Johnny. He's young. A baby will hold him back. He'll find out and then what do you think will happen? His life will be over. His ambitions thwarted.'

Above them Mrs Kolinski began to play. She was practising scales, running her fingers effortlessly up and down the keys. The scales transformed into a beautiful piece and they both looked up. Connie thought Dorothy must be as taken by the sound as she was, but when she glanced back, the woman's face was blank, as unaffected by music as she was by art. It was hard to believe that Johnny was her son.

Dorothy spoke again. 'You must understand that I am Johnny's mother and his interests come first.' She leaned forward and picked fluff from Connie's sleeve. 'But that's not to say I don't care about you. The thing is, sometimes men and boys need to get on with the important things in life and we must deal with these other decisions – these female matters – ourselves. Why don't you come back with me this afternoon?' She leaned a little closer. 'I told you there are options. If you don't want to take the medication, there are other things you can do.'

Connie moistened her lips. Why wouldn't this woman leave her alone? If only she hadn't spoken to her in the first place. She should have found someone else to confide in.

Dorothy was still talking. 'There are couples who are desperate for their own child. Good people who will give your baby a far better life than you could. They have money, status, all the things that people like us don't have.'

People like us. Connie stared back at her. She didn't feel remotely connected to Dorothy.

'I only ask that you think about it,' said Dorothy. 'Please don't shackle my son.'

She turned, clearly deciding she'd said her piece, and headed down the stairs. Instead of following, Connie opened the door to the flat and stepped inside; the shop and her father would have to wait. She leaned against the wall, heart thumping. A film of sweat had gathered on her forehead. In the last few weeks, her inner temperature had rocketed. The vomiting had stopped, but smells still set her off: sour milk, Victor's aftershave. The sickly scent of Dorothy's breath. She sat down, head in her hands. Dorothy's loyalties lay with her son. A mother would do anything for her child.

Closing her eyes, she tried to conjure Johnny's face. The image blurred even though it had only been a few months. That last time, the day before he left, it was incredible to think she had been pregnant. Cells multiplying. Her body creating while she had lain motionless beside him. She groaned, feeling her loss as a wrenching pain. She *had* to see Johnny. He would write. She *knew* he would, but in the meantime, she must find a way to buy a ticket to Paris. Rousing herself, she went into her bedroom and took out her mother's jewellery box.

The bell jangled as she went inside the shop. Harry was balancing on a stool behind the counter. He wore a black jumper, his usual drainpipes and a checked flat cap.

'Connie,' he said, almost toppling from his perch when he saw her. 'I've missed you.'

He dragged off the cap and held it over his heart. He was known for his hats. His father had been a hatmaker. A gambler too. When Harry was small, the shop had gone bust. Harry's father had disappeared and the bailiffs had come. But wily Harry had hidden a stack of the hats and when his mother had begged and borrowed and built up a grocer's to replace the hat shop, Harry had worn them to remember.

His mother emerged from the back. Short and round,

the reverse of her son, she shot Connie a suspicious look before asking after her father.

'He's not too bad, thank you for asking, Mrs Hachette.'

'Glad to hear it.' She busied herself, stocking a shelf with tins of corned beef, eyeing Connie through the display.

'She thinks you broke my heart,' Harry whispered across the counter.

Connie hoped she hadn't. Harry didn't deserve that. They had only been out once, to the pictures – but he'd brought her chocolates as well as a bunch of violets.

She asked for half a pound of cheese. Harry sliced and weighed, laid the cheese on waxed paper and popped in an extra piece. 'Anything else?'

'Half a dozen eggs.'

He fetched them, juggling to make her laugh.

The bell jangled and a woman with a small child anchored on her hip came in. She was brandishing a bottle and wanting vinegar from the barrel out the back. Forced to leave her post, Mrs Hachette frowned and disappeared.

Connie took her chance. 'I need a favour,' she said in a low voice.

Harry looked at her. 'What is it?'

The customer set down her toddler.

'I've got jewellery.'

'Again? You're not serious.'

'Please, Harry.' She put her hand on his arm. The necklace she'd asked him to pawn last time had been to raise money for Johnny's ticket. Now she had to pay for her own.

He shook his head in exasperation. 'Why? What's happened?'

'Nothing.'

He packed the eggs, frowning. 'Then why are you pawning your mum's jewellery? You'll regret it.'

'I won't regret it,' she said quietly, 'because I'll get it back.'

He narrowed his eyes suspiciously. 'It's not her wedding ring, is it?'

'No, of course not. That's at home.' Safe beneath a floorboard in her room where she'd once kept her childhood treasures.

'But I don't understand. If you're not in trouble, why do you need so much money?' He eyed her suspiciously. 'Are you ill?'

'Do I look ill?'

'No,' said Harry, softening as he took the opportunity to admire her. 'You look lovely.'

Despite herself she smiled. Harry gave her straightforward compliments. Johnny had only ever talked about the line of her neck or the curve of her cheek, as if she were a painting or a sculpture.

Harry wasn't giving up. 'Are you going somewhere? Is that what you need the money for?'

She shook her head.

He leaned forward. 'You are. I can tell. Where are you going?'

It was hard lying to Harry. She lowered her voice. 'It's only for a short time and you mustn't tell.'

'Is it to do with Johnny?'

She looked away guiltily.

'You're going to Paris, aren't you?'

She bit her lip and nodded.

'What about your dad? It's not as if he won't notice.'

'He'll be in Whitby.'

'You won't go with him?'

'He's better off without me . . . Just him and his sister.'

'Has he agreed to that?'

She shrugged. He hadn't said yes yet, but he would eventually, after she had convinced him. Besides, she genuinely believed he would relax if he didn't have to worry about her.

'Still. I can't believe you're going behind his back,' said Harry.

'Don't say that.'

Maybe he heard the hurt in her voice because he stopped speaking. She touched his hand again. 'Come on Harry, you've always been a good friend and right now I need your help. Please trust me.'

He sighed. 'I suppose I'll have to.'

'Thank you.' She slid the bag across the counter.

Opening it up, he gave a low whistle. 'All of this?'

Harry's mother reappeared, brandishing a bottle of vinegar. Taking the bag, Harry stuffed it under the counter. Connie counted out the money she owed him for the groceries. Harry took it, holding her fingers for too long.

'When?' she asked quietly.

'Day after tomorrow, maybe.'

She nodded. 'Thank you. I owe you.'

'Best not say that.' He smiled, but the sparkle had gone from his eyes and as he rang open the till and tucked her money away, she felt a snag of regret, a memory of violets. He was a good sort, Harry.

19

Marina

January 1992

Marina broods about Kenneth Quip coming into her flat and rooting amongst her things. Not that she has evidence, but still, she has an imagination and in her mind's eye she sees him clawing through her drawers, yanking open cupboard doors, scanning greedy eyes across her desk.

She telephones Wayne and asks him if the landlord has got any further with sorting the heating. She doesn't mention her suspicions and nothing he says suggests he knows that Quip has been already. On the contrary, he is apologetic and promises to hurry him up. Maybe she's got it wrong – although if it's *not* Quip who's been in the flat, that's even more worrying. Still, despite everything, she wants him to come. It's the perfect excuse to have contact.

Marina continues with Agata's manuscript. Agata has escaped to England via Kindertransport. Her parents are in the concentration camp and Marina's heart breaks as she pictures the little girl alone on a train, clutching her belongings in a single bag. On impulse, she decides to learn more about the subject. She takes a quick look through the Yellow Pages and finds a library a short drive away.

Grabbing her coat, she leaves the house and jumps

into her car. The engine takes coaxing before it splutters into life, but she sets off, driving to the end of the street and joining the traffic. The common is ragged today, grass patchy, trees bare. The weather is dull, the sky colourless. She has a yearning for home and its wide-open spaces, the sight of the horse on the hill.

Fifteen minutes of being in traffic and she pulls into a side road. The library is a dusty Victorian building. Inside, Marina enquires about past copies of newspapers and is sent to a room along the corridor. It has high windows and cracked linoleum and reminds her of an old classroom. Here, another woman gives her a quick explanation of how to use microfilm and shows her the filing cabinets where the reels are stored in boxes.

There are hundreds to choose from and Marina dithers. How far back should she go? Finally, she selects October 1936, slots the reel into place, loads it correctly, brings up the images and adjusts the focus, using the buttons to scroll. It's a local paper dealing with local issues, but still, there's plenty of mention of Hitler and the threat of war and the rise of Oswald Mosley and the Blackshirts. She comes across an article about the march in Cable Street and reads about barricades and local men fighting with makeshift weapons and women flinging debris from their windows. It reminds her of a castle under siege and she feels a thrill imagining these people routing the fascists, and then a sadness understanding what Agata had faced.

She returns the reel, selects another and this time she reads about the Second World War, the bombing and the Blitz, brave boys and D-Day, references to concentration

camps and refugees. She reads about the Jewish popula-
tion in London. She thinks of Natalia Kolinski and Eva
as well as Agata, and tries to understand what life would
have been like for them.

Her stomach growls. More than an hour has passed.
She glances around. Most of the visitors are older than
Marina, but she catches the eye of a young woman with
braids and they exchange a complicit smile.

Next, she picks out a reel from the 1950s. Now she
reads about rock and roll and a new dance hall. She
reads about the Windrush generation, the hostility of
signs on boarding houses and hotels – *No Blacks No
Dogs No Irish*. It's the same old discrimination, the same
old hate-filled speech. History lurching forwards, repeating itself. She glances at the girl with braids and sees that
she is looking at the same period. Another complicit
smile – although it's more of a grimace this time – and
Marina pushes into the 1960s. If only it was so easy in
real life to swipe away the past.

She chooses more reels. Demonstrations, Beatlemania,
women's rights. Local crime, a burglary or two, a story
about a sixteen-year-old boy called Peter who had a pen-
chant for pickpocketing. Marina smiles at the alliteration.
She is still smiling when she reads about a spate of robberies in south London – a post office, a jeweller's, a
builder's yard, a bank. The last apparently went badly
wrong: a security guard had disturbed the gang and was
viciously attacked. The offenders were subsequently
caught. There are three captioned mugshots, and Marina
recognises Kenneth Quip. He seems older than the other

men. The first has short cropped dark hair, the second has lighter hair and ears that stick out like handles.

Marina leans forward examining this second man and another memory chimes, from reading through various newspapers when she was younger, trying to find out what happened to her mother: a body pulled from the lake at Tooting Common. She remembers staring at the photo of the victim – a mugshot, an ex-prisoner. She'd reread the story many times, like all the stories she'd found then, searching for some kind of connection. Now she feels a link between that memory and the man in the picture before her. What date had that been? It must have been some time in 1964 because that was the year she'd been researching.

Quickly she grabs another reel and scrolls through. Finding nothing, she tries again and this time she comes across the headline. *Body Found in Lake Identified*. She leans closer and stares into the face of the victim. Frank Dennis. Was his death an accident, the paper asks, or was he murdered? There are details of the robberies he'd been involved in, including the bank job. Frank had initially been charged with attacking the guard, but afterwards the accusation had been rescinded. All three members of the gang had done time, and one of them had died in prison. Most of the money had been recovered, but not all of it. What had happened to the rest?

Marina rubs her eyes. Maybe she needs glasses. Neither Ruth nor David have bad eyesight, but of course, that is irrelevant. Two out of three men dead. What are the chances of that? The facts coincide with what Victor told her, although he didn't mention the possible murder of Frank Dennis. What had he actually said? That his death had been *convenient*.

The woman in charge announces that there are thirty minutes until the library closes. People get ready to leave. Quickly, Marina positions the article correctly and prints.

On the way home, Marina takes a detour and parks close to Crystal's shop.

Inside, there is a smell of burning incense. Crystal is sitting at the counter reading a manuscript, but when Marina comes in, she greets her warmly.

'Have you come to teach a class?'

Marina smiles. 'Not exactly, but I did think about it.'

'Wonderful,' says Crystal, her eyes glinting. 'Why don't I make you a cup of tea while you get acquainted with the classroom?'

She gestures to the ceiling, and Marina does as she's been bid, making her way to the far end of the shop and climbing the staircase to the first floor. There is a table in the centre, surrounded by plastic chairs. Two of the walls are lined with shelves of battered books. A further bookcase is laden with teaching materials. It's a possibility she thinks, running the fingers of one hand across the spines, returning to teaching, or at least combining it with her editing, and Crystal seems like a genuine person. It would be a reason to stay, to throw down roots in London. Is that what she wants?

She moves to the window and spots Mrs Hyde hurrying past. What a strange woman she is, scurrying like a mouse. Victor hadn't liked her. What had he said?

Vinegary and sly. Kenneth's right-hand woman. Going into people's flats without permission. Does she still have spare keys? It strikes Marina that it might have been Dorothy who had been inside her flat that time, not the landlord at all.

Marina goes back downstairs. Crystal has been waylaid by a customer, an elderly man. She has a book in her hand and is clearly recommending it to him. She slips a packet of biscuits into his bag along with the book. 'No charge,' she says.

While she is busy, Marina examines the collage of postcards on the wall. *Welcome to York. Greetings from Whitby.* If the postcards weren't trapped behind glass, she would love to turn them over and read the writing on the back. Who sent them and to whom? There are several arty postcards amongst them, which seems incongruous. Leonardo and Raphael. Christ with a crown of thorns. The Madonna in prayer. Marina breathes in the scent of incense and has a sense that she is missing something.

'Quaint, aren't they?' says Crystal, appearing beside her. Marina turns. The elderly man is ensconced on the window seat drinking a cup of tea.

Marina agrees. 'Were they part of what was left behind?'

'Yes, along with the photos and the sign.'

'Strange to leave something so personal'

'Too much like hard work to get rid of it all, I expect. It's interesting though, after you mentioned it the other day, I started trying to remember why there had been the delay – with the will, I mean. I'm pretty sure it was something to do with a missing family member who

JENNY QUINTANA

should have inherited, but I can't remember who it was or why they didn't.'

Marina is intrigued. Maybe at some point there *was* someone living with Thomas. How can she find out? Somerset House perhaps. She could find out if he was married.

Another customer comes in and Crystal goes to serve her. While they are talking, Marina looks more closely at the art postcards. The colours have dulled but she can still appreciate something of their original richness. She touches the glass and a tingling sensation travels through her fingers and along her arm. Stepping away, she laughs at herself. She has never been religious, despite trips to church with David, and there's no danger of her converting now.

Still, the pictures resonate. Especially the one of the Madonna. She recalls a school trip to the National Gallery. What had they learned about religious art? The artists had used the most expensive colours when depicting the Virgin Mary. That blue. What was it called? Ground from a precious stone, lapis lazuli. Even on a faded postcard, its beauty is obvious.

The original must be spectacular.

20

Connie

June 1964

The basement was worse than Connie had imagined.

Victor was out, thank God, and she hoped he wouldn't return before she could at least sluice the black-stained walls and sweep and mop the floor. He had already removed the mouldy carpet, rolling it up as if there was a body inside and dumping it at the front of the house.

Harry had failed. When she'd gone to the shop to ask him whether he'd pawned her jewellery, his mother had sent him to the back and served Connie herself. Cutting the cheese, her movements were rapid – slicing, stinting – and then, lips thin, she had pushed the packet across the counter, taken the money and muttered, 'Leave him alone. Girls like you.'

Girls like you. The words had stung. Had she hurt Harry that much? Tears in her eyes, she had hurried away. Halfway along the street, Harry had come running. 'Connie, wait, you're killing me.' Only this time there had been no smile to go with the joke, just an explanation. The owner of the pawn shop had apparently disappeared, along with his haul, including, Connie realised with a wrench, the necklace she had originally pawned. Now Harry had to find another contact, and that would take time.

The problem was, she didn't have time, which was

why she had agreed to clean the flat for Victor, so long as he paid her the going rate. Every little would help.

She stood in the dismal front room, dressed in an old apron. The only view was of the metal stairs leading to ground level. Connie could see the foot of the maple tree, the railings, and the legs of people in the street: first a pram, followed by a mid-length skirt, tights and brogues; then the hem of an emerald coat, smart shoes with buckles, which stopped for a few moments before moving quickly on, just as Mrs Kolinski's pencil skirt came into view along with Eva's purple dress, the one that used to be hers.

In the kitchen, Connie looked in a cupboard and wrinkled her nose at a scattering of mouse droppings. They were on the floor too, running along the bottom of the skirting board and in the corners. Victor was going to buy a cat, apparently. Kenneth had agreed to bend the rules.

The smell made Connie retch. She twisted the key and opened the back door, which led onto a square of cement and a set of crooked steps to the garden. She flung the windows wide, trying to at least air the place, then filled a bucket with water, grabbed the Ajax and started cleaning the walls in the front room.

Late afternoon, she heard the voices of Victor and Kenneth. They were standing on the steps, discussing the abandoned carpet.

'It's an eyesore,' said Kenneth, tapping his stick to the rhythm of his words. 'It attracts attention, the wrong kind of attention. Tramps. Slackers. Criminals. They'll think this place is empty and in they'll come, as free as you like.' On he went, exaggerating.

They were still talking when Connie emerged. Squeezing between the two of them, she mumbled to Victor about finishing off tomorrow and then hurried inside. Her father would be home by now, reading a book, waiting for his tea. She would make toad-in-the-hole from her mother's recipe book and maybe a fruit flan.

Still. A few more minutes would do no harm. Passing the flat, she climbed the next set of stairs. Mrs Kolinski's door was ajar. Connie could hear her calling to Eva. The door clicked shut.

Opening the door to the attic, she went up the steep staircase. Johnny had stored his paintings behind an unwanted chest of drawers. Jam jars containing brushes with stiff bristles and paint-splattered handles were stacked against the wall. Connie put the latter in the chest for safekeeping.

Light glinted on a fragment of glass embedded in the floor. She bent to prise it from the wood, remembering how it came to be there. Johnny had wanted Connie to model for his version of *The Virgin in Prayer*. She'd agreed but, restless, had moved too often. Frustration had turned to anger and Johnny had yelled at her to keep still. When she forgot and moved again, he'd flung a jar against the wall. The glass had shattered and Connie had been the one to clear away the pieces while Johnny had begged her to forgive him. 'It's my mother's fault,' he'd said. 'We had a row earlier. She doesn't understand me. She hates my art. All she wants is for me to cut up carcasses and decapitate cows.' He'd sat on the floor with his head in his hands, pulling at his hair like a child.

At night, Connie lay in bed imagining the house wrapping her inside its walls. During the day, she kept busy, cleaning the flat, washing and ironing, trying new recipes for her father. She finished cleaning Victor's rooms and took her payment, but of course it was nowhere near enough to buy a ticket to Paris. She hid the money with her mother's wedding ring beneath the floorboard in her room, away from temptation. She would find the rest, but first she needed Johnny's address. Each day she checked the post box and each day her stomach churned with disappointment.

To distract herself, she gathered together a bundle of postcards – some she had bought with Johnny at the National Gallery and some her father had sent her on his quests for rare books. He had travelled to Oxford, Durham, Harrogate. Once he had gone as far as Edinburgh. She made a display of the postcards in the shop, pinning them on the wall by the door.

One day, she pulled on her polka dot dress and struggled to do up the zip. Dragging it off, she threw it on the bed and then sat down in her underwear, touching her belly. The change was slight but undeniable. She groaned and leaned forward with her head in her hands. Her predicament was becoming visible. People would notice and what would they say? She thought of Harry's mother, and imagined her pointing a finger and muttering words like *tart* and *whore* and *girls like you*. No one would understand.

She took an old sheet from the cupboard, cut it into strips and wound them around her body. Slipping on a different dress, she smoothed the material at the front and thought that it would do. She would wear some of her mother's larger dresses if she needed to, and avoid seeing people as much as she could, especially Harry who knew her well and might catch her out.

The weeks passed and she kept on binding her belly, only letting herself free at night. The fluttering inside grew stronger. One time, standing at the side of the road waiting to cross, she felt a movement so pronounced that she cried out and passers-by looked at her in alarm.

She wasn't sure what was worse: the fear of discovery or the waiting. She had to do *something*. So, she wrote Johnny a letter. Perhaps once she had his address, she could send it to him and he would get used to the idea of the baby before Connie arrived on his doorstep.

In her letter, she told him how much she loved him, that she hoped he loved her too, and that nothing mattered but being together, the three of them. At times, she pictured a happy ending with Johnny in the shop, working alongside her father, but the image never stayed long. Johnny would hate to be confined to four walls. Even the attic, with its view of the sky, had stifled him. Perhaps in Paris he had found a place where he could breathe.

One morning, after a particularly restless night, Connie got up late to find her father slumped in the armchair, face grey, still in his dressing gown.

'Dad! What's wrong?' She ran to him. 'Has something happened?'

He shook his head, moistened his lips.

'I'll get you some water, an aspirin.'

She rushed to the phone box, called the surgery and booked an appointment. Then she gritted her teeth and rang Victor, who was still at his boarding house, and asked him to take them in his car.

By the time she came back, her father looked a little better. She helped him get dressed, and when Victor arrived, they were ready.

At the surgery, Victor and Connie stayed in the waiting room. A few patients sat on the chairs, noses buried in magazines. Connie sat too, picking up a copy of the *Reader's Digest* and leafing through. Victor was uncharacteristically quiet, pacing the room, stopping to study a painting – very modern, all bright colours, splashes and sweeps; Johnny would have loved it – with his hands clasped behind his back. She expected Victor to announce the painting was terrible, like a child had done it, but he stayed quiet. He was subdued, not even flirting with the receptionist, as he normally would have done, although she had greeted him by name when they arrived, which seemed odd, now Connie thought about it, since it was she, not Victor, who had made the appointment.

Ten minutes later, her father reappeared, looking brighter. 'False alarm,' he said, buttoning his coat.

Later, Connie went to the shop alone because despite her father's protests, she'd insisted that he rest.

She was sitting at the counter, reading through the

letter she'd written to Johnny, when the door opened and Harry walked in. Folding the paper in half, she slipped it into a poetry book.

'Connie!' he said, opening his arms and grinning as if it was a surprise to see her there. She smiled back at him, glad that she was hidden behind the counter and had taken her time to apply lipstick and rouge before coming to the shop. Did Harry detect a difference? She didn't think so. His eyes were fixed on her with the same soft admiration he always had, mixed with a sort of hurt.

'Did you know that the shop next door is closing down?' he said. 'If you want that Remington, you'd better hurry.'

Connie looked at him fondly. She'd only mentioned the typewriter to him once, casually, but Harry had remembered her dream of buying it and becoming a writer. To her, now, it seemed like a long-gone childish fantasy, and she felt a sudden, acute pang for the carefree girl she'd once been.

'I can't afford it,' she said.

He patted his pocket and winked. 'Are you sure?'

Hope rushed through her. 'Have you pawned the jewellery?'

'Might have.' He grinned.

She clapped her hands. 'But that's wonderful. Come on, Harry, tell me. How much did you get?'

He scratched his chin. 'Well now, let me see . . .'

'Harry!'

Relenting, he produced a paper bag from his pocket and pushed it across the counter. 'It's for a necklace and three bracelets. I can sort out the rest, but I thought this might be enough.'

'Thank you,' she said more quietly, although her heart surged with gratitude. 'I appreciate it, honestly.'

'I know you do.' His voice caught a little. From his other pocket, he pulled out a bag of toffees. 'Your favourites,' he said, holding them out for her.

She took one, enjoying the sweetness on her tongue.

'They won't sell those in France,' he added.

She laughed. 'No, but they'll have other treats.'

He regarded her for a moment. 'Aren't you nervous going all that way on your own?'

'Of course not! And even if I was, it wouldn't stop me.'

'No, Connie, I don't suppose it would. But you can't blame people for being worried about you.'

She looked at him sharply. 'You haven't told anyone else, have you?'

'Not a soul, cross my heart!'

The grandfather clock struck midday.

'Listen,' she said quickly. 'Would you do something else for me?'

Harry's eyes lit up, hopeful.

'Will you check on the shop when I'm gone?'

His face fell and he shrugged. 'Course.'

She reached beneath the counter for the spare set of keys. Handing them across, their fingers brushed and she drew away quickly, flushing.

'There's a key for the flat on there too,' she said. 'You can use it if you want a bit of peace.'

'Thanks,' he replied. 'But it won't be the same without you.'

He sounded wistful. She looked away, her resolve weakening, but she pushed down her feelings and a few minutes later he had gone.

21

Marina

January 1992

The man with the cane is in the garden. Marina spots him as she stands at the kitchen window, eating toast for breakfast. She bolts her food and then dashes outside, rounding the path and catching him before he disappears through the bushes.

It is quiet in the garden at this hour. The morning is misty. Blades of wet grass brush her shoes, damp air clings to her hair. Clothes hang limply on the washing line, forgotten overnight.

'Mr Quip,' she calls. The harsh rattle of a magpie answers.

He stops but doesn't turn. Like an echo, she calls again and this time he moves to face her. He has yellow, rheumy eyes. An overcoat hangs loosely on his body and he wears a trilby. He reminds her of a bird – thin like a heron or a stork.

He has an odd way of standing, leaning awkwardly on the stick as if he both needs it and doesn't, and she makes an assumption that he is using it as a prop. It *is* eye-catching – dark wood with a polished silver top. He has a strange way of looking too – his eyes resting on hers for a second before slanting away and scanning the rest of the garden.

Now is her chance to bring up the neglect of the

house, to mention the mould beneath the windows, the poor state of the kitchen and the bathroom, the dodgy boiler and the falling plaster. She should confront him too about potentially entering the flat without permission. More than anything though, she should take this chance to lead him into talking about the past.

She draws herself up and steps forward, closing the gap between them. 'Zoe,' she says, holding out her hand. 'I'm your new tenant.'

A moment's hesitation and then he extends his own. His palm is powdery and dry. His bony fingers are gnarled like claws. He has a string of crudely tattooed numbers on his knuckles.

She lets go of his hand and her desire to complain diminishes. He is so frail, she is sure he must be ill. His left eye weeps; his skin droops. It's as if he is wasting away. She imagines his body crumbling until there is only a pile of clothes.

'I was wondering,' she says, refocusing, 'when the boiler would be fixed.'

He looks at her blankly, and despite her sympathy, she feels a nudge of frustration.

'I'm sure Wayne has explained the problem. Maybe you've had a look already.' It's the closest she can come to accusing him of entering her flat and she pauses, waiting for him to confirm.

He is frowning. His face is gaunt, skin stretched so tight, Marina can see the shape of his skull. She thinks of Death. She thinks of Tarot cards. She thinks of Kenneth with a scythe instead of a cane.

The gate creaks and Mrs Hyde appears at the side of

the house holding her empty laundry basket and heading for the forgotten clothes, which, in this weather, can surely be no drier than when they were first pegged out. She halts when she sees the two of them, blinks, mouth open, white breath misting the air. Marina raises her hand, but the woman ignores them both, hurrying to the washing line and pulling down the clothes. The rattle of the magpie comes again. Marina spots the bird in the magnolia tree. One for sorrow. She searches for another. No joy.

Quickly, Mrs Hyde loads the basket with her damp washing and, still without any acknowledgement, scurries away, disappearing around the house.

Kenneth, meanwhile, has barely moved. He coughs and pulls out a handkerchief that he holds to his mouth.

'I'll get it fixed,' he says. His voice is hoarse, the words rasp on his tongue. Marina is reminded of a saw on wood.

'Do you know how long it will take?'

He pauses. 'A few days. I'll do it myself.'

She wants to keep him there, press him further. The boiler is one thing, but Kenneth Quip and the knowledge he has is another. Too late. He is walking away from her, towards the end of the garden, using his stick to part the long grass.

'I'd like to paint the flat,' she calls out. 'The estate agent said it's all right, but . . .'

He cuts her short, waving his handkerchief, signalling no objection. She can hear him spluttering as he disappears from sight.

*

Ron is bounding up from the basement as she rounds the front of the house. He stops, surprised to see her.

'What are you doing out so early?'

'I was on a mission,' she replies. 'Spotted the landlord in the garden and chased him.'

Ron grins. 'What did you say to him?'

'I asked him to fix the boiler and he agreed.'

'Bloody hell. How did you manage that? Charm?'

She grimaces. 'Not exactly.' She takes in Ron's clothes – his casual jacket, shirt and trousers. 'Off to work?'

'Yes, but I intended to stop off and tell you the news. I've spoken to Eva.'

'Oh?'

'I told her about your article and she said she'd be happy to speak to you. In fact, she was interested.'

Marina's stomach churns. 'That's great. When?'

'This afternoon, at about five?'

She nods eagerly. 'Perfect. It's good of her.'

'Yeah.' He is blushing. She suspects the candle he holds for Eva has been reignited.

She spends the rest of the day settling on blue as the colour for the walls and driving to the nearest DIY shop to fetch the paint.

When she gets home, she prises off the lid and considers where to start. She knows she should lay a groundsheet and prepare the walls by washing them down and putting masking tape around the edges. This is the method David uses, but David is methodical. Marina is more like Ruth – haphazard. Besides, right now she can't be bothered. So, she replaces the lid on the paint and digs out a cigarette from the packet she has buried in the wardrobe. As she smokes, she considers what questions to ask Eva.

She settles herself in the armchair and flicks through her notes. She is building a picture of these people from the past: Victor, Kenneth, Eileen, Dorothy. She has met the men and Dorothy, but Eileen is an enigma. Marina knows she is beautiful because she has seen her photograph. She knows that she threw parties with her boyfriend, Leonard Crisp, in the place where Marina is sitting now. Closing her eyes, she pictures a smoky room crowded with people, narrow trousers and short dresses, white boots and floppy hair, dancing in that jerky sixties fashion to the Beatles. Then darkness comes. A punch is thrown. Eileen staggers. Blood drips from her nose.

Marina's eyes snap open. She is prone to daydreams, but this is something different: sharper – more real; the violence almost visceral. She shudders and jumps up and, to take her mind off ghosts, sets to decorating after all. Not bothering with the preparation, she drags the furniture away from one wall and slaps on paint with fierce, haphazard strokes.

All the time she works, she is thinking. Her mind takes her to the attic, and she visualises the brushes, the jam jars, the pictures hidden behind the chest of drawers. The copies of sunflowers and sunsets and starry nights. Had Dorothy's son painted them as she suspected? He had disappeared to Paris. Had he made it as an artist? His paintings – if they are his – are haunting. Marina recalls the girl in the unfinished sketch, so delicately drawn. A memorable image. She has seen it before. Where?

Marina keeps going until the lower section is complete, then climbs on a chair and starts again at a higher level. She doesn't stop until the whole wall is covered with an uneven coat of dark blue paint. Just as she finishes, it clicks. The bookshop. There was a postcard in the display on the wall. *The Virgin in Prayer*.

It is dark when Marina steps into the hall. The piano has been playing all afternoon, stopping and starting with varying levels of skill as pupils come and go. Now Eva is playing. The music swells and draws Marina up the stairs.

When she knocks, the piano stops and the door opens quickly. Eva Kolinski must be around thirty, but she seems younger. Dark-haired and olive-skinned with dark circles beneath her eyes, she is dressed in a simple green tunic. She has an entrancing beauty. No surprise Ron is captivated although she is thin, too thin, with tiny, fragile wrists. Marina is unnerved. Perhaps it's because of the intense way Eva is looking at her. Or perhaps it's because Marina has built up this meeting in her mind.

They greet each other and Eva motions to Marina to sit on the sofa. It's soft and sagging and tired like the rest of the room with its rich combination of muted colours.

The room is cluttered, with old-fashioned furniture, embroidered cushions, dark tapestries, a burnt-orange rug and lamps. A pair of brass candlesticks stands on the mantelpiece beneath a gilt-edged mirror while a silver samovar sits beside the fireplace below. The wallpaper is dark green and the curtains are red velvet. A polished mahogany piano stands against one wall, stacks of sheet music piled on top of it and heaped in a basket next to it. A circular, dark wood table with sculpted legs occupies the middle of the room, and sports a vase with a single, wilting rose.

'Tea?' Eva offers.

'Thank you.' Marina sits and listens to Eva moving quietly in the kitchen. She notices the bookshelves. There are volumes of poetry and other works written in Polish. Before Marina is tempted to investigate further, Eva reappears carrying a yellow-flowered teapot, matching cups and saucers and a plate of sweet pastries on a tray. She sets the tray on the table, next to the vase, and takes a seat at the piano stool.

'Thank you for agreeing to see me,' says Marina.

Eva bows her head elegantly and looks at Marina with eyes the colour of chestnuts. 'Ron said you were writing an article about the abandoned baby.' She speaks quietly, but there's an eagerness underlying her tone.

Marina feels a pang at not telling the truth and as with Ron she is tempted to explain to Eva, but something is holding her back, a desire not to prejudice people's view of her. 'That's right.'

'What made you decide on it as a topic?'

'Well, I'm interested in moving into journalism. I heard about this story and thought I might be able to come at it from a different angle. I hoped you would be able to help.'

'I was three, so I'm not sure what use I can be.'

'Yes, I know,' says Marina gently, 'but perhaps you

heard your parents talking about it through the years. It must have been a huge story in the house.'

'My father had died by then.' Eva speaks simply, clasping her hands together.

Of course. Ron had told her that. 'I'm sorry.'

'I don't remember him, actually. He had an accident. A car knocked him down. We were in Oxford Street at the time.'

'You witnessed it? That's terrible.'

'Yes, but it's all right. I don't remember that either.'

'Even so. How tragic.'

'It was worse, obviously, for my mother. They were trying to make a new life here . . . You know, after the war.'

Marina takes a breath. 'Where did she meet your father?'

'In London. They were in a similar situation. They married and had me.'

'Do you have brothers or sisters?'

'No, my mother had a miscarriage shortly after my father died.' Eva hesitates. 'Apparently, I saw that too.' She gives a hollow laugh. 'Bad timing.'

Marina looks at her curiously. Eva is more talkative than she had expected from Ron's description.

'It sounds upsetting,' she says, and waits for a few moments before leading Eva back to the abandoned baby, asking her if she recalls anything at all about the day they found her.

Eva frowns and shakes her head slowly. 'I know the story because everybody did and I expect I listened to people gossiping, but as you say, all that came later.'

Marina is quiet, sensing that Eva has more to say.

'What is strange, though . . .' She stops. She is staring across the room at the bookcase. Marina follows her gaze. There's a rag doll propped on a shelf.

'Yes?'

She shakes her head. 'Nothing.'

Marina lets go of her disappointment. Then, in return for Eva's honesty, she offers a personal detail about herself. She tells her that one reason she is interested in the case is that she was adopted.

Eva's eyes widen. 'Adopted?'

Marina nods. 'I suppose that's why I've always been interested in people's origins. It's a bit of an obsession. Recently I've been editing the memoirs of a Jewish lady who had to leave her parents behind in Poland. It's an awful story.' She stops talking, aware there is nothing she can say to Eva because she already knows.

There is a silence. Then Eva throws up her hands. 'I'm sorry! I forgot your tea.'

She hurries across to the tray, pours rapidly and hands Marina a cup and saucer and a pastry. Eva's hand shakes, the tea spills into the saucer, and she apologises again. Marina tells her not to worry, but she is intrigued: she senses a complexity about Eva which she would like to understand.

Instead of sitting down, Eva paces the room. She stops in front of the rag doll on the shelf. 'Have you ever wondered,' she says, 'how reliable your memories actually are?'

'Definitely. Memory is peculiar.'

'Do you think we make up things?' Eva takes the doll and holds it to her face. 'Do you think we piece together bits of information that other people give us and form stories to suit ourselves?'

Marina shifts in her seat. She can sense a change in Eva, but she isn't sure what it means.

'Take this doll, for example. I remember that somebody gave it to me, but I can't remember who. Yet it feels significant for some reason.'

'Was it your mother?'

'No, I don't think so.'

'I had a rag doll like that once upon a time. They must have been all the rage when we were girls. I called mine Jemima. How about you?'

Eva tilts her head. 'Sarah.' Her eyes light up. 'That's just come back to me. I'm sure I didn't know that five minutes ago.'

'I bet you did,' said Marina. 'You just haven't thought about it for a while.'

'Maybe.' She sets the doll back in its place.

'But you don't remember where it came from.'

'No. But I think it was from someone important.' She returns to her seat, frowning. 'And that makes me feel strange.'

Marina raises her eyebrows. She has never met anyone like Eva. A mix of openness and reserve.

'Chopin,' she says suddenly, swivelling around and playing a few bars. 'My mother's favourite piece, and yet – I know this sounds odd – it scares me.'

'Maybe you associate the music with a bad experience.'

'Yes. I've considered that.' She plays a few more notes and then turns again and smiles. 'I'm sorry. I'm being maudlin.'

They talk for a while longer. Marina shares more about herself, telling Eva about her teaching job in Bristol and when she lived abroad. 'Actually, I was in Poland for a while.'

'You're lucky,' Eva says wistfully.

'Have you visited?' says Marina gently.

'No.'

'Your mother didn't . . . ?'

She shakes her head. 'There was no one there for her, you see.'

Marina nods, understanding. A terrible sense of sadness floods through her. 'Still. It's not too late.'

'Perhaps.' Eva looks at her watch and grimaces. 'I'm afraid I've got another pupil coming. I should get ready.'

'Yes, of course.' Marina stands. 'Thank you for talking to me.'

'I haven't been much help.'

'It's not a problem. It's been good to meet you.'

Eva smiles warmly. 'It's been good to meet you too. You should come again.'

'I'd like that. I think we have a lot in common.' Marina says the words to be polite, but as she speaks, she realises she means them, and that she would like to see Eva again. Taking one last glance at the rag doll, she heads back to her flat.

22

Connie

July 1964

Connie stopped looking at herself in the mirror and undressed in the dark, unwinding the strips of sheet, grateful that she had made it through another day with no one knowing the truth.

She checked the post each morning and often passed Dorothy on the stairs clutching hers.

A letter arrived for her father with a postmark from York. Connie inspected the envelope and stared vainly into the box for more. What was the point of having the money to buy a ticket to Paris if she didn't have Johnny's address?

Despite the hour, music blared from Flat 2.

Kenneth came along in his dressing gown and slippers. Ignoring Connie and muttering about the noise, he rapped on the door with his cane. Eileen appeared, glamorous in a pale green dress, surrounded by a fug of smoke.

'Turn it down,' growled Kenneth. 'The whole bloody street can hear you.'

'Sorry, darling.' She gave him a beguiling smile. 'It's the end, you see, and we're celebrating.'

The end of what? Their West End show? Or maybe their relationship. If she were Eileen she would get rid of Leonard sharpish, Connie thought.

'Well, celebrate more quietly,' snapped Kenneth. 'I've told you before.'

Eileen smiled sweetly again. Seeing Connie, she waved.

'Did you get your audition?' Connie asked.

Eileen grinned and nodded. Lucky her, getting away from this place, this house. Imagine travelling all the way to America, to Broadway. Maybe after Paris, when they had saved up some money, she and Johnny could go to New York. There were so many places she would like to visit.

She made breakfast, cracking eggs and sizzling bacon, and frying a slice of bread in the fat as her father preferred.

'Not eating?' he said, shuffling into the kitchen.

Despite Doctor Franklin giving him the all-clear, he looked even more tired than usual. Sitting heavily, he tucked his serviette into his collar. He hadn't shaved properly and wore yesterday's clothes. Connie's stomach twisted with guilt as she bent to kiss his cheek, breathing in the scent of the cologne her mother had bought him, and another, medicinal smell. Maybe the doctor had given him a prescription after all. It would be just like her father to pretend nothing was wrong.

'I'll have toast,' she said, eyeing the runny yolk of his egg and placing the letter from York on the table.

His mood lightened as he picked up the envelope and sliced it open with a knife.

'Good news?'

'The book has arrived and it's mine if I want it.'

'What is it?' asked Connie, leaning forward to see.

'It's a first edition copy of *Wuthering Heights*.' He smiled at her. 'Emily Brontë. One of your mother's favourites.'

She nodded, remembering, and a lump formed in her throat. The book would be expensive and hard to sell in the shop.

'What's the condition?'

He scanned the letter, reading out extracts. 'Two twentieth-century inscriptions of ownership, in pencil . . . joints and spine ends expertly restored . . . front board professionally reattached . . . altogether a very good copy.' He looked up, eyes sparkling. 'How about that?'

'Sounds perfect,' said Connie, pleased to see him animated. 'When are they planning to sell?'

'The owner is away. So, the beginning of August.'

'In that case, you could combine fetching the book with a visit to Aunt Maud like we said. Imagine! You could take three weeks off.'

'I was thinking about that,' he admitted, peering over his glasses at Connie. 'Although I'd much prefer it if you came with me.'

She bit into her toast. If her calculations were correct, the beginning of August was two months before the baby was due. Even if she could hide her condition from her father, she'd never be able to avoid the eagle eye of her aunt.

No. She would time her trip to Paris to coincide with his visit, leaving Harry to look after the shop. The plan was sorted. All she needed was for Johnny to write.

*

The postman might not have guessed Connie's condition, but he'd reached his own conclusions about why she was so eager for his arrival each day, and made regular quips about beaus and boyfriends and billet-doux.

One morning, he turned up grinning.

'You're in luck.' He handed her a parcel. *Miss Connie Littleton*, it said, *24 Harrington Gardens*. She recognised Johnny's beautiful blue calligraphic writing – the hand of a proper artist – and her heart soared as she ran straight up to the attic. Taking her time, she examined the return address: a boulevard in Paris. An *address*; at last.

Slowly, heart pumping, she tugged at the string and peeled off the sticky brown tape. Inside she found an envelope and a package wrapped in silver paper. She set aside the envelope and opened the gift.

She unfolded a shawl, the colour of the painting in the gallery. *The Virgin in Prayer*.

That blue. It was lustrous, more vivid than any colour she had ever seen.

Johnny had told her about the paint. It had once been more precious than gold, and had come from the most prized stone in all the world, lapis lazuli, mined from deep within the earth. It was millions and millions of years old, revered by kings and queens and pharaohs. It had decorated masks and jewellery and been kept inside palaces and pyramids. It had been ground into a powder called ultramarine – the finest of all blue pigments, favoured by Titian and Vermeer and Perugino.

One day Johnny had said that his art would be recognised and then he would give her as much gold as she wanted. She had told him that she didn't care about gold, that she only wanted him, and perhaps a shawl, the colour of the lady's shawl in the painting. And now he had sent her that shawl.

Tears pooled in her eyes as she took the letter, drew out the single sheet of paper and read.

At first, she registered only fragments of sentences and odd words. She reached the end of the page and took a breath, looked up at the windows set in the roof. Clouds drifted across the sky above her and shafts of light picked out the dust. She heard the piano playing in the flat below, the faint scrabbling of mice. The scratch of a pigeon on the roof.

She studied the letter again and focused more clearly. He wrote about the beauty of Paris, Notre Dame and the Sacré Coeur. He talked of climbing the Eiffel Tower and walking in the Tuileries and visiting the Louvre. He had met so many talented artists, he said. Most of them were men, but there was a woman too who painted the most beautiful sunsets he had ever seen.

Connie read and reread this part over and over, feeling the needle of jealousy. Who was this woman? It was only at the end of the letter that he told Connie he missed her. He made no mention of coming home or of her coming to see him. A shadow passed overhead. A bird, wings outstretched, gliding through the air. It disappeared and left no trace.

Slowly, Connie walked downstairs. On the first floor, she paused outside Dorothy's door. Should she share Johnny's address with his mother? No. She would keep this to herself, for now; she couldn't risk Dorothy interfering.

Not yet. If all went according to plan, there would be plenty of time to let her know their whereabouts. She gave a smile at the thought. *Their* whereabouts. Her and Johnny and their beautiful baby.

Eva appeared, clutching the rag doll. Connie let the little girl smooth the shawl with her fingers and then gave her the silver paper and told her how to cut out stars and hang them from the ceiling.

Even the presence of Kenneth and Victor in the front room didn't dampen Connie's mood. In her bedroom, she hid the shawl beneath the floorboard.

She had power because she had knowledge and money and could make choices and decisions. No one would stop her now.

23

Marina

January 1992

Marina wakes the next morning thinking about Eva.

She decides to distract herself by spending the next few days decorating. She paints the rest of the living room blue and it is soothing, like waves lapping on a shore. She trawls around shops and markets and buys blue cushions with gold piping and a pair of green second-hand curtains. The place starts to feel like home – even the bathroom once she's painted it coral and bought a new bath mat to cover the stains. She imagines she has created the sea. She is Marina, floating beneath the surface. She is suspended in time.

She finishes Agata's manuscript and visits her in Tooting Bec to talk through the next step. Marina makes calls on her behalf and eventually finds a small independent publisher who agrees to buy the book. It's not a huge sum and there are no promises of far-reaching readership, but it means Agata's story will be heard. They celebrate with sweet pastries and cakes.

Marina is sorry the project is over and considers what to do next. Realising the state of her bank account isn't great, despite her cheap rent, she looks more earnestly for work. Since she has no definite idea, she applies for a variety of jobs – a position in an art gallery, a museum, a publishing house. She buys a *TES* and leafs through the newspaper. A French teacher is required at a large comprehensive school in Tower Hamlets. Another is wanted in Hackney. She draws a circle around each advert. There's no harm in enquiring about both. She spots another job at her old school in Bristol. She hesitates then circles that one too.

She returns the design book. While Selena is in the kitchen making tea, and the baby sleeps in the cradle, Marina slots the book back in its place. Absent-mindedly, she takes out the dusty book of poetry she saw before. Carefully, she turns the brittle pages and thinks again of the lines she remembers from school.

> *Though I must go, endure not yet*
> *A breach, but an expansion,*
> *Like gold to airy thinness beat.*

A fine brown dust has settled on her hands. It tickles her nose and she sneezes. Instantly, the baby stirs and gives a cry. Selena appears with the tea.

'Sorry,' says Marina, closing the book. 'My sneeze must have woken her.'

Selena sets down the tray and picks up the baby lovingly. 'No worries. It's feeding time anyway.' Settling in the armchair, she glances at the book in Marina's hands. 'I don't know why I kept it.'

'Where did it come from?' asks Marina curiously.

Selena sits in the armchair. 'Pete found it underneath a loose floorboard in the small bedroom.' She nuzzles the top of the baby's head, and adds, 'He was sanding them.'

She pushes up her top and the baby feeds. 'There was money too, inside the book, a bundle of pound notes.'

'Interesting. Anything else?'

'A collection of shells in a box, a fossil, an exercise book with scribbled stories inside.'

'Sounds like a child's treasure trove.'

'Yes, although the book's a bit adult, don't you think? Do you want it?'

'I'd love to borrow it.'

'Keep it. Poetry's not my thing.' Selena soothes the baby and changes the subject, drawing Marina's attention to an abstract painting on the wall. 'Local artist,' Selena says. 'It's good, isn't it?'

Marina agrees, but is only half listening. When she was small, she used to put her treasures in a tin for safekeeping, which she hid in the wardrobe. She kept special stones, pictures of animals she cut out from magazines, gonks with different coloured crazy hair.

'How long did you say you've lived here?' asks Marina when the subject of the painting is exhausted.

'About ten years,' says Selena. 'Can you believe that? I came first actually and when I met Bill, he moved in.'

'And you said the previous tenant died.'

'That's right.' She adjusts herself as the baby finishes its feed. 'Although that was a long time before. The flat was empty for years.'

'I wonder why.'

Selena shrugs. 'I can't really remember.'

Marina is silent for a moment and then she says, 'I was talking to the owner of Crystal's Books.'

Selena strokes the baby's head. 'Crystal's Books? The shop off the High Road?'

'Yes. Apparently, Thomas Littleton . . .'

'Who?'

'The previous tenant here.'

'Oh right.'

'Well, he owned it.'

'Maybe. I don't know.'

'She said that the reason there was a delay with the sale was because there was a missing relative. A relative who was supposed to inherit.'

'Hmm. It rings a bell.' Selena is distracted, buttoning the baby's cardigan.

'Do you know anything about that?'

Selena finishes securing the buttons, smooths the tiny cardigan and frowns. 'No, I don't think so. Although now you're talking about it, I do recall the estate agent making an excuse for the flat being in a state because the landlord hadn't been able to rent it out. He said something about the previous tenant's possessions, though I'm not sure why they couldn't have gone into storage. Maybe there was more to it.'

'Right.' Marina massages her temples, thinking. 'I was just wondering about the stash you found. It sounds like it belonged to a little girl, doesn't it?'

'I suppose so. Yes.'

Marina knows she is asking too many questions, seeming too interested, and has to make a conscious effort to back off. The baby is asleep again. Selena crosses the room and lowers her gently into the cradle. She stands looking down, a faraway smile on her face, and then chats about feeding habits and sleepless nights. 'I dream of having six hours of straight sleep. Five would be enough, even four,' she says.

'Absolutely,' Marina replies absently. Her mind is still in another part of the flat, imagining a little girl hiding treasures beneath a floorboard, keeping them safe just as Marina herself used to do. Could it be that Thomas had a daughter who wasn't mentioned in the newspapers? Perhaps that was the missing relative Crystal spoke about?

Selena is still talking. Marina refocuses. She is being crazy, thinking like this. She doesn't know for sure whether this relative was male or female. How can she find out more? Who can she ask? Victor comes to mind. Perhaps it's time to speak to him again.

24

Connie

1 August 1964

'Are you sure you won't come?'

Her father was leaving for York. His suitcase was packed and ready by the door. Victor had offered to pick him up and drive him to King's Cross.

'Yes,' said Connie, brushing a speck from his waistcoat and handing him his jacket. 'You'll be better off alone.'

'Are you certain?' he asked again.

'I'll be fine.'

Besides, soon she would be in Paris. She had bought her ticket and would be leaving London on 7 August, returning a week or so before her father was due home. It meant she had time to execute the list of chores her father had left her for the shop.

Five days with Johnny. Her heart beat madly each time she thought about what would happen when she saw him. How would he react? Would he pull her into his arms, delighted to see her again? She tried to imagine their reunion, but she couldn't get past boarding the train to Dover, taking the ferry across the Channel. After that it was a blur.

'You can ask Victor for anything you need,' said her father, slipping on his jacket. 'Kenneth too. Though maybe you should try Victor first.'

'Why?'

He raised his eyebrows. 'Kenneth's behaving oddly. I mean more oddly than usual.'

'How?'

'He thinks there's been an intruder in the house.'

'He always thinks that, doesn't he?'

'I know but he said things have been moving around.'

Connie laughed. 'Maybe we've got a poltergeist. Mum always said the house was full of ghosts.'

'Yes, she did, didn't she?'

They looked at each other wistfully, as they always did when one of them mentioned Sarah. This time Connie couldn't stop the tears gathering.

Her father took her hand. 'I'm so sorry, Connie,' he said.

'Don't be. It's not your fault.'

'I've let you down.'

'No, you haven't, Dad.'

She couldn't bear her father's sadness or his guilt. He looked so tired, standing there in his old coat, his face lined, his eyes tearing up behind his glasses.

'You've been such a good girl since . . .' He stopped and shook his head, searching for the right words. 'Since she left us.'

Connie hung her head. If he knew the truth, he wouldn't think that. He would be disappointed and worried, not proud at all.

He carried on talking. 'I wouldn't have survived without you.'

'Don't be silly, Dad. Of course you would have done.'

'No,' he insisted. 'You've kept me going when it should

have been the other way around. I should have been taking care of you. I'm sorry, I really am. But things will be different from now on. I promise you. When I get back from this trip, I'll be my old self again.'

'You don't need to change,' said Connie.

'Yes, I do.'

He patted her hand and did up the buttons on his coat, his fingers fumbling. She reached out and did them for him, speaking too brightly. 'Tell me about Kenneth,' she said, 'and these things which have been moving around.'

He laughed. 'There was the carpet that disappeared from the front.'

'It was stolen!'

'Yes, but apparently, there was also a tea towel. It turned up inside when it should have been out.' His lips twitched. 'You wouldn't believe how much he ranted about that.'

Connie grinned, pleased to see her father smiling. It must have been the tea towel she'd dropped outside Dorothy's door ages ago. 'What else?'

'Someone stole a rose.' He looked at her suspiciously. 'I don't suppose *you* know anything about that?'

She widened her eyes. 'Me? No. I'm innocent.'

'Innocent of what?' Victor appeared in the doorway.

Connie ignored him. Brushing away another speck from her father's coat, she leaned in for a hug, breathed in the familiar scent of his cologne.

'Things *will* change – when I'm back,' he said in her ear. She didn't reply, not trusting her voice. 'And if you decide to come after all, I've left some money in the tea caddy. You can use it for a train ticket.'

She kissed him on the cheek. 'Enjoy yourself, Dad, don't worry about me.'

He smiled sadly and then he was gone.

The next morning, Connie stumbled out of bed. The baby had kept her awake for much of the night, moving and kicking. She got ready slowly and left the house, walking heavily, conscious of a dragging sensation, a pain around her pelvis.

Outside, she spotted a woman in an emerald coat heading rapidly towards the High Road. Connie shaded her eyes. The coat was familiar. And then it clicked. There'd been a woman wearing one just like it, heading towards that dreadful house. And then again outside her own house. Connie had seen her through the basement window. Maybe it was a coincidence. From this distance, Connie couldn't tell if she was pregnant or not.

Mind you, the way Connie was dressed, in her shift dress and a coat, despite the heat, and with her belly bandaged, she didn't think people would guess that she was pregnant. Either way, the woman was certainly moving at a faster pace than Connie, who dawdled along, reluctant to get to the shop, where she knew she would just spend another day brooding.

Beside her, a bus pulled up. Impulsively, Connie clambered on. She could afford a morning off. She asked for a single to Tooting Bec, and the conductor took her fare. When they got there, she followed the crowd into the Underground, and felt glad to be hidden amongst so many people, despite the jostle and the lack of seats.

At Charing Cross, she emerged from the Underground

into a bright morning light that slanted over Trafalgar Square. She crossed to the National Gallery and sat on the steps taking in the scene: the early-bird tourists, the statues and Nelson's Column; the hum of people, the rush of fountains, the flutter of pigeons. She felt soothed and filled with a sudden hopefulness. It was good to be here, away from the darkness of 24 Harrington Gardens. She sometimes thought the house was malign, determined to cast a shadow over anyone who lived there.

They were wild thoughts, though, and Connie shook them off as she climbed the wide steps into the grand entrance with its vaulted ceiling and bustle of visitors and echoing voices. Closing her eyes, she imagined her hand on Johnny's arm, her excitement quickening as they walked across the wooden floors of the galleries.

She looked for *The Virgin in Prayer*, but had forgotten where it hung. One gallery led onto the next and she passed row after row of religious paintings, all depicting suffering in a way that was repellent and fascinating in equal measure. At last, though, she walked into a room and spotted the painting. She stared at it for ages: the rich red and deep blue, the Virgin's face in shadow, her straight nose and thin lips, her pink cheeks and blunt nails. Connie had hated having to sit for Johnny. What had it been like for this model? She must have stood for hours at a time.

Maybe that was the problem, she thought now in a kind of revelation. She didn't want to stay still. She wanted to move through life, causing a ripple, making a difference. Yet so often people left no trace unless they created a masterpiece, like a sculpture or a painting. Or could it be something intangible? A memory held in a heart? Or a child. A child that then had a child themselves. Generation following generation. She thought of her mother, and the child in her belly.

Suddenly, Connie wanted to be home. Gathering herself, she left the gallery and retraced her earlier footsteps. At Tooting Bec, she missed a bus, so walked slowly home. Her feet were sore, her shoes too narrow for her swollen feet. They rubbed and chafed and she would have slipped them off if the pavement had been cleaner. What would it be like in Paris? She imagined the city glittering like a mirror. But she had based her ideas on photos and paintings and knew it must have its fair share of dusty corners like any other place.

Her head ached and the pain in her pelvis had come back. She would take an aspirin and lie in a darkened room once she got to the flat.

She paused for breath and a woman hurrying out of a shop nearly collided with her. As they both apologised a newspaper on the stand caught her eye. Bending, she read the headline: *Body Found in Lake Identified.* Connie looked more closely. There was a photo of a man. Middle-aged with light-coloured hair, unremarkable save for his ears, which stuck out like two handles of a teapot. She frowned. It was the man she'd seen with Kenneth in the garden. The caption even named him: Frank Dennis. She bought a copy of the paper, then tucked it under her arm and headed for home.

*

Connie's first thought was that the gathering crowd near number 24 had something to do with Frank Dennis, but as she got closer, she saw debris covering the ground. An empty suitcase, clothes, books, a smashed reading lamp, a statue of Buddha. Eileen appeared at the window waving what looked like a script, which she proceeded to scatter, page by page.

The front door opened and Leonard appeared half-dressed in jeans and a vest. Zipping his flies, he leapt down the steps. The crowd laughed as he shook his fist.

'What the hell are you doing?' he yelled.

'I'm throwing you out!'

'You can't throw me out. It's my flat.'

'No, it bloody isn't. I pay the rent!'

'Mad bitch.'

'Stupid bastard. I should have got rid of you months ago.'

She carried on throwing his belongings into the street.

'I'll kill you!'

'Touch me again and you're dead!' she said.

The crowd cheered. Leonard threw his hands up in defeat, snatched the suitcase and filled it with whatever he could grab before stalking off, trying to be dignified with no shoes and no shirt.

'And don't come back,' Eileen yelled after him.

She caught sight of Connie and waved. Connie waved back and laughed as Eileen gave a bow along with a flourish to the onlookers.

*

Indoors, Connie settled down to read the article. The body had been dragged from the lake on Tooting Common. Frank Dennis, a low-grade gangster, had done time for robbery including assault. However, the assault charge had been revoked – just as Connie's father had said – and Frank had been released. Three months later, he had turned up dead. He might have been drunk, the paper speculated, and fallen into the lake, or he might have killed himself. Or had he been murdered? It turned out he had significant debts.

Connie folded the paper, brows drawn. Did Kenneth know that this man was dead? Her father had talked about a rift. How serious had that been? She shivered and blew on her hands. She wished her father was here now, to talk the story through.

To distract herself, she went into the kitchen, opened the fridge and surveyed its contents. She should go shopping. There was hardly anything here. In the end, she had bread and butter and stood at the window eating. It was almost dark, and the bushes and trees appeared ghostly in the twilight. As Connie gazed out, Kenneth came around the side of the house and walked across the lawn. He stopped halfway and turned. Instinctively, Connie stepped to the side and then moved further back.

That night, unease curled around her as she drifted in and out of sleep. As well as the usual noises, she imagined she could hear others: the beating wings of an owl; the flitter of a bat. Flowers in the garden closing their petals, the leaves curling, the trees stretching their branches.

A high-pitched sound made her jump. She swivelled her legs onto the floor and got out of bed. In the kitchen, she poured a glass of water. The screech came again. Leaning forward, she pressed her face to the glass. A creature scrambled over the fence and dropped onto the ground. It ambled across the lawn and stopped in a pool of moonlight. Sticking one leg up, it began to lick its fur. Socks. Her heart lifted. She'd come home. Connie rapped on the glass, but the cat took no notice, carrying on with its routine. Without thinking, Connie pulled her coat over her nightdress and slipped on her shoes. She grabbed her keys and let herself out of the flat.

Leaving the light off, she fumbled her way downstairs. In the hall, she hesitated. A glow from the street lamp showed through the window. The baby kicked and she grasped the bannister. Jazz music played quietly in Eileen's flat. The sound of a chain rattling into place came from Kenneth's.

Quietly, she opened the front door. The return of Socks was a sign. Connie would entice her inside, and in the morning, she would ask Eileen to take care of her until she returned from Paris.

She hurried round the side of the house. Surprisingly, Kenneth had left the gate unlocked. She pushed through and regretted not bringing a torch, but the moon was bright and she spotted Socks still sitting on the lawn patiently licking her fur.

Connie called out softly and the cat's eyes glittered yellow. The shriek came again, sounding closer. Not Socks, but a fox perhaps, or could it be an owl? The cat reacted, hackles raised. Connie crept closer and was rewarded. Socks padded to meet her, purring loudly. Her face had thinned, but her belly hung low and she had a wild air and a fetid smell. Connie bent, stroking the cat, and, as she did so, she saw a movement, a kind of rolling inside her. She stepped back, surprised. Socks was pregnant too.

Maybe Connie's touch had broken the spell, or else Socks recalled a primeval urge warning her to avoid humans, because she suddenly shot away, disappearing through the hidden part of the garden.

Connie followed, but stopped abruptly. A man was shovelling earth into a hole. Victor. He had taken off his jacket and it lay on the ground next to a duffle bag.

'Oh,' she said, before she could stop herself.

His head snapped up. 'My God. What are you doing here?'

She backed away. There was a flash of fur as Socks disappeared behind the shed. 'I was looking for the cat.'

'What?' He got to his feet.

'Socks. The cat we used to feed.'

'You nearly gave me a heart attack.' He threw down the spade and advanced.

Frozen to the spot, she babbled about not being able to sleep, but he wasn't listening. He stood before her and rested his hands on her shoulders like weights. The baby moved. Thank God for the darkness. It veiled the heat of her face and the shape of her body beneath her coat.

'Were you spying?' he said, his face inches from hers.

His breath was cold. It smelled of stale whisky and smoke. But she held still, willing him not to move his hands. If he grabbed her anywhere else, he would surely guess the truth.

'I'm not,' she said. 'I told you. I came to find Socks.'

The animal cried again. Victor jumped and let her go. 'Are you sure?'

She nodded.

'Fine. I want you to forget what you've seen. Do you understand?'

'Yes.'

He leaned towards her. 'Say it.'

'I've forgotten what I've seen.'

'Good girl.' He straightened, satisfied. 'Because if you tell anyone, it could be life or death.'

He spoke dramatically. Wiping his hands on his trousers, he stepped away, back to the patch he'd been digging. He stamped on the loosened soil and when he'd finished, grabbed the duffle bag. Reaching inside, he pulled out a wad of money, peeled off several notes and held them out. 'For your silence,' he said.

Connie curled her fists. 'No thanks.'

'Why not?'

'Because I don't know where it's come from.'

He batted a rose bush. 'Right here. Kenneth thinks nobody knows about his buried stash, but it's so obvious. He's such a fool.'

He laughed unpleasantly and Connie thought about Frank Dennis. Victor was playing a dangerous game. 'Why are you taking it?'

'Let's just say I need it more than Kenneth does.'

'What do you mean?'

Victor hesitated. 'Let's also say that I won't be knocking on your door for a while. I'm otherwise engaged. Literally.'

'I don't understand.'

'For God's sake, Connie. It isn't difficult. I'm engaged to be married.'

'Who to?'

'My former landlady's daughter. She's pregnant and doesn't want to get rid of the baby, or leave me alone for that matter. Haven't you seen her hanging about the house?'

The woman in the emerald coat. Of course. 'Don't you want to marry her?'

He shrugged. 'I'm getting used to the idea.' He indicated the money. 'And extra cash may not give me a happy journey, but it will certainly oil the wheels. Come on. Take a share. You know you want to.'

'But, it's . . .'

'What? Stealing?'

Connie nodded, but her resolve was weakening. How much could she buy for the baby?

'How do you think Kenneth and his pals got it in the first place? And how many people did Kenneth betray to keep it all for himself?'

Connie had a vision of Frank Dennis flailing in the lake.

'Come on,' said Victor, shaking the notes, 'I haven't got all day.'

Heart thumping, she took the money and walked as fast as she could to the house. Climbing the steps at the front, she felt a stab of pain. It must be a stitch. She waited for it to pass. Breathing heavily, she pressed on, closing the door behind her and returning to the flat.

Later, her dreams were full of random images: Socks's belly, heaving with kittens; Frank Dennis's body being pulled from the water; Kenneth's roses blossoming but with banknotes instead of petals.

25

Marina

January 1992

Victor lives in a sixties block of flats, ten minutes from the High Road. Marina presses the buzzer on the intercom and he opens the door without checking who is there. She had called him again and, this time, when he suggested she come to his home, she agreed.

She avoids the lift and climbs the concrete stairs to the third floor where she finds the door to his flat is ajar. She steps inside and calls out his name.

'In the living room,' he shouts back.

The corridor is narrow with parquet flooring which is shabby but well-swept. Glancing through the first open door on the left, she sees a small and tidy kitchen. The next room must be Victor's bedroom. The curtains are closed and she makes out the shape of a bed and a wardrobe. There is a further closed door which she guesses is the bathroom and, at the far end, the living room.

Victor is less well-groomed than before. He wears a white shirt, but there's a stain on the front and he needs a shave. His eyes are bloodshot and Marina suspects he has either started drinking early or has kept it up extremely late. In contrast, she has gone for a no-nonsense image again. Her hair is scraped back and she wears jeans, a jumper and her thick furry coat. She is well and truly covered.

He gestures for her to sit in the armchair and offers tea, insisting when she refuses. While he is gone, she looks about the room. There is a single armchair, a bulky TV, a plain table and two hard-backed chairs. The colour scheme is bland – brown carpet and curtains, beige walls and a yellow lampshade, although one wall is covered in a glamorous array of black and white photos of women with chandelier earrings and mini-dresses and men in suits. It's a shrine to the sixties. She recognises Diana Ross and Cilla Black. There are a couple of men who resemble gangsters.

Victor returns with one cup and saucer which he hands to Marina before fetching a chair from the table and setting it in front of her, too close for comfort. He sits and folds his arms.

'So,' he says, 'to what do I owe this pleasure?'

'I wanted to ask you about Thomas Littleton. I know that you worked with him, so I wondered if you could help me with some details.'

He leans back in his chair and takes out a cigarette. 'What about him?'

'Was he married?'

'He was when I met him.'

'What happened?'

'His wife died. Cancer.' He lights his cigarette.

'When?'

He shrugs. 'I can't remember exactly, early sixties.'

'What was her name?'

'Sarah.'

Marina blinks. Where has she heard that name before? 'Did they have a child?'

In an instant, Victor's expression closes. He produces the hip flask from his pocket and takes a swig.

'Ah yes. Connie.'

Marina feels a shot of excitement. She was right. There *had* been a girl living in that flat, hiding her treasures beneath the floorboards – a girl called Connie. She lets the revelation settle and drinks her tea, which is strong and surprisingly good.

'You knew her,' she says, setting down her cup.

'You could say that.' Victor's manner has definitely changed. He is guarded, looking at her with lidded eyes as he smokes.

'Was she away when they found the baby?'

He frowns. 'Yes, she was. You really are interested in this case, aren't you?'

She regards him steadily. 'I'm interested in writing an article.'

He nods slowly, raising his eyebrows as if he doesn't believe her.

She swallows and continues. 'So, where was she?'

Victor waits a beat. 'Paris.'

It's her turn to frown. 'Didn't you say Dorothy's son, Johnny, went to Paris?'

'Yep.' Dislike creeps across his face.

Now she understands. Connie must have run off with this boy and Victor was jealous. 'How old was she?'

'Seventeen.'

'And when did you say she left?'

'I didn't.'

She blinks. 'All right. When did she leave? How long was it before the baby was discovered?'

'I don't know exactly. Days, maybe.'

Marina stares at him. 'In that case . . .'

'I know what you're thinking and no, Connie wasn't pregnant. Definitely not.'

She continues to look at him. How can he be sure?

'I saw her just before she went. I was this close to her.' He indicates the distance between them. 'She wasn't pregnant. Impossible.'

Nothing is impossible, but Marina focuses on the facts. 'So, Johnny was waiting for Connie to join him.'

'I suppose.' He gets up and walks to the table to use the ashtray. 'Why are you so interested in this story? It strikes me that people aren't interested in much unless there's something in it for them.'

'I told you. I'm writing an article.'

He stays standing, regarding her coolly. He's a big man, powerful, far too large for the small room. Marina wishes he would sit down.

'And there's money in that?'

She guesses what he wants. 'There might be.'

'So, you won't forget your informers.'

'You mean contributors. Yes. I'll pay you if the article gets published.'

He grins knowingly. 'I'm kidding.'

She doesn't believe him. She tries again. 'Thomas Littleton was away at the time, wasn't he?'

'That's right. Visiting his sister in Whitby. I remember because I took him to the station.'

'So, Flat 4 was empty.'

'Bloody hell, you have done your homework.'

She ignores his comment, speaks slowly, piecing

events together. 'So . . . Connie was abroad. Did her father know, or did she run away?'

'She told a couple of people, but not Thomas. He got home from his trip and she was gone. It was cruel of her. He died not long after that and she didn't even come back then.'

'Is that what she was like?'

He is quiet for a moment. 'No, actually. She wasn't like that.'

There's a sad note to his voice. Has she misjudged him? Maybe he cared a lot about Connie.

She considers this and then says, 'If she was in Paris, she might not have heard about her father's death.'

Victor doesn't seem convinced. He takes the hip flask from the table and polishes it on his sleeve before untwisting the cap and taking a swig.

Marina carries on. 'Connie must have been pretty young when her mother died.'

'Sarah. Yes, she was.'

Sarah. Suddenly Marina remembers where she has heard the name. Eva's doll. It must be a coincidence, though: Sarah is a common name.

'What was Connie like?'

He fiddles with the cap from the hip flask, taking his time, before he answers. 'She was a good person.'

Again, Marina sees the heart beneath Victor's bluster.

'How did she cope with her mother's death?'

He shrugs and looks away. 'She had friends, I suppose.'

'Do you remember any of their names?'

He takes another furtive swig and closes one eye. Marina realises that he's actually quite drunk.

'There was a boy called Harry.'

'Harry?' Her heart thuds. It's another name she hasn't heard before.

'Yep. Skinny boy that had a crush on her.'

'How old was he?'

Victor shrugs. 'I don't know. Her age, maybe.'

'And they were friends, not lovers?'

'Definitely not lovers.'

'Where did he live?'

'Above a grocer's shop.'

'Where exactly?'

Now Victor grins. He's back to his old self, enjoying the fact that he has information she wants. 'Near Thomas Littleton's bookshop,' he tells her finally.

'Is the grocer's still there?'

'Yes, but he isn't. That shop must have changed hands at least three times since then.'

'Oh.' Marina tries to hide her disappointment.

He is looking at her shrewdly. Marina detects an intelligence in his eyes. She is rapidly changing her opinion of Victor. There is more to him than she first thought.

'How long do you plan to stay in the house?' he asks suddenly.

'I don't know. It depends.'

'On what?'

He has turned the tables and is questioning her. She keeps her voice neutral. 'Work. Money. I'm applying for jobs. I might do a bit of teaching.'

'You're hoping to sell this article,' he says directly.

She flushes. 'Yes, well. I'm going to try.' Moving away from the topic, she talks about renting a different flat.

'The house isn't the most . . .' She stops. Is it prudent to be critical when Victor knows Kenneth?

He understands. 'I get you. Kenneth is a lazy bugger.'

She looks at him. 'You were friends back then?'

He shrugs. 'Not particularly.'

'Tell me something. What did you mean last time when you said he didn't notice what went on under his nose?'

He observes her as if weighing her up, and has another drink. 'Money.'

'What about it?'

'He had a whole load of money that he'd stolen. I mean stolen twice. Once in a raid and once from his gang.'

'And?'

Victor grins. 'Actually, I should say it was stolen three times.'

'Three?' Now she guesses. 'You mean you stole it?'

'Some of it.' He looks pleased with himself. 'Kenneth didn't miss it. Well, if he did, he never suspected it was me. I had personal problems. Things needed paying for.'

He is rambling, justifying himself, drinking again. She thinks that if she keeps quiet he'll explain. She is right. He talks about his girlfriend – the daughter of his land-lady, who he'd got pregnant. 'I had to marry her. I didn't have a choice.'

Marina pricks up her ears at the mention of a baby. Do the dates work? She thinks they might – although her excitement is tempered by the thought that this man could be her father. Surely not. She regards him beneath lowered lids. They have nothing in common, physically or personality wise. Besides, he hasn't finished his story.

She wants to press him further, but suspects he'll either clam up or become suspicious. She'll bide her time, try a roundabout route. 'And the money?'

'I needed to support her, didn't I? I remember giving a few pounds to Connie.' He frowns. 'I guess she used it to fund her escape to Paris.'

'Why are you telling me this?' says Marina suddenly. 'Aren't you worried Kenneth will come after you?'

He gives a laugh. 'You are joking? Kenneth couldn't go after anyone. He might have done then, true, but not now. He's . . .' He pauses thinking of the right word. 'Diminished.'

Marina remembers the frail old man she met in the garden. 'Maybe it's guilt,' she says.

She expects Victor to laugh at her, but instead he looks serious. 'I'd hazard a guess his mind is full of scorpions.'

'Pardon?'

'Shakespeare, my dear. *The mind of guilt is full of scorpions*. Kenneth must see them everywhere, which can't be good for the soul.' He takes yet another drink. 'Whereas I'm more inclined to see pink elephants.' He laughs again as if to cover the cleverness of his remark.

It doesn't work. Marina is impressed. Victor has surprised her again.

He lifts his flask in a gesture of cheers, stops with it halfway to his lips and says, 'Mind you . . . It's always best to be careful. I assume I can rely on your discretion.'

'Of course,' says Marina. 'I never reveal my sources.'

He smiles with a touch of uncertainty. Takes out another cigarette, eyes her and then says, 'Actually, I know where Harry has gone.'

'Oh yes?' Marina feigns nonchalance, but her heart is beating rapidly. First the mention of the pregnant girlfriend; now this. 'Where?'

'He crossed the river. I heard he had a rather bijou shop in Angel. Did well for himself in the end, it turns out.'

'A grocer's?'

'Hats.'

'You kept in touch.'

'No. My wife – ex-wife that is – her mother knew his mother or something. Sent Christmas cards every year.'

She thinks again about the baby Victor's wife was expecting, tries to calculate the dates. It must have been born around the same time as her. 'Does your ex-wife still live in this part of London?'

Victor grimaces and looks down at the carpet. 'She moved to Liverpool with the bloke she met after me.'

'That must have been difficult for you, not seeing your son or daughter.'

'Didn't make it.' He raises his head and his eyes shine. Marina understands. 'Oh God. I'm sorry.'

He clears his throat. 'The irony was that at first I wanted her to get rid of it. When she told me she was pregnant, I tried to persuade her to have an abortion, even encouraged her to go to a backstreet clinic. Terrible place it was.'

There is a pause. Marina speaks gently. 'But she wanted to keep the baby?'

'Yep. Persuaded me and I married her. Got used to the idea. Five months in and she lost it.'

'I'm really sorry.'

'Yeah. I was too – by then.' His eyes glisten again. 'Funny how things end up,' he says, grinding his cigarette in the ashtray.

His loss seems almost tangible to Marina; she feels it too, but isn't sure whether she's relieved or otherwise to learn that Victor isn't her father.

26

Connie

3 August 1964

In the morning, it was as if the scene in the garden with Victor had never happened. Normality had been restored. Tea towels and aprons flapped on the line, flowers bloomed, light sparkled on the windows of the church.

But Connie had the stolen banknotes.

Why had she taken them and put herself in debt to Victor?

She bound her belly as usual, slipped on her dress and applied her make-up carefully. Once again, she had been kept awake for most of the night – not just by splintered dreams, but also the baby kicking and turning and, in the early hours, a dull ache that had come and gone. Rummaging amongst her mother's clothes, Connie found a fringed shawl and draped it over her shoulders.

On the way out, she stopped at her father's desk and rolled back the lid. In a few days' time, she would be gone. She would pack later, but now she wrote the note she planned to leave for her father, just in case he came home early or she was delayed. She worded it carefully, making no mention of her pregnancy, but telling him how she had left to find Johnny. *I love him*, she wrote at the end, and *I hope you understand*. She signed off and left the lid of the desk open, the note visible on the blotter.

Eileen was collecting her post, and when Connie asked

for a word, invited her into the flat. The front room reeked of stale smoke; clothes were draped over the furniture or dropped in suitcases that had themselves been left open on the floor. Despite the warmth of the day, the fire crackled. Connie could see the blackened edges of burning papers. More of Leonard's things, she guessed.

Sweeping a pile of magazines from an armchair, Eileen indicated that Connie should sit, while she perched on the sofa. 'You must have wondered what was going on the other day,' she said. 'I guess I looked like a crazy woman.'

She said the word *crazy* in an American drawl with a long, lazy vowel. Her voice was warm like her personality. Connie glanced at the open suitcases. Eileen was obviously leaving soon.

'Broadway here I come,' she said, following Connie's gaze.

Connie sighed, sinking further into the chair, turning her face to the heat of the fire. She would miss her. The ache in her belly had increased. She arranged the ends of the shawl more effectively to cover herself and tried not to show her discomfort. Maybe she *should* tell Eileen about the baby and her plans to go to Paris. Eileen wouldn't be shocked. She'd come all the way from America so she had to know something of the world.

She was talking about Leonard. 'Never stay with a man who wants to control you,' she said. 'Freedom is everything and you need to fight for it.'

But what if you couldn't be free? What if you were captured by circumstance because you had no money, or you had lost a loved one, or were pregnant when you were only seventeen?

Connie imagined the words on her lips, but somehow, when she opened her mouth, they just wouldn't come. Instead, she told Eileen about Socks, asking her to look out for the kittens, at least until she left for America.

'Yes, of course I will, darling,' Eileen replied, 'but where are you going?'

'France.'

Eileen's eyes widened.

'Paris,' Connie added. 'I'm going to see my boyfriend.'

'That's very brave,' said Eileen gently. 'Does your father know?'

'Yes,' she lied.

'And he doesn't mind?'

Connie shook her head.

'Well, that's modern of him and independent of you. Well done.'

The baby kicked and Connie felt another urge to confide, but then somebody hammered on the door and Eileen leapt up. 'If that's Leonard,' she said, 'I'll . . .'

It wasn't, but it *was* a friend of his, and Connie suddenly felt awkward and unwelcome as Eileen invited him in. She introduced him as *Leonard's pal*, but she clearly knew him well too, and even though there didn't seem to be anything between them, Connie was uncomfortably aware of how young and gauche she must appear. As soon as she could, she left them to it and headed out into the garden.

The flowers on the magnolia tree were past their best. The petals were brown-tinged and drooping at the edges. Connie felt the pain again – sharper now, more prolonged. The sensation grew and she put her hand to her belly until it disappeared. Trying to ignore her misgivings, she stepped through to the end of the garden. Victor had done a good job of flattening the earth.

Nettles and brambles choked the space between the shed and the wall. Covering her mouth and nose against the stink of moist earth and decomposing plants, Connie peered into the gloom and spotted Socks lying on a patch of flattened undergrowth. At first, she thought the cat was dead and the squirming creatures around her body were fat maggots feeding on her flesh, but then she saw a pair of yellow eyes staring back at her. The writhing bodies were kittens. She counted five of them, ravenously pawing at their mother's flesh, and a sixth, motionless amongst them.

She tiptoed away, leaving Socks to it, hoping Eileen would remember to look out for the kittens. At the side gate, she put her hand on the latch, stopping abruptly as the pain – almost like cramp, but more crippling – returned, stronger this time, lasting longer. Breathing deeply, she waited for it to go.

At the front of the house, she stood beneath the maple tree. She felt an odd sense of finality, a feeling that she might never see these things again. Frowning, she fixed her eyes on the familiarity of the street, touching the bark of the tree, running her fingers along the roughness of the railings.

The cramp came yet again. She must have eaten something that disagreed with her – it was too early for the baby to be due. But the pain grew fiercer and she gripped the railing. Food poisoning, she told herself, as it sub-sided. Staggering to the steps, she climbed them slowly. Gritting her teeth, she made it into the hall.

Music flooded from Eileen's flat. Connie couldn't tell whether she was alone or if Leonard's friend was still there, although she could make out Ella Fitzgerald and Eileen's voice singing along. Should she tell her that Socks had had her kittens? Softly she knocked, but nobody heard. From the top of the house came the sound of the piano. Connie gritted her teeth at more pain, seething and hot.

Ella Fitzgerald stopped. Sweat beaded on Connie's brow. She raised her hand to knock a second time, but her legs were trembling and she felt sick, and when she touched her forehead, it was clammy. Slowly, she allowed herself to drop, sliding down the wall. She was struggling to focus, and somewhere – although she couldn't work out whether it was real or not – she sensed a presence. A figure gliding down the stairs like a ghost. If only it was her mother come back from the dead, but that was impossible – it couldn't be her.

Shifting, Connie searched for the strength to stand, to knock on Eileen's door. She pushed down on her hands and struggled to rise, but her body was like lead, her limbs unresponsive. Defeated, she groaned and breathed deeply, battling to stay conscious – because the figure coming towards her, she suddenly realised, was not a figment of her imagination at all, but a woman. A woman with a bright pink lipstick mouth and a scent of eau de cologne.

Sickness rose in Connie's throat as the woman took hold of her arm.

27

Eva

January 1992

Eva stands in front of her door with one hand on the latch. Any moment now and she will do it. She will step out onto the landing. A few intakes of breath and she will take the stairs, one at a time, holding onto the bannister as she goes. Two flights down to the hall and she will knock on the woman's door. *Zoe*. She said her name was Zoe, and the name means *life*.

It has been a while since Eva has had a life, at least outside her flat. How does she survive? Through the kindness of strangers. Well, the kindness of *almost strangers*. When her mother died, Selena had brought flowers and food and run errands, buying stamps and posting letters; Giovanni had brought music. And then, of course, there was Ron, the kindest of them all, never pushing, only enquiring. Are you all right? Fancy a takeaway? Need any milk?

Opening the door, she pushes the light switch and the mechanism whirrs. The stairs are steep. She clamps her hand on the bannister. From here she can see the first-floor landing and the doors of the flats below. But she is teetering on the edge of a memory. Shadows are flitting, people are whispering, voices are rising, loud and angry.

She concentrates, takes one step at a time. She goes down slowly and by the time she reaches the first-floor landing, the light fizzles and goes out. Fumbling in the darkness, she finds another switch and pushes it hard. BAM. There is light and now she looks upwards and it feels as though she is peering through a tunnel of time.

In her imagination, Little Eva stands at the top of the stairs. She wears the purple dress. She holds the rag doll loosely in her hand. But her face is stained with tears. Why is she sad?

Listen. Little Eva's voice is whispering. *Shall I tell?*

The air thickens in a heavy, malevolent swirl.

In the present, Eva presses her hands to her head and takes deep breaths. She closes her eyes to force away the memory and when she opens them again, the whispering has ceased, the voices have quietened, the ghost is gone. It's 1992. She is standing on the first-floor landing. She can hear the hum of a washing machine, the buzz of people talking, the sound of a baby crying.

What is real and what is not?

She continues slowly, all the way down the next flight of stairs to the hall. Her body is trembling, her skin slick with sweat. A few more steps. Tensing her muscles, she forces her legs forward and knocks on the door.

The woman answers quickly. Zoe. She is wearing her black coat and fingerless gloves and has a long, black scarf wound like a python around her neck.

She stares at Eva. 'Are you all right?'

Eva smiles back weakly.

'Please. Come in.'

'But you're going out.'

'It's not important. Come in. You look terrible.' She takes her arm and Eva allows herself to be led.

Eva has never been inside the flat before, but she guesses Zoe is responsible for the vibrant colours and textures.

'Would you like to sit down?'

'Thank you.' Eva walks unsteadily across the floor and takes a seat.

Zoe perches on a chair and unwinds her scarf. Her dark eyes are large with concern. She offers a drink: tea, coffee, water.

Eva declines. She has a headache and pushes her fingers against the hammering pain.

'Are you sure you're all right?'

Eva blinks and concentrates on Zoe's hair – the way it falls forward, curtaining her face. She closes her eyes, but when she opens them again, the floor is still tilting. Her mind is still sliding.

Zoe leaps from her seat. 'What's wrong?' she says.

'It's nothing.' Eva tries to focus. 'I just feel . . .' She slumps in her chair.

'What do you feel?' The voice is gentle.

'It's nothing really,' she murmurs. 'It's happened before.'

Zoe kneels at Eva's feet and takes her hand. 'Tell me.'

'I can't explain.'

'Try; it might help, you know, to confide in a stranger.'

Eva nods slowly and when she speaks again the tension starts to drain. She talks about when she was a child and lost whole chunks of time; how she refused to leave the house. She recounts her mother making appointments for her to see doctors and psychologists.

'They said I was having blackouts, brought on by the trauma of witnessing my father's death and my mother's miscarriage. I can't remember either of those events, but I suppose that's the point.'

'And this is one of those episodes?'

'Yes.'

'What happens exactly?'

'The world goes black. Everything around me disappears. Then a flash of memory comes. It's like a white light splitting the darkness. I see myself as a child standing somewhere high up and I have a sensation of falling, like vertigo. I'm watching something that makes me feel awful.'

'What is it?'

'I don't know. Faces. Figures. But they're blurry.'

'What else?'

'There are sounds – a tapping, a whispering, rising angry voices. A flash of light, a sudden noise like a door slamming and then crying. It's a deep memory. I want to reach inside my mind and claw it out, but each time I take hold, it slips away.' Eva takes a breath.

'Does this happen all the time?'

'It comes in phases.'

'Do you know what triggers these episodes?'

Eva shrugs. 'A scent, a sound, a person.' She frowns. 'You.'

'Me? How?'

'I saw you. That night when you came to the house. I watched you from my window. I thought I was looking at a ghost. I couldn't believe it when you moved in.'

'So, what is it about me?'

Eva pauses. 'Your hair.'

Zoe touches it. 'What about it?'

'The colour. The thickness. I'm not sure. I only know that from the moment you walked in that door, I didn't want to walk out.'

Zoe stares at her. 'Do I remind you of someone?'

Eva shakes her head in frustration. 'There's somebody that I see in my memories. She's pretty and kind and . . .' She stops.

'Yes?'

'She's in trouble. I'm frightened for her.'

Zoe reaches out her hand and takes Eva's. Her face is drained of colour, her eyes huge and dark. She looks frightened and yet her gaze is warm and her expression is kind.

There is a name inside Eva's head that she just can't reach.

She makes herself a promise. She will work out what that name is. She will force herself to remember. She will find out what it is exactly that unnerves her about this woman who is kneeling before her now.

28

Connie

3–4 August 1964

When Connie opened her eyes, she was lying on a bed in a darkened room. For one moment, she thought she had died. But then the pain came. A wild animal seizing and ravaging her, tearing her apart. She arched her body, waiting for the cramp to build and swell and climax and then leave.

She relaxed, breathing heavily. How had she got here? Her mind trailed backwards. The arrival of Dorothy. Her grip on Connie's arm. The laborious climb up the stairs. She had made it into Dorothy's flat before the liquid flooded from between her legs. Stumbling into this room, she must have fainted.

It smelled sour, of sweat and bile. The curtains were drawn. Connie felt panic rising from the pit of her stomach and spreading through her chest. There was a noise, a whimper, and Connie realised the sound came from her. In the dim light of a bedside lamp she could see flowered wallpaper, a heavy wardrobe, a chest of drawers.

The door opened and a figure appeared. Connie opened her mouth to call out, but the pain came again, rising and sharpening, taking her breath. She writhed and groaned, grabbing hold of the bedstead, trying to haul herself up, but she was too weak, and before she could stop herself, she leaned over the bed and vomited straight into the bucket that Dorothy held.

The pain subsided and she lay back, wiping her mouth with her hand, wishing the room would stop spinning. A few minutes lapsed and it began again. She wanted to scream, but in the back of her mind she knew she must be quiet: this was her secret; she wasn't ready for it to be discovered. Yet the baby was coming, even though it was too early. How could a baby survive coming into the world so soon? It was her fault. All the times she had considered getting rid of it, and the times she had tried, shifting the furniture, running as hard as she could, taking that hot bath.

The pain faded and she found that she was clutching Dorothy's hand. Letting go, she turned away.

'Did you do something?' said Dorothy. 'Did you take something to bring this on?'

'No,' moaned Connie. 'I want my baby.'

'Hush,' said Dorothy, and as the pain came again, she pushed something hard and wooden inside her mouth. 'Clamp down,' she said and Connie did, grinding her teeth, tasting the darkness and earthiness of what? The handle of a brush, a wooden spoon? She wanted to choke.

On and on came the pendulum of pain. There were longer periods of hell. Shorter and shorter reprieves. Dorothy's face loomed as Connie slipped in and out of consciousness. When she was awake, and a contraction began, she flailed and thrashed, grunted and moaned. Her hair stuck to her neck and forehead with sweat. But she didn't scream. She bit obediently onto the wooden handle.

'I'm dying,' she said between gasps of agony.

'You're not,' said Dorothy. Her voice was matter-of-fact, but Connie could see something else. Fear, perhaps.

'Do I need a doctor?' she said in a moment of calm.

Lips pursed, Dorothy shook her head. 'I can do this.'

'But it's too early,' Connie wailed. 'I don't want my baby to die.'

Another contraction was coming. 'Clamp down,' Dorothy instructed.

And she did, biting the wood, pushing her fists into the mattress, trying to resist the nausea that swept through her.

'Don't fight it,' said Dorothy.

Connie tried to trust her.

A soft rain pattered against the glass. The pain raged on. In her lucid moments, Connie imagined being with Johnny, walking hand in hand through the streets of Paris. If only she had gone sooner. If only she had sent him her letter. What would happen to her now? What if the baby died?

Suddenly she felt a searing as if her body was splitting apart.

'It's coming,' said Dorothy. 'Keep going. Push now.'

She tried: she pushed and pushed, and when the next contraction came, she pushed again.

'It's coming,' Dorothy repeated. 'Do you want to see?'

Connie was exhausted, spent, but somehow – somehow – she found the strength to press her hands against the mattress, force herself upwards, and there, between her legs, she saw a crown, a head. In another instant, a shoulder and a chest, a whole body, arms, legs. It was a tiny naked being, smeared in skin and blood and mucus, and it was the most incredible sight Connie had ever seen. She reached out, but the pain kept on coming.

Dorothy was busy: clamping and cutting and checking the baby. 'It's a girl,' she said. Connie felt emptied out and desolate, as if her body had given something up, but then Dorothy wrapped the baby in a blanket and placed the bundle into Connie's arms and, as she looked into her child's face, love replaced the loss. She bowed her head as her tears swelled. A girl. A daughter. *Her* daughter.

Dimly, she heard Dorothy swear, saw her face contort as she reached between Connie's legs and drew out a lump of gristle and flesh, which she dropped into a bowl. She was only half aware of Dorothy examining her, frowning and mopping and pressing and prodding. Because how could she concentrate on anything other than this beautiful baby in her arms? How could she concentrate on anything else ever again? Gently Connie touched the damp mass of hair that was black, like her mother's.

Sarah.

She whispered the name in the baby's ear.

She slept and when she woke, her arms were empty. It was dark in the room. There was an ache inside her and a sharp pain between her legs. She could feel a wetness there too, and put down her hand and touched blood. Struggling to sit, dizzy and frantic like a child who'd lost her mother – yet this was the other way around. Where was her baby? Where was Sarah?

Connie's panic grew wild. She flung out an arm,

knocking the lamp, fumbling for and finding the switch, and then spotted a blanketed bundle on the floor.

Relief became desperation. She must reach the bundle. She must pick up her baby. She must keep her close and warm. She tried lowering her legs over the side of the bed, but pain stopped her. Desperately, she gripped the bedside table, twisting her body, using it as leverage. The lamp fell. The baby let out a cry. The door opened and light sliced the room.

Dorothy rushed in, picking up the bundle and placing her in Connie's arms. The baby burrowed close, her tiny face screwed up with concentration as she suckled.

How long did they stay like that, mother and baby? Connie could not tell. She fed the baby and dozed and fed the baby again. From time to time, Dorothy appeared like a nurse, or a gaoler, with a glass of water and a pill to take away the pain, with pads and towels to soak up the blood. Occasionally Dorothy took the baby away and while she was gone, Connie felt hollow and bereft. When the baby came back, she smelled of soap and Connie clutched her greedily to her breast. *Sarah*, she whispered time and again. She hoped the name would summon her mother and bring her close. Perhaps she was looking down on them both.

In moments of clarity, Connie wondered where Dorothy had found the clothes she dressed Sarah in. Had they been Johnny's? An image of his face came to her so intensely, it was as if he had come into the room. For the rest of the time, she slipped into a dreamy darkness where time ceased and nothing mattered.

*

'How is she?' A woman's voice. Dark and familiar.

Through closed eyelids, Connie sensed light.

'She's lost a lot of blood.' This was Dorothy. 'But it seems to be stopping and I'm keeping an eye on it. The baby's fine. Early but no complications.'

Connie opened her eyes a slit. Dorothy on one side of the bed. Barbara on the other in a dark orange coat and matching hat.

'Have you spoken about what we discussed?'

There was a pause. Connie focused on keeping entirely still. Her throat was dry, her lips cracked and she badly wanted to lick them.

'Not yet,' said Dorothy. 'She's drowsy. I've given her painkillers.'

'Where did you get them?' asked Barbara sharply. 'Have you told anyone?'

'No. They're mine. For my back. I've told no one.'

'Do you think she'll agree? I can easily find people. No questions asked.'

Pause. 'I don't know. Come. Not here.'

They moved away. A moment later, the door clicked shut and the room dropped into darkness. Connie wanted to call out and ask them what they meant, but her mind felt dull and confused. She closed her eyes and drifted into sleep.

When she woke again, Sarah lay beside her and Dorothy was back in the room. She held a bowl of soup. Connie shook her head. She had no appetite. She was drowsy, her body was sore, her head thick with confusion.

'I brought your nightgown,' said Dorothy, indicating where it lay at the foot of the bed.

Connie didn't ask how she had got into the flat. She remembered the keys she had seen on Dorothy's sideboard. The thought of the woman rooting through her things made her shudder, but she said nothing.

In the haze of her muddled thoughts she wondered how much time had passed. It must have been a day and a night at least since she had gone into labour. Dorothy was at the window peering through the curtains at the street. Bright light slid through the gap. Connie wondered if she ought to see a doctor. But Dorothy was a midwife and, besides, going into hospital would raise questions. Her father would have to be contacted. It would delay her trip to Paris – although she realised she was in no state to travel anywhere. Not now, at any rate.

Dorothy sat down on the bed. Instinctively, Connie lifted Sarah to her breast. They stayed in silence for a few moments before Dorothy reached out and took her hand. Connie endured her touch, sitting rigidly with Sarah perched uncomfortably in her other arm.

'We need to talk,' said Dorothy quietly.

A feeling of dread crawled down Connie's spine.

'You want the best for her, don't you?'

Still Connie didn't reply.

'And you want the best for Johnny.'

There was a pause.

'Have you considered the other option we discussed?'

'What do you mean?'

Dorothy smoothed the bedspread. 'Adoption. Do you remember, when you said you didn't want the medication?'

Connie had a vague recollection of Dorothy mentioning that, but they had never discussed it, she was sure. 'No. I'm going to keep her.'

Dorothy moistened her lips and plucked at the bedspread again. 'It would be for the baby's sake.'

'Her name's Sarah.'

Dorothy blinked. 'Yes. For Sarah's sake and for Johnny's as well as yours.'

'But I don't want to do that. I'm keeping my baby.'

'It isn't only about you, though, is it?' said Dorothy. She leaned over and picked a stray hair from Connie's nightgown. 'Barbara has done this before. She knows lots of people who are desperate for a baby. Good people who can give Sarah a better life than you can. You can't bring her up alone. Imagine what people will say about you.'

'But Johnny might . . .'

'He won't! I know my son and he won't want to be saddled with a wife and a baby. Not at his age. He's probably not given you a second thought since he left. Think about it, Connie. All this time, and he hasn't written to you once.'

Connie wanted to tell Dorothy that he *had*, actually – he had even sent her a gift, and she was planning to go to Paris to see him – but she kept quiet. Instinct told her that Dorothy would try to stop her. All she wanted was for her son to come home, and preferably to stay well away from Connie.

Dorothy was still talking. 'It can be done privately, discreetly. A little money passing hands. Nobody needs to know.'

'But I don't want . . .'

'Shush now. You'll wake the baby.'

'Sarah. Her name's Sarah.'

'You want the best for her, don't you?' said Dorothy again. 'And for Johnny too.'

'Yes, but . . .'

'We want the same thing. We want Johnny to come home. That's all that matters, isn't it?'

'But . . .'

'Sleep now. You'll feel better later.'

Swiftly, Dorothy lifted the baby from Connie's arms and left the room.

29

Marina

Harry's Hat Shop isn't difficult to find. A scan of the Yellow Pages and there it is.

Outside, the walls and window frames are beautifully painted in a deep red, while the door is a glossy black. The windows are illuminated by spotlights and there is a tasteful display of hats on stands – women's on the left side, men's on the right.

Marina stands outside, looking through the polished glass. There are no customers inside, but she can see a young woman sitting at the counter, reading. She hesitates for a moment and then pushes open the door and steps inside.

There is a delicate smell of lavender. The shop gleams. The walls are red here too and there's a red patterned rug on the dark wood floor. The woman at the counter is in her late teens perhaps, with sandy-coloured hair that's cut short and tucked behind her ears. Her face is small, her skin has a smattering of freckles. She gives Marina a brief smile and an equally quick *hello* and, when Marina indicates she's happy to browse, is then immediately absorbed in her book.

The walls are lined with shelves that are in turn laden with hats, and several tables are artfully dotted about the room, each with their own display. The lighting is soft and well positioned. There are paintings on the walls – old-fashioned portraits, a London skyline – and a rectangular gilt-edged mirror with an intricate pattern.

Marina scans the array of bowler hats, flat caps, pork pies, stylish fedoras, bell-shaped cloches, elegant fascinators. There is every type of hat conceivable, each carefully arranged to show it to the best advantage. She pauses at one of the smaller tables to examine a chocolate brown pillbox with a bow and a tiny veil. Marina has no knowledge of the art of millinery but she can see that the hat is exquisitely stitched, the material expensive, the netting fine. While she is bending to admire it, a middle-aged man appears from the back of the shop, carrying a top hat. He bears a remarkable resemblance to the girl – same colouring and freckles, same slight build. They must be father and daughter. He stops short when he sees Marina as if somehow it's a surprise to see a customer, then he smiles and greets her before continuing to the main table where he places the hat on a stand.

Marina touches the hat she has been examining with one gloved hand. She would like to pick it up, but doesn't dare. Anyway, she doubts it would fit properly over her thick hair.

The young woman calls out, 'I'm off now.'

The man is standing, arms folded, contemplating the hat he has just set down. Looking up, he asks, 'Where?'

'To meet some friends,' she says vaguely.

'What time are you back?'

Marina listens while taking an interest in a beautiful crimson beret.

The door shuts and the man appears beside her. 'I think that would suit you,' he says.

She checks for signs that he is flirting with her, but his face is serious. He wants to sell her a hat.

'I'm not sure,' she says. 'Do you think so?'

'Try it,' he says, gesturing to the mirror. He picks up the beret and passes it to her. She takes it and crosses the room. Placing the beret on her head, she gazes at her reflection and adjusts the fit. In the glass, she can see the man staring at her, yet she doesn't find it intrusive.

Quickly, she removes the beret and turns. 'I'm not sure,' she says again.

'It suits you,' he replies.

She glances at the price tag. It's too expensive.

'We have a sale.'

'Do you?' She looks around for evidence, signs offering discount, but there is nothing.

He offers her thirty per cent off. When she raises her eyebrows, he says, 'Come on, you'll be doing me a favour. I haven't made a sale today.'

She regards him suspiciously. It seems like special treatment, but the hat is lovely. She peels off one glove and touches the soft wool. 'All right. Thank you.'

At the desk, he wraps the beret in tissue paper. His fingers are long and deft and he takes great care. While he works, he asks her casually if she is from the area. She hesitates before telling him she lives in Streatham.

He stops what he is doing. Is it her imagination or is his face paler than it was before? 'I used to live in Streatham,' he says.

She swallows. So, this is Harry. No doubt about it.

They complete their transaction. It is quiet in the shop with only the faint buzz of traffic from the street. Marina doesn't move.

'Is there something else?' he asks.

She breathes out, long and slow. 'Yes, actually.'

He raises his eyebrows. They are thick, she notices, and he has laughter lines and soft, brown eyes.

'I'm writing an article about a local story. I mean a story local to Streatham.'

'Are you a journalist?' His voice is suspicious now.

'No,' she replies hastily, 'I work in publishing. But I'm interested in local history and specifically about an event that happened in the 1960s.'

He frowns. His manner is changing. 'What event exactly?'

'There was a baby that was abandoned in 1964 in a house – 24 Harrington Gardens. Do you remember that?'

His eyes widen, but he speaks carefully. 'Yes,' he says, 'I do recall that story.'

Despite the rising sense of guilt that she has somehow tricked this man, Marina continues. 'I'm searching for the tenants who lived there at the time. I've spoken to several already, but . . .' She pauses. 'There is a particular person I'm interested in tracking down.'

'Oh?' He tightens his lips. 'Who's that?'

'There was a young woman called Connie Littleton. She moved abroad before the baby was found. I was told she had a friend called Harry. And . . . I'm guessing that's you.'

He stares at her, his eyes narrowing. 'Yes,' he says shortly. 'Who told you where to find me?'

'Victor. Victor Wallace.'

'Oh.' He studies her for a second and then frowns as if trying to place her. 'Tell me again who you are.'

'My name is Zoe . . .'

'Zoe?'

'Zoe Alexander.' She pauses, wondering what to say next.

A woman appears from the back. She is about Harry's age, rosy-faced and cheerful. She seems surprised to see the two of them standing there and glances from one to the other in turn. 'This is my wife,' he says, 'Belinda.'

The two women smile at each other. Then, reaching inside her bag, Marina pulls out her notebook and a pen. She tears out a page, scribbles down her phone number and hands it to him. 'Would you call me if you think you can help?'

He takes the paper with no response and she leaves quickly, clutching her beret in its elegant bag, walking rapidly away from the main road, in no particular direction. Her face burns. She has been too hasty mentioning Connie to Harry. She should have built up a relationship, gone into the shop a few times, established a rapport.

She is halfway along the street when she hears a shout.

'Wait.' Harry in a coat and trilby is hurrying towards her.

Her heart lifts and she stops. He catches up.

'What did you say your name was?'

'Zoe Alexander.'

'Zoe.' He scrutinises her. 'Let me buy you a coffee.'

He walks away, hands in his pockets, as if expecting her to follow – which without hesitation she does.

They go to a cafe and find a seat in one corner. The cafe is elegant with Art Deco lamps and dark wood tables. Harry takes off his trilby and lays it on the table.

'Tell me about your article,' he says. 'Why are you writing it?'

She clears her throat and speaks quickly, seizing her opportunity. 'I'm a teacher by profession, but I'm working in publishing and I'd like the chance to write articles, for magazines. When I moved into 24 Harrington Gardens . . .'

'You live there?'

'Yes. There was a room free and I . . .' She falters.

'Go on.'

'Well, I found out about the abandoned baby and it occurred to me to use it as a springboard for an article about historical events in the area.'

The practised lies fall easily from her lips, but Harry is unsmiling. Victor had humoured her. This man most likely will not.

He fires questions at her. 'Do you expect to find the missing parents? Are you planning to speak to the person who was abandoned? Have you asked them if they mind your delving into their life?'

Flustered, she suddenly regrets coming to this cafe with a man she hardly knows. She considers leaving her coffee, apologising for wasting his time and making a bolt for it, but there is nothing to lose by fronting it out.

'I'm sure the person in question won't mind.'

'And why do you have so much interest in Connie Littleton?'

'Because she disappeared to Paris and never came back and . . .'

She loses her thread, takes a gulp of hot coffee, scalds her mouth and splutters. He hands her a paper napkin and she can tell that he doesn't believe a word.

'Why don't you tell me who you really are?' he says finally. 'If you *are* a reporter, I'm not in the least bit interested in speaking to you.'

His tone is dismissive, coldly angry, his gaze piercing, and now she understands. His invitation has nothing to do with wanting to help her with research. He has created a trap, and his gaze, which didn't bother her earlier, is now definitely intrusive. In fact, it's downright annoying.

'I'm not a reporter,' she says, pushing her chair back and standing. 'I'm a teacher, an ex-teacher, and an editor – and I'm interested in this story and . . .' She trails off. 'And I'm grateful for your advice about the hat . . . the beret . . . and the discount . . . but can you please stop looking at me like that!'

She fumbles in her bag for her purse. He leans forward and grabs her arm.

'What the hell . . . ?' She pulls away, but then stops. He is staring with such intensity, she has no idea what he wants.

'I believe you,' he says, 'at least the part about you not being a reporter.'

Her heart slows.

'And I didn't mean to stare.' He lets go of her and puts his hands to his face. 'It's just so strange. I mean . . . you came here talking about Connie Littleton and . . .'

'And what?' Even to her own ears, her voice sounds slow and far away. Her limbs feel light and Marina puts one hand on the table for balance.

'You look so much bloody like her.'

She sits slowly, not taking her eyes off him. There is a churning inside her stomach and she is struggling to focus her mind. 'What do you mean?'

'Exactly that.' He leans back, frustrated. 'You look so much like her, you could be her daughter.' He frowns. 'Are you?'

'What?' Her voice is no more than a whisper.

'Connie Littleton's daughter?' His mood changes; his voice is desperate now. He shoots out a hand and grabs her wrist. 'If you are, you must tell me where she is.'

'What?'

'Where's Connie? Tell me. I need to know what happened to her. Why didn't she come home?'

30

Marina

January 1992

The truth pours from Marina and Harry listens, looking from her face, to his hands, to the pavement outside the window.

She tells him her real first name and about being abandoned at 24 Harrington Gardens. She tells him she has been through phases of searching for answers, but that she has always given up. She tells him it's only now she has lived inside the house that she has found the courage to keep trying.

At the end of her speech, he stays silent, brow furrowed. Then he says, 'But you're so much like her.' His voice is incredulous.

'What did she look like?'

'She was beautiful,' he says. 'She had thick dark hair which hung about her face – like yours.'

Marina feels dizzy. It's the second time someone has talked about her hair. She grips the table again, steadying herself. Has she found her mother at last?

'But . . . she wasn't pregnant,' Harry continues. 'You are so much like her, but you can't possibly be her daughter. Maybe you have her blood. Maybe that's it – maybe you're related; perhaps by a cousin or something.'

'Did she have a cousin?'

He scratches his head. 'No. No, she didn't.' He speaks

more slowly, carefully. 'But she wasn't pregnant when I saw her a few days before she went away.'

'Before she went to Paris to join Johnny?'

Harry sighs and Marina detects the ghost of an emotion: envy. Harry, Victor and Johnny. All of them in love with this Connie.

A silence falls between the two of them and, for want of normality, Marina reaches for her coffee and takes a sip. It's cold but she finishes it and replaces the cup on its saucer. The cafe has quietened around them. The waitress has switched on more lamps.

'What kind of person was she?' Marina asks.

Now Harry smiles. 'She was clever and kind. She read books and poetry. She dreamed of buying a typewriter. A black and silver Remington. When the shop closed down, I bought it, only I never had a chance to give it to her because by that time she had gone.'

'But,' says Marina slowly, 'if Connie left only days before I was found, isn't that a coincidence?'

He interrupts her. 'If Connie was pregnant, then no one knew about it and that's just not possible. I would have known. Her father would have known and so would other people. The police asked questions, obviously, but they didn't pursue it. Why would they? Everyone said she had gone to Paris. She left a note for her father. She told people. Me. Eileen Clarke. And she looked the same as she ever did. She couldn't possibly have hidden a full-term pregnancy. I mean, at the start she might have done, of course – but I saw her about a week or two before the baby was left in the house.'

Marina, though, has read stories about girls who hid

the truth from their families out of shame or fear, binding their expanding bellies, eating less to keep down their weight. Girls who gave birth in hotels, or in car parks, or in woods, all alone. How terrifying must that be?

'Are you certain that she actually left?'

'Yes,' Harry says firmly. 'I remember, her father was staying with his sister at the time. In Whitby. I helped her . . .' He hesitates. 'I pawned some of her mother's jewellery so that she could buy the ticket to Paris. I promised I would check on the bookshop and she gave me the keys. She trusted me. She would have told me if she was pregnant.'

'How do you know she actually went? Maybe it was all a ruse and she was in her flat. Hiding.'

He looks away guiltily. 'She gave me her keys and said I could spend time there if I wanted. So that's what I did. It made me feel close to her . . . You know, sitting in the space that she used to sit in, touching the things she touched too. I know, it's odd . . . But I loved her. I missed her.' He shrugs. 'She definitely wasn't there. She was gone.'

Marina sighs. She pulls at her hair, releasing a strand and swirling it about her fingers.

Harry smiles sadly. 'But you do look so damn like her.'

A lump rises in Marina's throat. She speaks slowly, deliberately. 'Do you believe that if Connie *had* been my mother she would have abandoned me?'

'Honestly? I could no more see her doing that than I could see her abandoning her father. But who knows? She left – left him – and she *didn't* come back. Not even for his funeral . . .'

Outside, the streets lamps are flickering on. One by one their yellow light struggles to brighten the dusk. The waitress turns the sign to closed.

Later, when she gets home, Marina passes Mrs Hyde on the stairs. If she looked small before, she seems positively shrunken now, clutching at the bannister for support.

There is something distasteful about Dorothy and the pink lipstick that bleeds into the crevices around her mouth. After an initial nod of greeting, Marina steps into her flat, closes the door with relief and breathes deeply.

That night she wakes, disturbed by a sound. She lies for a moment, listening. It's freezing in the room, worse than usual. The curtains flare and she realises she's left the window open.

Getting up, she stares into the darkness, searching the garden for a clue, but there are the same shrouded shapes as always. Nothing has changed. She closes the window and moves into the living room. Here she finds the source of the noise that must have woken her. Another sizeable chunk of plaster has fallen, clattering onto the table below. Marina glances anxiously at the ceiling for signs of more damage.

For once, the house is silent. Marina pictures Eva, gazing from her window. She thinks of the strange Mrs Hyde, and Selena and her family, and the Italian musician, Giovanni, who she still hasn't seen or heard. He must have gone away. No one can stay hidden for so long.

Thoughts like these skate through her mind and

knowing that she won't sleep now, Marina heats milk, takes it to bed and settles beneath the covers. Her mind is aflame with the story of a young woman who ran away to be with her boyfriend, leaving one man heartbroken, and maybe a second too, if her intuition about Victor is correct. She was loved by so many and yet she stayed away even when her father died.

Connie Littleton. Marina says the name out loud and it has a rhythm to it, a sound of the past. She is building a picture. Connie Littleton who once upon a time lived in this house, in the flat above her now. A young girl whose mother died from cancer, whose mother's name was Sarah, whose father sold books. She wanted to write and to travel. She loved poetry.

Poetry. Her mind turns to the volume that Selena gave her. She would like to fetch it, but she is too cold and soon she is drifting into a glassy, shivering kind of sleep.

In the morning, she meets Giovanni Gaetti at last, the mysterious occupant of Flat 1.

She has run out of milk and is on her way to the shop. He is coming into the house as she is going out. Late-thirties, dishevelled, in a rumpled black suit and white shirt and an empty space where his concert bow tie should be. He has black hair and dark eyes and deep lines on his forehead.

Their eyes meet as they pass on the steps. She wears her old coat and fingerless gloves. She has messy hair and smells of sleep. They murmur a greeting and she thinks *he exists*, which for some reason gives her a huge sense of relief.

Home again, she makes coffee and toast and stands at the window watching the street. It's a windy day. Leaves chase each other across the pavement. Branches whip and snap. A mother passes with her small daughter, the two of them running, laughing. They have identical hair, Marina notices, a golden-brown, the colour of autumn. Poetry is on her mind. Keats's ode 'To Autumn'. She recites a few lines. It's a mournful poem about death and regret.

She finishes her toast, turns away from the window and sits in the armchair thinking about Connie. What if Harry was wrong and she *was* pregnant? Did he know her that well? Her gaze dwells on the photo of Ruth and David. Her parents. Yet not her parents. She remembers Ron commenting that she looked like David. People see what they want to see. If Harry loved Connie, and was jealous of her relationship with Johnny, the last thing he'd want would be for her to be pregnant. The last thing he'd want to *see* would be her pregnancy.

Truth and how we see – or fail to see – it. Marina smiles wryly. The poets all had a go at trying to explore truth. She leans across, picks up the volume lying on the table in front of her and holds it carefully, imagining Connie leafing through.

Those lines again, running through her head.

> *Though I must go, endure not yet*
> *A breach, but an expansion,*
> *Like gold to airy thinness beat.*

She finds Donne in the contents page and then runs her fingertip down the titles of the poems, searching,

JENNY QUINTANA

until one of them chimes – 'A Valediction: Forbidding Mourning'. Turning to the right page, she reads the words to herself and then selects other, equally familiar poems and murmurs them aloud.

The brown dust has settled on her fingertips again and it occurs to Marina that the dust is like ashes and that the book is decaying. She turns the pages more carefully and reaches the end. An envelope is stuck to the inside of the back cover. No name on the front, the paper is yellowing. Did Connie put this here? Gently, she opens the flap. Carefully, she slots her fingers inside. Slowly, she pulls out a single sheet of folded paper and her stomach roils.

And now.

She opens the sheet of paper.

She smooths it out on the table.

It's a letter, blotched and smudged, written in blue ink with a fountain pen.

She starts to read.

By the time she has finished, tears are streaming down Marina's face.

She sits stock still in the tatty armchair.

Away in the kitchen, a tap drips into the porcelain sink. Above her Selena is pacing. There is a scratching at the window. Laughter in the street.

A letter. A letter from Connie to Johnny explaining she is pregnant. A letter that, after all these years, confirms who Marina is.

She draws a breath that turns into a sob. She wipes her face with her sleeve, but it isn't enough. She rises, fetches tissues, resumes her place, tries to make sense of what she has read. So many questions.

How hard it must have been for Connie to keep her secret. Yet her mother was dead, her lover absent. Who could she have confided in? Who would have known her well enough to spot the signs, if she were determined to hide them?

In the hall, Marina hears a door opening and a cough. Giovanni is on his way out – to a concert, presumably. She goes to the window. He walks slowly as if in pain. Has he been ill? Is that why she hadn't seen him before? Had he been in his room all this time?

Marina's breath catches inside her throat. People may not have seen Connie in the house, but it didn't mean that she wasn't there, or at least somewhere close. What is it they say? Hiding in plain sight. Perhaps Connie was doing precisely that. Not in the flat, because Harry had visited, but the attic, maybe. It was a perfect hiding place.

And what does it mean – the fact that Connie wrote but didn't send the letter to Johnny? According to the letter, she planned to travel on 7 August. Had she hoped to have the baby in Paris? Or to have the baby and *then* travel to Paris? She wouldn't, presumably, have booked a ticket near to the baby's due date, but that was assuming she knew the due date. Marina has always been told she was a small baby, born early.

As the questions multiply in Marina's mind, fresh tears rise, thinking about Connie alone and pregnant. Frightened, not knowing what to do. Marina scrubs at her face with the tissues. Connie is her mother. She is certain. It's simply the logistics she needs to work out. And she *will* work them out and then she will find her. She will search the whole of Paris, if necessary. She imagines the record offices she will scour, the town halls she will enter, the officials she will talk to, the red tape she will work through until she unearths an address, a boulevard, an apartment. Then she will knock on the door.

She stands abruptly and strides to the window. Somebody must know something. A baby can't be born and survive even for a few days without help. Who had been there for Connie? Her mother was dead. Her aunt lived on the other side of the country. She had no siblings and no cousins according to Harry, and no grandparents as far as Marina knew.

What about on Johnny's side? What about *his* mother? If Connie had been desperate, might she have confided in her? And then it strikes Marina. Harry saw the resemblance. Who else has seen it too? Victor? She thinks back to when they first met. She remembers that he held her hand a little too long, but can't recall a flash of recognition. So perhaps not Victor – and, besides, if it's all about her hair, she had deliberately worn it up both times they met, wanting to appear business-like. But Dorothy . . . She remembers the woman's – what was it? Hostility? Shock? – when she first saw Marina. Yes. Dorothy is obvious. She definitely reacted oddly and was also the mother of Connie's boyfriend.

Another thought comes to Marina. Dorothy is Johnny's mother, which means, of course, she is also Marina's grandmother.

Strange how she has always assumed that she would

know her family if she met them, that she would look into their eyes and feel a warmth. There is nothing warm about Dorothy. She has the air of a woman eaten up by disappointment – or is it guilt?

31

Eva

January 1992

Eva looks at the clock. It is eight o'clock and she calculates that she has had approximately two hours' sleep.

She yawns and gets up, makes hot chocolate and sweetens it further by eating Turkish Delight.

The petals from the rose have fallen now. She gathers them in the palm of her hand. They are brown-tinged, but still beautiful. She touches them gently, and without warning, she is struck by a flash of memory.

Little Eva pressing flowers: pansies and violets and dahlias. Someone is showing her how to do this, but it's not her mother. The face of a young woman appears, smiling and kind. Dark-haired like the woman downstairs.

Eva shakes her head, sips her drink, eats more Turkish Delight. The woman downstairs had been kind. What was it about her that had caused Eva to confide?

Moving to the window she spots a figure approaching and recognises the landlord, Kenneth Quip. She shivers as if cold.

Kenneth stops outside the house. His gaze moves from the basement all the way up to the gables and the finials. Eva feels as if she is inhabiting his mind. Seeing what he sees. Living vicariously.

Precariously.

She clutches the windowsill. Her fingers press into the wood as if her life depends on it.

Life depends on it. Whose life?

She closes her eyes. The memory comes. Little Eva is jumping on the stairs. The young woman gives her a rose. A perfect rose. *Watch out for the thorns.* Suddenly, the name comes to her. It slips into her head like a detail in a dream. *Connie.* It's Connie who is leading her home to where her mother is playing Chopin. It's Connie who gives her the rag doll called Sarah. It's Connie who helps her press flowers and who hands her the rose when they reach the landing. And it's Connie who whispers *Don't tell anyone. Not a word. It's our secret.*

The reel of memory leaps. Little Eva is skipping out of her flat. She is standing at the top of the stairs and looking down. There is a man. He is leaning over Connie. Something is wrong. Connie is frightened. She thinks of her mother when the boys threw stones. She thinks of her father stepping in front of a bus. She thinks of her mother again, crying on the stairs when the woman with the bright blue eyeshadow delivered a lump from her body. A tiny baby. Too small to live in the world.

There is no blood now, no nasty boys, no red buses, but Little Eva feels the same cold fear.

From her position on the landing, she sees Connie looking up at her. She wants to call out, but Connie's eyes say no.

She puts her hands over her mouth and traps her words. Warm liquid runs down her legs. Tears trickle down her face. She runs inside and to her room where she changes her knickers and her dress.

Later her mother will find the wet clothes, but she won't shout because she never shouts. Even when Eva wets herself for many nights after that, her mother will change the sheets and wash them and tell her not to worry.

Eva misses her mother. You can never get over losing your mother. Her grip on the windowsill loosens as she gives in to the dizziness and slips to the floor.

32

Marina

February 1992

It's a misty day; the sun shines weakly through the window; yet Marina has an urge to be away from the claustrophobic house. She pulls on her coat and goes into the hall, pausing for a moment as the familiar prickling crawls across her skin. Shaking off the sensation, she opens the front door and heads around the building towards the garden gate. Considering she has been here for a month, she has spent little time outside. From the lawn, she can see into Ron's kitchen window. There is no sound or movement. He must be sleeping still, or perhaps he is with Eva. Marina has a feeling they will be back together soon.

It's quiet beneath the white-grey sky, and mist curls eerily around the bare trees. Silvery spiderwebs glitter amongst blades of grass. At the far end, beyond a tangled curtain of shrubs, a dilapidated shed leans against a moss-covered wall. A flat patch of ground is covered in grass and weeds and dead rose bushes.

Marina is surprised to see an arched entrance set into the wall. She guesses it leads to the church. Idly she turns the handle and the door opens easily. She steps into silence and what looks like the oldest part of the graveyard – ancient tombs with cracked stones and faded inscriptions. She wanders along the overgrown paths briefly, and is about to return the way she has come when a figure appears. It's Dorothy holding a bunch of flowers. She frowns, surprised, perhaps, to find the door left open, and then she walks slowly, skirting the graves, and disappears to one side of the church.

On impulse, Marina follows her. The paths and graves here are equally unkempt, the ground uneven. Crosses lean precariously and headstones crumble.

Dorothy stops midway along the side wall and stands head bowed. Her lips are moving, as if she is talking to herself, or praying. Marina watches only for a moment before she walks quietly away and round to the front of the church.

She waits in the cold stone porch. There is a notice-board set behind cracked glass. Absent-mindedly, Marina reads. There is a list of services, an out-of-date advert for the Christmas fair. There's a rota of women who clean the church and sort the flowers. Dorothy's name is among them. There is a list of other roles too: the vicar, the curate, the treasurer. The last: Kenneth Quip. Marina smiles wryly. They have enlisted the help of an ex-thief to take care of the money.

It seems as if their names are forever linked: Kenneth and Dorothy. She was his spy, perhaps his one-time lover. And now this. They've known each other for years, yet it occurs now to Marina that when she was speaking to Kenneth in the garden and Dorothy appeared, the two of them hardly exchanged a glance.

Marina leaves the porch and returns to the side of the church. Dorothy has gone but the flowers lie against the wall. Marina looks around, curious. Does Dorothy have a relative buried here? She scours the graves, but they are all so old and weathered that the inscriptions are almost gone. Besides, why would she put the flowers all the way over there?

A crow calls. Marina glances up as it flies from the roof of the church. Still curious, she crosses to where the flowers lie, and kneels on the ground. Ivy and something that might be bindweed reaches from the wall, curtaining the earth. Gently, she sweeps the plants aside and there, right at the back, she finds a tiny wooden cross. She leans back, frowning. It must be a pet. Yes. A beloved pet that Dorothy has buried. How complex she is. A woman estranged from her son, and seemingly utterly without charm or warmth, yet she cherishes her cat or dog or whatever else it is hidden beneath this earth.

Impulsively, Marina leans forward and takes the cross from the ground. No name. No date. It is simply two small pieces of wood nailed together. Not much of a marking for a grave. She replaces it gently.

Sardine appears as Marina steps into the main part of the garden. He winds around her legs and she stoops to stroke his fur. Ahead of her the house looms darkly.

She has made up her mind. She will go straight to Dorothy and ask her what she knows.

But Kenneth Quip is at the foot of the front steps when Marina rounds the corner. He wears the same dark and shapeless suit that he wore before, and has a battered briefcase clamped beneath one arm. If anything, his body is more wasted than it was last time Marina saw him. He is unshaven and his eyes are bloodshot. He looks like a man who hasn't slept.

At last, Marina thinks, he has come. Dorothy can wait. Now she will question Kenneth.

'Are you here to fix the boiler?' she says, innocently.

He stares back at her and bows his head.

It starts to rain. 'Shall we go inside?'

He bows his head again.

She leads the way. It's as cold inside as it is out. Behind her, Kenneth closes the front door and the hall descends into darkness.

33

Connie

5–7 August 1964

Another day passed. Connie lay fretfully in the darkened room, but she was resolved. She was going to leave for Paris as she had originally intended. It would be a struggle, she knew that – she was still bone-tired and sore, and so far she'd barely left the room, let alone the house. Travelling across London and then on to Paris with a newborn child was insanity – but Connie had no choice. She couldn't risk whatever it was that Dorothy was planning.

Dorothy had said nothing more about adoption. Perhaps she had changed her mind. Sometimes, Connie caught her looking at Sarah with a fixedness, a fascination. Yet that afternoon, Connie had woken to hear voices outside the room. Barbara again. Panicking, she had struggled upright, but her daughter was still asleep on her makeshift bed on the floor.

Was she a prisoner? Were they plotting to keep her there and steal away her baby? Connie didn't think so. Dorothy brought her food and drink. She helped her wash, sponging the blood from her legs. She helped her change her stained nightdress. She helped her to look after Sarah. From time to time, she went out, to collect or deliver laundry. The door wasn't locked, or at least Connie didn't believe it was. She could leave at any time, only she was too weak. She had lost what seemed like an awful lot of blood, but she didn't know if that was normal or not.

She focused on recovering, eating everything Dorothy brought her. When Dorothy went out for provisions, Connie left Sarah sleeping and eased her legs onto the floor. When the room stopped spinning, she hobbled to the kitchen, drank water and felt better. She had two more nights. Then she would go to Paris.

The day passed and then another. Connie could keep track now. She was stronger, fitter. Better. The enormity of the task ahead still daunted her, but she was determined. The seventh of August came. The day she must leave.

In the morning, Dorothy appeared. 'I won't be long,' she told Connie. She was dressed to go out, her handbag hooked on one arm. She had applied her make-up, bright as always with a thick slash of crimson on her lips.

Dread unfurled like smoke. 'Where are you going?'

'I'm meeting Barbara.'

'I told you,' said Connie. 'I don't want this to happen.'

'I know and it's hard, but you need to think more clearly. Imagine what your father will say when he finds out. Imagine how people will judge you.'

'I don't care.'

Dorothy adjusted her coat, seemed to consider. Then she leaned down, so close that Connie felt her breath on her cheek. 'I was alone with Johnny,' she said. 'I know how it feels to have fingers pointing, tongues wagging.'

Connie stared at her. 'But I thought Johnny's father . . . I thought he . . .'

'You thought wrong,' she snapped. 'Johnny's father took off the moment I told him I was pregnant. He disappeared as quickly as this.' She snapped her fingers.

'So, who was the man who came here?' Connie asked, remembering the man who had abused Mrs Kolinski when her mother had been alive.

Dorothy shook her head impatiently. 'Not his father. My ex-husband. And he never thought of Johnny as his own.' She stopped, as if she'd said too much.

'Why did you marry him?'

'Because I thought my son needed a father. It was a mistake. You have no idea what he was like or what I went through. So, listen to me. I know what it's like to have a baby on my own and I am telling you it's hard.'

'But Johnny . . .'

'There is no Johnny.' His mother raised her voice. 'He's gone and he won't come back if he thinks there's a baby here to weigh him down. And if he doesn't come back, what will I do? You have your whole life ahead of you. I have nothing. Except him.'

Connie turned her head away. She wanted to say that she would have a grandchild, but Dorothy was bitter. Angry and bitter. She wouldn't listen, or care.

'Barbara has found a couple,' she continued. 'They're coming here this afternoon. I think when you meet them, you'll agree that it's for the best.' She spoke firmly but Connie heard the catch in her voice and saw the colour flaming in her face. Was she trying to convince herself as much as Connie?

The door banged shut. Sarah whimpered. Connie fed her and knew it was now or never. She waited for Sarah to finish, for her breath to slow, her body to relax. She waited for the trickle of milk to slip down her tiny chin. Then she kissed her daughter gently, laid her down on the sheet, and with both hands for support, pushed herself out of bed.

Pain weaved through her. The ache in her belly, the soreness between her legs, the strain of her breasts. Her keys were in amongst her clothes at the foot of the bed. Connie picked them up, then limped from the room, Sarah in her arms. Slowly, she opened the front door. She listened carefully: a drip in the pipes; a creak in the joists. Tip-tap. Kenneth doing his rounds. She moistened her lips. She needed to drink or else she would faint. Shuffling across the corridor to her flat, she unlocked the door, feeling a wave of relief and something like triumph as she closed it quietly behind her.

In the kitchen, she drank water. In the living room, she set Sarah on the settee. In the bedroom, she busied herself looking for the baby clothes that her mother had saved. She lifted the loose floorboard and pulled out the shawl. She found her ticket to Paris and the extra money from the jewellery, which she had hidden inside the poetry book. The letter to Johnny was folded away in a makeshift envelope which she'd stuck onto the back cover. She didn't need it now because she was going to see him herself. Taking half of the money, she left the rest inside the book, tucking it beneath the floorboard. When she came home, she would give the money to her father to use towards the rent he owed to Kenneth. Next, she slipped on her mother's wedding ring. Travelling with a baby would be easier as a married woman. Fewer questions. Less unwelcome attention.

It was hard to wash and dress with the pain gripping her insides. Connie gritted her teeth, moving clumsily, fixing her make-up with shaking hands. In the living room, she sat for a moment, recovering, before wrapping Sarah in the blue shawl. She soothed her, fed her and, when she was ready to go, her eyes lit on the money that Victor had given her. She would take it to the basement, put it into his post box. She had Sarah now and wanted nothing to do with his dirty cash.

Opening the door, she heard the tip-tap of a stick. Kenneth. Hastily, she stepped back inside. The tapping paused on the landing. She held her breath. A minute more and he carried on, doing his rounds. Tip-tap up the second flight of stairs and all the way back down.

Voices in the hall. Kenneth had been joined by Victor. Her heart sank. How would she get past them? At last, she heard a slam. They had gone. She must get out of this house, or else she never would.

Mrs Kolinski was playing the piano. The familiarity of the music gave Connie courage. Wincing, she picked up her suitcase, slung her bag over her shoulder and, with Sarah clasped to her chest, stepped onto the landing. There was a noise above her. She looked up. Little Eva in her purple dress, on the stairs, clutching her doll. Connie waved and then she put her finger to her lips.

Setting the suitcase on the floor and turning to lock the door, she rummaged in her pocket for her key. No luck. Feeling hot, she put Sarah down inside the flat, to the side, hiding her from view. She searched her bag. She plucked out her purse, her passport, the ticket. Nothing. Any minute Dorothy would be back. She'd stop her from leaving. Maybe she'd come with Barbara and the couple who wanted to steal Sarah.

Sweat dripped down Connie's side. She scrabbled through her things. Almost crying, she pulled out the bank notes. No key.

And then she heard a voice.

'Connie. Where are you going?'

She swung round. Kenneth. At least it wasn't Dorothy. She leaned against the doorpost.

He was staring at her, his eyes travelling from the suitcase to her face, to the money in her hand. Slowly she tucked it into her pocket. Please God he hadn't realised.

'What's that you're hiding?'

'Nothing.'

His eyes hardened. 'Is it money?'

'Yes, but . . .'

'Your father owes me rent and you're running around with that?' His face darkened. 'It's not mine, is it?'

She stared back at him.

'Have you stolen it?'

'No, I . . .' She stopped. What excuse did she have?

He raised his voice, spoke deliberately. 'All this time I've been searching for intruders and the little thief has been right here, under my very nose.'

He leaned into her face. His breath stank. Rearing back, Connie pulled the door half closed.

'No,' she said again. 'I was going to give it back. I was on my way now.'

He ignored her. 'Haven't I helped your father enough?'

'But . . .'

'You've been spying, haven't you? Watching from your window. I've seen you looking out at night. You found my little cache and you've been filching. That's right, isn't it? I expect you thought you were clever. Have you any idea what happens to thieves in my world?'

He was glaring, waiting for her answer.

'No,' she whispered, but she thought of the man with the sticking out ears whose body had been dragged from the lake. Was that how it ended?

He gave her a smile that nowhere near reached his eyes. 'Well,' he said, 'I can tell you, they don't do well. They don't do well at all.'

'But I didn't steal it,' she said desperately. If she didn't go soon, she would miss her train. She would be slow anyway, carrying Sarah, and she was still bleeding: she could feel it draining through her even as she stood there.

Kenneth straightened up. 'I was convinced it was Victor rummaging about in my flower beds, but when I accused him, he had no idea what I was talking about.'

Why did you believe him? Connie wanted to scream. But no words came out.

'But if I wasn't sure who it was then,' Kenneth added, 'I certainly am now.'

'Did he say it was me?' she asked, keeping her voice level.

'No, because he obviously didn't know.'

Connie's shoulders slumped. How had he got Victor

so wrong? She pressed her lips closed. If she could get rid of this money and get away from Kenneth, she could take Sarah and leave and still be on time. But she felt so weak. Pain pierced her stomach.

Kenneth carried on. 'I find this very disappointing after everything I've done for your father.' His eyes dropped to the suitcase on the floor. 'I'm guessing that's full of my money too.'

'No. I promise . . .' She blinked, trying to focus, but Kenneth's face had blurred.

'And now you want to disappear. Where are you going?'

'Paris,' she said, but her voice sounded far away. Blood had soaked the towel. She was sure it was spilling at the edges. She needed to change. Did she have time?

'Please. I have to get a train.'

He shrugged. 'You can get whatever train you like, my dear, but first you can give me my cash.'

She could hear Sarah softly whimpering and felt the painful rush of milk. She made to go inside.

Kenneth, oblivious, grabbed her arm, pushing her off balance. 'My money,' he said. She staggered against the door and it slammed against the wall.

'Give it to me, now, and we'll say no more about it.'

'But I need . . .' *What?* A doctor, painkillers, more towels to staunch the blood?

She stepped into the flat. He grabbed the suitcase and followed her, as she backed away further, hoping he wouldn't see Sarah.

'Please,' she said, to an empty space.

He was on his knees, surprisingly agile, opening her suitcase, muttering and cursing when he found no money. Had he registered the baby clothes?

She looked at him, but her sense was dulling. His words were simply noise. His body just an outline.

Blood ran down her legs. Like heavy drops of rain on the rug. Sound amplified. The blood. Kenneth's breathing. Her own heart pounding.

'I need a doctor,' she managed, her words slurring as she fell.

Somewhere, her baby made a sound. She moved her arm, reaching for the whimper, but the pain sharpened and her eyes filled with tears.

She would never be able to get up from where she lay and walk across the room to pick up her daughter, who must be so cold even though she was wrapped in the shawl.

It was blue. More than blue. Better than blue. Like the colour of the paintings in the gallery.

What was it called? That colour? That blue?

He had told her. He had told her everything as they had wandered through the different rooms, her heels clattering on the wooden floor. He had talked about artists: Sassoferrato – the name had fallen from his lips and whispered through the gallery. Botticelli. Whistler. Van Gogh. He knew so much. She had listened in awe.

All the paintings in the gallery had been beautiful, but the one of the lady in blue had been the best: *The Virgin in Prayer*. They had lingered there and he had told her how the blue paint had once been more precious than gold, and that one day his own art would be recognised and then he would give her as much gold as she desired. But she hadn't cared about gold. She had only wanted him, and a shawl – the colour of the lady's in the painting. That blue. What *was* its name?

Music drifted through the house and she closed her eyes. It was Chopin. She had heard it many times as she had lain in bed late at night or leaned against the doorway of the flat listening. But she couldn't reach for the name of the nocturne any more than she could remember the blue.

The baby cried again and the sound was like the keening of the wind, or the call of a lost animal. If only she could move, but her body wouldn't obey her brain's commands, and the pain in her stomach grew along with her sorrow and, because she could do nothing else, she started to weep. Maybe, she thought, each tear would be one fewer that her baby would shed after she had gone. It wouldn't be long now. She felt that instinctively. Darkness was falling, like fog descending.

34

Marina

February 1992

Kenneth gets as far as the centre of the room before he stops. He pokes the rug with his cane as if roughly tracing the pattern.

'The boiler?' Marina says.

He looks up. His face is grey, devoid of colour, eyes almost hidden in their pouches of skin.

He has no toolbox. The observation flutters in Marina's mind like a fat moth.

'I am meticulous,' he says at last, 'in checking facts and figures, financial and personal. I am meticulous.' He stops, clears his throat. 'I realise this is partly what I pay the estate agent for, but at the same time . . . At the same time, I like to do it myself. I like . . . I like to be certain about the details of my clients. You might say,' he adds, 'that it's my hobby.'

Marina shifts on her feet. A pulse throbs at her temple. She presses her fingers to her skull. She is wrong-footed. *He has no toolbox. He is not here to fix the boiler.* What then?

'The thing is,' he continues, resting the cane against the side of a chair, 'it has come to my attention that there's been a mistake. Yes, a mistake.'

There is a beat. 'What do you mean?'

He is shaking as he balances the briefcase on the chair and awkwardly snaps it open. He pulls out a sheaf of papers with trembling hands, selects one, and brandishes it at her.

'I have your name down on the contract as Zoe Alexander. Yet, when I examine the photocopy of your passport, I see that your name is not Zoe Alexander. It's *Marina* Alexander.'

He looks at her directly, eyes watering.

She meets his gaze. 'Zoe is my middle name.'

He nods, grimaces. 'I know that. Yes. I can see that. The estate agent told me that you prefer to go by the name Zoe.' He taps the piece of paper with one gnarled finger. 'However, see here, the whole name needs to be recorded, not half. I don't like slapdash errors and . . .' He pauses, stares at the centre of the rug. 'I don't like being misdirected.'

A coldness seeps through Marina's body. Can he be serious? She studies his face and concludes he is. He has a certain arrogance. Isn't that what Victor had said? Paranoid too. Always thinking that people from the past are out to get him. Is that what is happening here?

'You are not what you seem,' he concludes, fumbling with the papers again, trying to get them back into his case.

She stays completely still, eyes fixed on his. 'It's a detail,' she says carefully.

'It's more than that, I'm afraid. It's a lie.' The papers flutter from his hands. He rocks on his feet, steadies himself, but makes no attempt to pick them up.

Her mouth drops open. 'That's an exaggeration.' She speaks quietly, still wary of upsetting him.

He closes his briefcase despite the missing papers. She considers gathering them up, but decides against it. She senses a change in his mood but can't identify what it means for her.

'I think you should leave my house.'

The air shifts about her. 'I have a contract.'

He picks up his cane and leans on it heavily. So heavily, Marina thinks it might snap. She is wrong about him not needing it: he might not need it physically, but he certainly needs it metaphorically; the cane is his prop.

'In my opinion, the contract is null and void on the grounds that you didn't disclose your information directly on the form.'

She opens her mouth, incredulous again. 'You are trying to evict me?'

'If you like.'

She laughs in disbelief. 'You are kidding.'

'I am not.' He looks around the room and his gaze falls again on the spot in the middle of the rug, lingers there before moving back to her.

She shakes her head. 'You can't do that.'

He shrugs. 'We'll see.'

Despite her instinct to be cautious, irritation is rising. 'I have rights. I won't go.'

'It's better if you do.' He tucks the briefcase beneath his arm and makes to leave.

Marina shivers. His voice is ominous. It veils a threat. Yet there is more to this, she thinks suddenly. He can't possibly believe that he can get rid of her on such a flimsy excuse.

'If you know my name is Marina,' she blurts suddenly, 'then you probably know who I am. In which case, you know why I'm here.'

He hesitates and stares back at her. 'I have no idea why you are here.'

'But you don't deny that you know who I am.'

'Marina is an unusual name.'

'So, it's obvious. You know that I was the baby that was abandoned in this house.'

He bows his head, conceding the point.

'I came here looking for my mother,' she says. 'I have information, but I need more.' She is bold now, moving in front of him, blocking his exit. 'Tell me about Connie. Connie Littleton. She disappeared in 1964 – ran away to Paris and never came back, even missed her father's funeral. Only I don't believe she ever went. I don't believe she would have just left me.'

'You.' He wipes his face with the handkerchief.

'She was my mother.'

He shakes his head. 'You are deluded.'

'I have a letter to prove it.'

'Prove it,' he says quietly.

She is not sure if he is throwing down a challenge or whether he is simply repeating her words. She exhales slowly.

He speaks again. 'You are out of your depth and should leave.'

Is he threatening her? She straightens, planting herself more firmly in his path.

'It would be better if you moved,' he says.

'First, I want to know what happened to my mother.'

'What makes you think I can help you with that?'

He is still water, she thinks suddenly – dead and quiet on the surface while underneath there's a mass of dangerous currents and tangled weeds. She wants to take a stick and stir things up.

'You knew her,' she says, finally answering his question.

His expression is impassive.

'Did you know that she was pregnant?'

He glances towards the door. There are familiar sounds, the sigh of the house, the creak of the stairs. Marina looks too and then back at Kenneth.

His face is hard and she feels a shiver of fear, despite his age.

'You should go.'

'I won't.' She steps forward, her face close to his. 'I told you. I have proof that Connie was my mother and I'm not leaving until I know what happened to her.'

He looks at her, eyes flashing. Marina remembers what Victor said about him. Kenneth is racked with guilt. Anger too.

'And I told you,' he says slowly, 'that it would be better for you to leave. Yet here you are still.' He thumps his cane in time to his words.

'Victor told me about the money.'

He is silent.

'Did she take it? Is that why you're so angry?'

He recoils. She has hit a nerve.

She goads him. 'She was young, wasn't she? How could you let someone so young get the better of you?'

He shakes his head. 'You don't understand.'

She grabs his arm, pulling him back. 'Explain then.'

Her touch ignites him. Suddenly he snaps and pushes her away. She takes a step backwards, colliding with the sofa.

'I gave you a chance,' he says, 'an opportunity to go without fuss. Get out of my house now or . . .'

'What?'

He raises his cane and light from the window flashes on the silver top. The Devil is in the detail. Time slows. Tap. Tap. The man in the lake. The voices arguing in Eva's head. The doll. The rose. Marina holds up her hand and it breaks the blow. With her other hand she shoves him, hard, in the chest, and he staggers.

'Victor said you were gullible. The two of them together cleaned you out.'

She is taunting him again, hoping that he will break. That he will crack open like a nut and tell her everything.

There is a sound. A figure comes into the room. Eva. Thin and shivering in her nightgown, pale as a spectre, like a little girl.

Something clicks inside Marina's head.

She *was* a little girl who saw something terrible – something so terrible that she has forced herself to forget. Only you can never forget. You can only compartmentalise. Shut memories away in a section of your mind and slam the door. Until along comes a trigger or a series of triggers, clawing like finger nails to open that door.

Eva speaks. Startled, Kenneth turns. Marina takes her chance, thrusting him away, moving out of reach.

'I saw you,' she says, her voice shaking.

Marina is watching, heart thumping. She understands what is happening. She understands exactly. Eva has remembered.

'You hurt Connie. It's your fault she didn't come back.'

Marina's chest is tight. She puts her hand to her throat. Kenneth is ashen. He is crumbling, she thinks, like an ancient statue. Soon there will be nothing of him left.

'You argued about money,' Eva says more calmly. 'You pushed her, and the door crashed against the wall. I was so small and so afraid, I went to find my mother, but she was playing the piano and crying, like she always did, so I went to my room because I had wet myself and I changed my clothes. When I got back to the landing, I saw you coming out alone, holding the baby. You did something to Connie and then you stole her baby.'

Eva stops and there is a stillness in the room.

Marina speaks to Kenneth. 'Is that what happened?' Her voice sounds far away. She clasps her hands together and feels herself shivering, teeth chattering.

His eyes are watering so badly now, it's as if he is weeping. 'No,' he says. 'I didn't kill her.'

Hope pulses through Marina. Her mother is alive. She can still track her down. 'So what happened?'

His body droops. 'She was dying, anyway.'

Dismay twists inside Marina's stomach. She is wrong. There is no hope.

He staggers backwards and drops into the armchair and Marina sees him for what he is: what he has become.

He is a man given up. Old and tired and plagued by guilt. He will confess, she thinks, but what will he confess to? What has he done?

'What happened?' Marina repeats. 'How did she die?'

Slowly he shakes his head. 'There was so much blood.'

Marina breathes slowly. 'Because you hurt her.'

He shakes his head. 'No. There was so much blood because . . .' He stops, starts again. 'I didn't see the baby at first. I was angry with Connie because she had my money. She was leaving, taking it away. She had no right to do that. Nobody did.'

'What did you do?'

He ignores her question. 'I knew if the police found her dead, they would accuse me and I didn't want to go back to prison. I couldn't risk that.'

'Why?'

'He had friends.'

'Who?'

'Frank Dennis.'

Frank Dennis. The dead man in the lake. 'Did you kill him?' she says, her mouth dry.

He stares back at her and she can see that he did. His guilt is palpable now, his expression unflinching.

'You killed him,' she says loudly. 'You killed Frank Dennis and then you murdered my mother.'

'No!' he snaps.

'Then tell me what happened.'

'She was dying. It was too late to do anything. She was bleeding so much. I tried to stop it, but I couldn't.' He looks at his hands, then at the ground as if he can see it still.

'Why would you be afraid of the police if you didn't kill her?'

'I didn't understand what was happening.'

'Yet you pushed her. Did you hurt her that way?'

He shakes his head. 'No. I told you. She was dying anyway.'

'Dying anyway?' she hisses. 'What do you mean, *dying anyway*? What was wrong with her? You could have called a doctor, they might have saved her. Instead you left my mother alone to die.'

Her voice breaks. The tragedy and injustice is too awful to bear.

'I had no choice. I took the baby and I put her in the hall. I would have taken her to a hospital, but there was no time. The baby was crying. And when I got back . . .'

Marina clenches her fists. 'What?'

'It was too late. I told you. Connie was . . . dying.'

Marina looks across at Eva. She is sitting now, head in her hands. 'She died alone,' Marina repeats.

'No.'

'Why did nobody find her?'

'They didn't search the house. They thought the mother had come in from outside.'

'You mean you led them to believe that. You said you had found the front door open.'

He doesn't need to reply. She knows it's true and from what she has read about the other tenants, they would have said the same. Hadn't Eileen Clarke talked about the open front door and how someone must have come in? Marina could almost hear her wanting to help like witnesses do. Kenneth would have backed her up, misdirected the police. At the same time, the other tenants would have said the same thing. Thomas was on holiday in Whitby and Connie had gone to Paris to be with her boyfriend. There would have been no reason to look in Flat 4.

The police had been scouring the streets when all along they should have been searching the house. Connie had been dying in her flat. And they simply hadn't looked.

'Where is she now?' Marina manages at last.

He is silent and she realises she has underestimated this man. He won't confess and she can feel her rage growing. Yet she will make him. She will force a confession. She hasn't come this far to fail now.

'What did you do?'

He looks away. She moves closer, reaches out to grab his collar. She will shake the truth from him. She will find out what . . .

She turns abruptly.

There is someone in the doorway.

Dorothy, wizened and tired, hands clasped, eyes cast down as if in supplication.

Her head still full of Kenneth's guilt, Marina takes a deep breath, willing her heart to slow.

'We buried her,' says Dorothy. 'But she didn't die alone. I was there.'

35

Eva

Eva remembers many things as she stands in the hall listening to Kenneth and the woman who she has now discovered is called Marina.

She remembers Little Eva changing her clothes. She remembers how she hid her purple dress and wet knickers in her room where later her mother would find them. She remembers pulling on a different dress. It was yellow, she thinks. Or maybe blue. The details are hazy. She remembers returning to the landing to find Connie, but she wasn't there. Instead, the door of the flat was closed and so she waited, uncertain, until the door opened and Kenneth appeared. He was holding a bundle, wrapped in blue. Eva crouched, making herself small, hoping he wouldn't see her, but he didn't look up anyway, because he was too set on creeping down the stairs.

Eva remembers many things. She remembers Little Eva watching the small woman with the bright eyeshadow hurrying up the stairs shortly after Kenneth had gone. She remembers her rushing into her flat, coming out with a bunch of keys on a ring and then fumbling with the lock on Connie's door.

She remembers the silence and the waiting and how she traced a pattern in the dust with her toes. She remembers a baby crying from all the way at the bottom of the house in the hall and then a voice exclaiming. She remembers recognising the lady who said words like *candy* and *sidewalk* and who gave her special chocolate bars that had come all the way from America. She remembers hearing Kenneth's voice and how it made her shudder and feel afraid because she was thinking that maybe he was like those boys who had wanted to hurt her mother, or maybe he was like the nasty husband of the small woman – the woman who had just gone into Connie's flat and still hadn't come out.

Little Eva has a rule. Her mother comes first. Besides, Connie has told her not to tell. She puts her finger firmly on her lips to remind herself, then slips into her own flat and shuts the door.

36

Marina

February 1992

Marina crosses Trafalgar Square. People are scurrying, dodging the pigeons. The midday light sparkles on the fountains. A child tosses a coin and makes a wish. A tourist climbs onto the plinth and has her photo taken with a lion. The scene is less dour than a Lowry painting, less glamorous than a Renoir. It is ordinary and safe.

She climbs the steps of the National Gallery and heads for the restaurant. It strikes her that until she moved into Harrington Gardens, she had spent little time in London beyond a few school visits or trips with Ruth and David.

And yet, London is her home. It was where her mother lived and where she was born.

Her mother. Connie Littleton.

She has said these words many times since Kenneth and Dorothy made their confessions and Eva remembered what she saw.

She has visited the place, marked by that simple cross, where they buried her mother in the churchyard, close to the wall. Kenneth and Dorothy had carried her body out in the dead of night. How hard they must have worked to clean up the blood so Harry didn't notice when he came. Marina tries not to think about that. Instead she clings to Dorothy's description. The blanket they had wrapped her in, the prayers they had said, the flowers Dorothy laid on the grave month after month. Year after year.

Dorothy held Connie's hand as she lay dying and promised to look out for her baby. She turned up at the hospital on the baby ward, found out who was fostering, and then adopting her. It wasn't hard with a criminal for a friend. Kenneth knew all the right people to ask. And then she appeared at significant moments. Not a figment of Ruth's imagination after all. Dorothy had kept her promise, tracking Marina's progress, making sure she was happy. How had she felt when Marina had turned up at the house? She must have recognised her immediately.

It will be a while before there can be a proper funeral. The post-mortem must be completed as they try to establish the cause of Connie's death. Dorothy thinks it was the placenta – that a fragment had been left behind and caused bleeding, slow at first, but steady. Like a dripping tap. Taking Connie's life drop by drop with an occasional gush of blood and then a massive haemorrhage. Is that what happened? Too late to prove it, but Marina believes that her mother's death was natural. She believes, too, that if Dorothy had realised, she would have called a doctor.

Harry came to see her when she called him to explain. After his initial shock, he had told her how much he loved Connie, described the things he'd missed about her after she'd gone. He gave Marina the typewriter he had kept for so many years, waiting for her return, and the rest of the jewellery too, which Connie had entrusted to him. And Dorothy gave her the ring which she had slipped from Connie's finger. Family heirlooms. It's something. And she has the paintings. Her father's paintings from the attic, including the one that shows a half-finished picture of her mother. She has spent a long time staring at the image, looking for a resemblance between them.

Dorothy confirmed that the paintings were her son's. She told Marina he had written occasionally over the years, but his letters had become few and far between. As far as she could know, he was still in France: despite everything, he had never come home. He had rejected his mother permanently and she had lived with that loneliness, staying in the house, hoping that one day he would change his mind, that she would return and find him in the flat.

At first, Dorothy said, when he'd asked after Connie, she'd told him that Connie had left London and that she, Dorothy, didn't know where she'd gone. Marina supposes that his feelings hadn't been strong enough for him to search. He hadn't loved her as Harry had done. She can't help but wish for Connie's sake that she had chosen him instead of Johnny. How differently everything might have turned out if only that had been the case. But Marina knows it's pointless to think like that; she might as well wish that Connie had left the flat just five minutes earlier, or later; or that there had been no haemorrhage; or . . . The list is infinite, the same as Marina's grief.

Dorothy will be prosecuted for the part she played in covering up Connie's death and not coming forward with the identity of the baby. Her complicity with Kenneth. She had made mistakes and she has admitted to them. She had tried to make amends and she had suffered years of guilt. Perhaps the judge will look on her favourably for that. In a strange way, Marina hopes so. After all, Dorothy is the only blood relative she has met. Naturally Kenneth will suffer his worst nightmare. Back to prison – at least for what happened to Frank.

In the restaurant, Marina chooses pasta from the menu and a glass of wine. It feels right to toast her mother here. Later, she heads towards the galleries. The calm and the quiet and the soft hum of voices reminds her of a church. She overhears conversations as she wanders through the different rooms, searching for the painting. She doesn't even know if it's still exhibited. She could ask, but she prefers to move slowly, pausing occasionally at a picture that captures her imagination, or hanging on the coat-tails of a guided tour.

The final gallery she walks into is packed. A group of people gather around a woman who is giving a lecture. Marina stays listening for a while. She is about to leave when she sees the painting, tucked in the corner. She moves across and sits on a bench opposite. The Virgin is leaning, head bowed, hands pressed together in prayer. There is a mystery about her. A sadness, too. Marina considers the shade and the shadow and the folds of her robes. Clothes like that would hide a pregnancy. Who would ever know?

And those colours. That blue. Better than blue. Marina crosses to read the card. The pigment is ultramarine. Its origins, lapis lazuli. She nods as if this information is the most important thing in the world and then she folds her hands and continues looking at the painting.

37

Connie

7 August 1964

The darkness was falling, like fog descending. Connie felt a pain so great she thought her heart was breaking. She knew she was going to die. There was no one here to save her. She was alone; even her baby had gone. Kenneth had taken her, wrapped in the blue shawl. What *was* that colour? It had a name, Connie was sure.

Questions filled her mind.

Who would take care of Sarah? Who would feed her and clothe her? Who would listen to her first words or witness her first steps? Who would take her to school and fetch her again? Who would teach her to be strong and fearless? Who would advise her to head for the horizon and not be satisfied with standing still? Who would love her as only a mother could?

She wanted to howl, but no sound came. She wanted to cry, but had no tears left. She wanted to live for the sake of her baby but she knew it was no longer her choice.

She reached again for the missing word, the colour of the painting, but it wouldn't come. It was as if every thought and memory were draining from her mind and every colour around her was leaking into nothingness. Soon there would only be grey left, and silence.

But she could still hear. A voice speaking gently.

I will watch over her.
Had she imagined those words?
I will watch over her. The voice came again.

And Connie's pain lessened. Because she believed these words. She believed this voice. She tried to smile as the woman's fingers curled around her own.

EPILOGUE

Marina

March 1992

It's early evening. The window on the top floor is open, but there is no piano music slipping through the gap. Eva is out. Marina can see her in the distance, walking with Ron, going slowly, heading for the common.

She smiles and takes the last of her suitcases to the car. She puts the bag in the boot, slides into the driver's seat and rolls down the window.

She is going home to Ruth and David, but then she plans to visit Paris. The vision she had of searching for her mother has changed, though the details are the same – the boulevard, the apartment. Only now in her imagination it's her father who will open the door. What will he make of her? Will he want to know? She hopes that he will because she would like to stay a while. But she will return to Ruth and David, because they are the people who have loved her unconditionally. They are the people who have taught her to be strong and fearless, to look ahead and not give up.

She turns the key and starts the engine. One last look at the house. Is it her imagination or does it seem calmer now that her story is done? Or are there more secrets lurking in the shadows? More hiding places not yet found? So many ghosts whispering their tales of sadness. It's impossible to listen to them all.

Marina releases the handbrake and then she pulls away. Away down to the High Road, away to the road home, away to pursue a life that stretches ahead of her like a distant horizon, while somewhere – somewhere – a young woman smiles because she has remembered the name for that beautiful, vibrant blue.

Acknowledgements

I am grateful to my agent, Sophie Lambert, for her energy, hard work and creative insight which continues to help me develop and grow as a writer, and to the whole team at C&W for their support. Thank you to my brilliant editor, Sam Humphreys, for her creativity and tactful approach, to Charlotte Wright for her patience and skill, and to all at Mantle and Pan Macmillan.

Thank you to early readers Alex Birtles, Amelia Walcott and Stephen Walcott, and to readers, authors, bloggers, reviewers, booksellers and librarians who have championed my books and given me confidence to continue.

Special thanks to family and friends who have encouraged me along the way, to my brothers, Peter, David, Christopher and Michael, and especially to my parents, Joyce and Jack Quintana who stay in my heart forever.

Thanks and love to my husband, Derick, who is the kindest and most patient person I know.

Finally, to my dearest, most wonderful and talented children, Stephen, Amelia and Olivia, to whom this book is dedicated. I am exceptionally proud of who you are and what you have achieved. Love always.

Selected for Waterstones Thriller of the Month

A stunning debut thriller, *The Missing Girl* by Jenny Quintana is a gripping novel full of twists and turns, and a desperate hunt to solve a decades-old mystery.

Anna Flores was just a child when her adored teenage sister disappeared.

Unable to deal with the pain, Anna took the first opportunity she had to run from her fractured family, eventually building a life for herself abroad.

Now, thirty years on, her mother has died, and Anna must return home to sort through her possessions.

In doing so, she has to confront the huge hole her sister's disappearance left in their lives, leaving just one question unanswered: what really happened to Gabriella?

Because not knowing is worse than the truth.

Isn't it?

From the author of *The Missing Girl*, Jenny Quintana's gripping novel, *Our Dark Secret*, tells the story of two girls, two deaths and two decades of silence . . .

As a teenager in the late 1970s, Elizabeth was clever, overweight and something of a loner. When Rachel and her family moved to town, though, Elizabeth was drawn to the bright and beautiful Rachel like a moth to a flame. She would do anything for Rachel. Anything.

Then the first body was discovered.

Twenty years on, Elizabeth wants nothing more than to keep the secrets of her teenage years where they belong: in the past. But another body has been found, and she can't keep running from what happened . . .

Can she?